She saw Charlie, then, no longer as a friend, not yet a lover, but as a soul mate.

Molly watched him with new eyes and new awareness over the next weeks and months. From the glider on the screened porch she would watch him do the yardwork for her family. Watch him peel off his T-shirt and use it to towel himself down in the blistering sun. She observed the play of muscles across his shoulders and back when he pulled the cord and started the old gas mower.

He was the embodiment of temptation. The devil in blue denim. She was a churchgoing lady, and she believed in the devil. Her mama had warned her about him. But if it had ever occurred to Mama that he might show up in tight jeans and cowboy boots, she'd neglected to mention it.

So Molly watched, waiting for the day when Charlie Cochrane would once again place his hand upon her naked breast.

Dear Reader,

Welcome back to another month of great reading here at Silhouette Intimate Moments. Favorite author Marie Ferrarella gets things off to a rousing start with *The Amnesiac Bride*. Imagine waking up in a beautiful bridal suite, a ring on your finger and a gorgeous guy by your side—and no memory at all of who he is or how you got there! That's Whitney Bradshaw's dilemma in a nutshell, and wait 'til you see where things go from there.

Maggie Shayne brings you the next installment in her exciting miniseries, THE TEXAS BRAND, with *The Baddest Virgin in Texas*. If ever a title said it all, that's the one. I guarantee you're going to love this book. Nikki Benjamin's *Daddy by Default* is a lesson in what can happen when you hang on to a secret from your past. Luckily, what happens in this case ends up being very, very good. Beverly Bird begins a new miniseries, THE WEDDING RING, with *Loving Mariah*. It takes a missing child to bring Adam Wallace and Mariah Fisher together, but nothing will tear them apart. Kate Hathaway's back with *Bad For Each Other*, a secret-baby story that's chock-full of emotion. And finally, welcome new author Stephanie Doyle, whose *Undiscovered Hero* will have you eagerly turning the pages.

This month and every month, if you're looking for romantic reading at its best, come to Silhouette Intimate Moments.

Enjoy!

Leslie Wainger
Senior Editor and Editorial Coordinator

Please address questions and book requests to:
Silhouette Reader Service
U.S.: 3010 Walden Ave., P.O. Box 1325, Buffalo, NY 14269
Canadian: P.O. Box 609, Fort Erie, Ont. L2A 5X3

BAD FOR EACH OTHER

KATE HATHAWAY

Silhouette®

INTIMATE™ MOMENTS®

Published by Silhouette Books

America's Publisher of Contemporary Romance

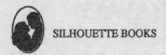 SILHOUETTE BOOKS

ISBN 0-373-07791-2

BAD FOR EACH OTHER

Copyright © 1997 by Kathleen M. Klemm

Printed in U.S.A.

KATE HATHAWAY

was born in Chicago and raised in California. She always wanted to write and, harboring that desire, obtained a degree in English literature. Reality intruded—the need to make a living!—and she spent a number of years as a registered nurse, working and teaching in the operating room. During that time she developed a deep appreciation for the courage, humor and selflessness people show at times of great crisis. The lessons gleaned from those years are the ones she most hopes to express in her writing.

Kate makes her home in Baltimore, Maryland, with her husband, John, a mathematician—yes, opposites do attract. She provides the flights of fancy in his life, while he keeps her solidly based. According to the oldest of their three children, "together they make up one pretty complete person." That's the best definition of a successful marriage Kate's ever heard.

For Mary

To the brave patients and dedicated staff of 3-South, the Bone Marrow Transplant Unit, the Johns Hopkins Hospital, Baltimore, Maryland. With special thanks to Terry Moorman, R.N., who generously shared the expertise gained from seventeen years of experience on this unit. She knows what she's doing; any mistakes are mine.

Chapter 1

Charlie "Kick" Cochrane shoved his Stetson back and rubbed a hand across his brow as he headed for the dressing room. God, he was bushed. He wanted a beer and a bed, in that order.

He needed a break. The whole band did. They'd been on the road, town after town, night after night, for months. But he hadn't been able to turn this gig down. It was for the hometown crowd.

When old lady Shanahan had approached him about a benefit to repair the high-school library that had flooded out when the Ohio breached its banks, she'd found his weak spot. His senior English teacher at that consolidated school, she'd been one of the few to see beyond the reckless, feckless boy he was, to the man he might become. Early on, she'd recognized the hunger, beneath the swagger and the grime. She'd caught on to his thinly disguised interest in anything by Tennessee Williams and quietly steered him to Faulkner and Thomas Wolfe. And there, immersed in the cadences and rhythms of the deep South, he'd found his voice.

He had a voice that was made to sing hurting songs. A

quality, an edge, that captured precisely that hollow hour of the night when the trees sighed and the wind moaned and the heart broke. It was to his great good fortune that hurting was the meat and potatoes of country music. From the moment he'd exploded on the scene, he'd been a star.

But Wheeling was home. His experiences here had molded him, its steel mills had forged his character and his resolve. These people were his people.

There were fans who believed the "Kick" came from that little jump he made with his hat in the air at the end of a show when things had gone especially well. Others, who'd known him longer, claimed it started with his days as the kicker on his high-school football team, when he'd led the Ironmen to the state championship. But you had to go way back to remember when his mother, pregnant with him, would roll her eyes and pat her abdomen saying this eighth of what would be nine children, whether male or female, would be known as "Kick." People in the audience tonight went way back.

Some had thought, when the recruiters came scouting, that he'd go on to college. But he'd followed his father and brothers into the mill. And he'd played the smoky, raucous bars in Wheeling and its environs at night. All he'd ever wanted to do was write his songs and sing them. He didn't need anybody to teach him how to do that.

"Hey, Kick."

He looked up to see Harlan Atkins, the drummer for the band, rounding the corner from the loading dock where he'd been seeing to their equipment.

"Yeah, Harlan." He wished he had a smoke. He was tempted to bum one, but resisted.

"You gonna make the party?"

"Nah. I'm beat. I'm gonna sneak out and spend the night with my folks." He gave a weary laugh. "Don't let it get around how the country star spends his wild nights." He started down the hall when another thought halted him.

"Keep an eye on Shooter." He referred to the man who played pedal steel and Dobro for the band. A class musician, but a nasty drunk. "That little lovely he was ogling is jailbait if I ever saw it. We don't want another ruckus like we had down in Bluefield."

"Will do. Speaking of jailbait..." Harlan indicated with a jerk of his chin the slight figure standing in the shadows at the end of the hallway near the dressing room door.

Squinting, Kick could just make out that the figure was female. The hips gave her away, even with the clipboard clutched to her chest. He turned back to Harlan.

"What's this?"

The other man gave an offhand shrug. "She wants to interview you for the high-school newspaper." At the scowl that quickly lined Kick's brow, he hurried to explain. "It's *your* school, too, Kick, or it was."

Hands on hips, Kick let out a long, disgusted breath. "Aw, hell, Harlan."

Harlan raised his hands, palms out, defensive. "Now, I had nothin' to do with this. Her daddy talked to your daddy. Nobody's gonna tell your father 'no.'"

Kick crossed his arms over his chest and leaned against the wall behind him, eyeing the girl from under the brim of his hat. She had edged closer in what could only be described as hopeful hesitancy. With a last, rueful shake of his head he made his decision. "Come on," he said, grabbing his friend's elbow. "You're gonna play nanny. You know how I feel about entertaining unchaperoned young ladies in my dressing room."

"You're not gonna need me," Harlan mumbled.

Kick sent him a sidelong glance as they approached the teenager. He extended his hand while Harlan made the introductions and the girl gave him the moon-eyed, tremblychinned smile he seemed to engender in much of the female population.

"What do you mean, I won't need you?" he muttered to Harlan under his breath.

"There's someone else waiting in your dressing room. Now, don't go off half-cocked! I didn't have anything to do with that, either. The manager let her in."

At Kick's questioning glance, he continued. "She told him you wouldn't mind. Guess she was convincing." He started to move away. "Lo-o-o-o-ong drink of water she is, too, and kinda plain. Not your usual type. Got breeding."

Kick's answer was a short laugh. He doubted Harlan would recognize breeding if it reared up and bit him on the nose. The other man's parting words caught him as he turned to open the door.

"Come to think of it, I don't believe I've ever seen you with a redhead."

As a warning, it wasn't much, but it was all he was going to get. He knew at once who waited for him beyond the door. There'd only ever been one redhead in his life. Molly Doyle had left Wheeling years ago. What brought her back now?

His hand tightened on the doorknob as waves of shock, anger and something akin to regret washed over him. Schooling his features to an impassivity he didn't feel, he pushed open the door, gestured for the girl to precede him into the room, and followed her.

"Hello, Molly." Deliberately, he shut the door behind him, buying himself time. "This is a surprise." Bombshell would be more like it, but he'd be damned if he'd let her know she'd thrown him. He only hoped he was better at fooling her than he was at fooling himself.

He watched her eyes flick from him to the girl—Sarah, was it? Sally? Something like that—and read the disapproval in her glance. Nothing changed there. She'd pegged him as a skirt-chaser a long time ago. Course, he hadn't figured she'd counted cradle-robbing among his many sins. But then, she'd know better than most. He'd been hot for her since she was fifteen.

"Charlie."

Nothing changed there, either. She had the same husky way of saying his name that brought to mind every time she'd breathed it in his ear, just that way, and he'd gone off like a Roman candle. That wasn't what she had in mind right now, though, he could tell. She wasn't aiming to get on his good side. Not with her hair skinned back like that, the way he didn't like it.

"I know this isn't a social visit. What's on your mind?"

Her eyes flew to the girl again. God, he should have bummed that smoke. Here she was back after, what? *eight* years and picking up right where she left off.

"We need to talk...privately, Charlie."

The years hadn't been kind to her. She was twenty-eight, he knew. Three years younger than him, but she looked older. There was strain around her eyes and a tight, pinched look, like she was barely hanging on. She was thinner all over. Still had a chest, though, and still trying to hide it. She'd never been what you'd call a flashy dresser, but her clothes had always been quality, not like this shapeless excuse for a dress she wore now.

His gaze dropped to the hands knotted in her lap. Still bit her nails, too, and he watched as she curled her fingers into her palms to conceal that. Despite himself, he felt stirrings of sympathy for her. He hoped she wasn't going to try to hit him up for money. Considering the animosity that had flared between them when they'd parted, that would be too embarrassing for both of them.

"I can't imagine what you'd have to say to me in private after all these years, Molly. You were never much concerned with privacy when you had a bone to pick with me anyway, as I recall."

He pulled a slatted-back chair away from a mirrored table and propped a foot on it, removing his Stetson and placing it carefully on the table. He rested an elbow on his raised knee and tunnelled fingers through his hair, ruffling it up where it had been flattened by the hat. When he looked at her again, she was more the Molly he remembered.

Her spine had stiffened and color flooded her cheeks. Heat simmered in her whiskey-brown eyes. He'd lost himself in those eyes before he'd ever tasted whiskey. It was more than a little unsettling to find they could still affect him.

"I need to ask a favor of you, Charlie." She darted another quick glance at the girl. "It's...personal."

This time *his* gaze shifted to the girl. ''Moon-eyed'' didn't begin to describe the look on her face as her eyes swung from him to Molly. He didn't kid himself that it was his charm that brought that look on, either. She was getting an earful. Probably saw ''scoop'' written all over this confrontation. Maybe he should get her out of here. Maybe if he hadn't been feeling so damn tired, put upon, and downright ornery, he would have. As it was, he straightened from the chair, crossed his booted feet at the ankles, hooked his thumbs in the frayed pockets of his faded jeans, and favored Molly with his best good ol' boy drawl, the one he knew would set her teeth on edge.

''You need money, Moll?''

She still had fire, no denying that. Her full lips flattened to a thin line as her color heightened even more. She shot a final glance at the girl, then pinned him with the accusatory look he'd seen countless times before.

''We have a son, Charlie. *He* needs you.''

Before he could manage a response, he heard the sharp intake of the girl's breath. He turned and watched her scramble to catch the clipboard as it slid down her body toward the floor. All the while his mind scrambled to make some sense of Molly's words. He'd been hit with paternity charges before—it came with the territory—and none of them had ever amounted to anything. But from *Molly?* What was her game?

Whatever, she was right about one thing. This demanded privacy. One look at the youngster's stunned expression and he knew he'd just given the fine people of Wheeling another juicy topic to chaw on over breakfast. Enough was enough. Taking her elbow, he summoned up his most fetching smile and murmured apologies as he hustled her from the room.

He leaned against the closed door, staring at the floor for just a moment before heading to the little refrigerator tucked under the dressing table. Pulling a bottle of beer from inside, he popped the cap and took a long swallow. He swiped a hand across his mouth, raised the bottle to Molly in wordless invitation, and nodded when she answered with a quick shake of her head. Of course not, not his Molly. What was he thinking? He took another swig, hitched his hip on the table, and tapped the long neck against his thigh, eyeing her.

"Okay," he said at last. "I'll play. What's this all about?"

Molly unclenched her hands and took a deep breath. The minutes he'd spent getting rid of the girl and swilling his beer had given her time to compose herself. And compose herself she must. She could *not* risk his wrath. She would do whatever it took to get what she needed from him. It wouldn't inconvenience him for long. He'd be back to his parties and his women in no time.

"Molly?"

She was wasting time. She took another breath and set her jaw determinedly. "I told you. We have a son. He needs—"

"Excuse me for being so crass as to mention this, Moll," he interrupted, "but you and I haven't been—" he made a suggestive motion with the bottle "—you know, in a long while."

Flustered, she reached for her purse on the floor beside her chair and withdrew Tobie's school photograph, taken the previous fall. She held it out to Charlie, making sure their fingers didn't touch when he took it from her.

Not that it mattered. She remembered his touch. It had only taken his crude remark to bring back with a rush the feel of his lips on her skin, his fingers in her hair, his tongue on that sensitive spot below her ear.

She studied him as he looked at the picture. She knew what he saw. The same thing she had seen when Tobie had brought it home so proudly all those months ago. The same laughing black eyes, the same unruly hair, even the same missing teeth. It could have been taken twenty-five years before.

And like an ambush, the past was upon her....

She sat on the tree stump in a sulky heap, chin resting on her fists, elbows planted on her knees, glaring at her dusty sneakers and trying to ignore the boy on the bike. Round and round he went, down the long gravel drive, over the warped one-by-twelve that spanned the little back stream off of Big Wheeling Creek, weaving under the crab apple and seckel

pear trees behind the house, across the railed footbridge and
back again. Just like he belonged there. *She* didn't feel that
way, and it was *her* house.

She heard his approach, turned her head to avoid the spray
of gravel as he came to a crunching halt in front of her. He
stopped just a foot or so away and toed the ground with his
scuffed boots as he straddled his bike. Pointy-toed boots like
the cowboys wore. He always wore boots.

"Hi, Red."

She scowled up at him. "Don't call me that."

He grinned. "Why not? Your hair's real pretty. I like it."

He smiles with his whole face, she thought. Ear to ear and
his eyes crinkling up into slits. She didn't know anybody else
who smiled like that. He was one of the Cochrane boys, but
she wasn't sure which. They all looked the same. Wild black
hair and wild black eyes. He was one of the younger ones.
A couple years older than she was. Eight, nine maybe.

"I don't like it."

He twisted the black rubber grips on his handlebars. "What
should I call you, then? Margaret Mary?"

She frowned even more fiercely at his shirtless chest.

Her momma called her Margaret Mary, and teachers the
first day of school. No one else. "Call me Molly," she said,
looking away into the dirt.

He shifted on the seat of his bike and toed the kickstand
down. *Why doesn't he just go away and leave me alone?* She
sneaked a peek at him through her lashes, but his gaze was
fixed above her head on the house behind her. When he
looked back at her, there was pity in his eyes.

"They fightin' again, Molly?"

Oh, fine. He didn't even know her name, but he knew about
her momma and daddy fighting. Everybody knew. There
wasn't a soul in all Wheeling her daddy couldn't get along
with. Except her momma. Especially when he was drinking.

Her throat felt tight and swollen. She hid her face in her
hands and willed him to go away.

She heard him sigh and drag his boots through the gravel.
He wasn't going to leave.

"So," he said. "You wanna go for a ride on my bike?"

She looked up at him, unable to believe her ears. "I don't know how to ride a bike yet."

He shrugged his bony shoulders. "On the handlebars, then. I'll take you."

She was so tempted. "I'm not supposed to go with strangers," she said, wavering.

He gave her half a grin, which was almost as nice as the full-face kind. "I'm not a stranger. My momma cleans your house."

She nodded her recognition. "You're Cleeve."

"Nah, not Cleeve. He's older. I'm Kick."

"Oh, Charles."

He slitted his eyes at her then, the first time he'd looked anything less than friendly. "I'm *Kick.*" He booted the kick-stand up. "You can call me Charlie, if you want. *Nobody* calls me Charles." He propped his foot on the pedal and challenged her with a jerk of his head. "You comin'?"

She had never been able to resist him, not from that first meeting on. He'd ridden her, laughing and squealing, over his favored path. That rickety board over the creek had been their undoing. He'd told her to sit still, quit bouncing, but it was too exhilarating, too exciting. They'd ended up on the rocks lining the streambed. She never did learn what happened to that bike. He'd carried her back to the house, scared, dirty and hurting, one of her brand-new permanent teeth broken off and poking through her bottom lip.

That was the first time folks had said they were bad for each other. It hadn't been the last.

"What's his name?"

Charlie's words brought her back with a start. He glanced up from the picture, his acceptance of the truth in his eyes. Unsnapping the flap over the left front pocket of his shirt, he slipped the photograph inside. Close to his heart, Molly thought, and wondered at the curious notion even as she did so.

"Tobias...Tobie." Behind his stony features, Molly sensed

his rage. Had it never occurred to him over the years that she might have borne the child he hadn't wanted, might have kept him, might love him? Apparently not.

"What else?" At her questioning look, he added, "Tobie what?"

"Doyle. Just Doyle. I didn't give him a middle name."

Charlie's eyes glittered hard as the steel tie-rods he'd spent years making. "Good. Doyle can be his middle name then, when I give him mine."

At his words Molly felt the first subtle inkling of uncertainty, the first vague suspicion that the situation was not exactly as she believed it to be. He seemed angry, not because she had come to him now to make demands for their son, but because she hadn't done so before. But that was impossible. Unless…

"What made you decide he needs me now, Molly?"

His question cut into her thoughts and she pushed her doubts aside, her concern for Tobie once more foremost in her mind. "He's sick, Charlie, seriously ill. A condition called aplastic anemia. He has to—"

"I've heard of that. Jase's sister—you remember Jase? Plays keyboard?"

Molly gave a quick nod of recognition. Jase was an original member of the band, with Charlie since high school.

"Jase's sister died of that, some five, six years back." He frowned and took another long pull on his beer. "Are you saying Tobie might die?"

The idea was one she hadn't been able to give voice to. Even now, with his question hanging between them, she couldn't say it. "He's very sick. He needs a bone-marrow transplant. I'm not a match."

"And you're hoping I am."

"Yes." She faltered just a little on the word. His voice was deceptively soft, silky, in contrast with his granite-hard expression.

"That's all?" He raised the bottle to his mouth again and drank deeply, then ran his tongue over his lips before he continued. "'We just need a little of your marrow, Charlie, thank you very kindly. We'll be on our way, and you can get lost again.' Is that what you had in mind, Molly?''

"I—"

"How could you *do* this to me?" He lashed the words at her. His hand closed around the bottle so tightly she thought the thick glass might crack. "You, more than anybody, always knew what family was to me."

That was true. In that moment she was reminded of the stories she'd heard of others with his heritage. The savage Scots, to whom clan was everything. Blood was all. Only what he was saying implied a betrayal of that blood so primal it left her speechless.

"Did you hate me so much?" His voice was barely a whisper, but harsh all the same.

"I never hated—'' She didn't go on. That wasn't what she had said when they'd parted that last time. Even now, the words echoed loud in her memory.

I hate you. Get out!
If I leave this time, I ain't comin' back.
I can't imagine any reason I'd want you back.

They'd been young, reckless, irresponsible, their quarrels as fiery as their love. Who would have guessed that this one would be their last? Who could have predicted that four weeks later, he'd be a star? And she'd be pregnant.

He turned from her and hurled the bottle into the trash. She flinched, bringing her hands up to cover her mouth. She'd seen him silly with drink, lazy after loving, lost in total concentration for the words and music he was creating, doubled over with laughter at some prank he'd pulled. She'd never, until this moment, been afraid of him.

She took a breath and opened her mouth to tell him the words that would exonerate her. The ones that would shift the blame to someone else. Someone who could never tell him of her regret. Someone who could never right this wrong. This would be a blight forever on a person precious to him.

She said nothing, and the moment passed.

He pivoted toward her, his hands curled around the edge of the table behind him. "Why, Molly? Can you give me a reason? Make me understand."

She shrugged, playing for time, struggling to come up with a reason it had never occurred to her she might need. "Pride, mostly. After the words we'd had, I just couldn't come to you, begging." She hadn't noticed the faint flicker of hope in his eyes until she saw it die and the bleakness that replaced it.

"Your damn pride."

Pride had come between them before, though mainly his, he had to admit. Much as he'd loved her, he'd never asked her to marry him. Not until he could measure up, in his own eyes at least, he'd told himself. Not until he had some degree of success. He remembered how it had humiliated him to come to her, his fingers still stained with the soot from the mill that had sifted through his canvas work gloves. How it had shamed him to touch her pale skin with hands no amount of scrubbing could clean. If she'd ever felt the same, she'd never showed it, never recoiled from his touch. He'd never have believed her capable of this duplicity.

"What do you want from me, Charlie?"

She had the gall to ask. "The years I lost with my son," he snarled. "Did you think you could be everything to him? One parent was enough? It's pretty obvious which parent he needs now."

She reeled as if he had struck her. "You wouldn't try to take him from me?" she whispered past bloodless lips.

Watching her, he felt his gut clench. Even now, angry as he was, he couldn't cause her that kind of pain. "No. I wouldn't do that. It would hurt him at least as much as you."

He walked over to the sink, turned on the tap and splashed

cold water on his face. He'd been tired before, but nothing like this. This weariness went bone deep, and no amount of rest would ease it.

"Where is he?" he asked, toweling himself dry.

"He's in the hospital, Greater Pittsburgh Metro. It's just a precaution right now," she added quickly, seeing his head come up, the concern—was it fear?—in his expression. "His resistance is very low. He's being isolated from anything that might be contagious. We live up there," she said as an afterthought.

He gave her a long look, his face unreadable. "I'll get some things together and we'll drive up." He tossed the towel over the bar alongside the sink. "We're gettin' married."

Molly went still at his words, unable to breathe. Why was he doing this? "We don't have to...I would never try to keep him from you, Charlie."

One corner of his mouth lifted in a humorless smile, a sad reminder of the ones he used to give her years ago. "You'll pardon me if I have a little trouble believing that." Before she could respond, he added, "What did you think, Molly? That I would donate my marrow and walk out of your lives?" He approached her then, leaning over her, his hands braced on the arms of her chair. "You know, like I did my sperm."

She searched his eyes, trying to fathom the reasons for his insistence. "Why marriage, Charlie? You don't want me." She shook her head, confused, floundering. "Because of what your fans will think? For the sake of your career?"

Her words only seemed to rile him further. "Don't throw the celebrity bit in my face," he cautioned her. "If you remember anything at all about me, you know that means less than nothing."

"*Why,* then? Tell me."

He appeared to hesitate for just a moment, and she sensed his motives weren't entirely clear even to himself. His words were slow, measured when he replied.

"The men in my family are *there* for their children, Molly. We marry their mothers. It's what we do. It's the way I was brought up."

She saw more in his eyes than he was aware he revealed. He was angry, yes. But he was hurting, too. What he thought she had done cut right to the core of what being a man meant to him. The truth would only hurt him more. She couldn't do that.

She felt his warm fingers under her chin, tipping her face to his. "Do you need a proper proposal, Molly?" His words were sarcastic, biting, but uttered with firm resolution. "It appears I should have asked you years ago. Will you marry me?"

There it was, stark and unsentimental. Not the proposal of her dreams. Still, it had come from Charlie, the man who had haunted her dreams. She had loved him as a child, and in the first blush of young womanhood. She had never loved anyone else.

And then there was the issue of the transplant. Without one, Tobie would die. That had been made manifestly clear to her. Though she didn't doubt now that Charlie would help regardless of her answer, marriage would strengthen her claim with his family, should that prove necessary. His demand seemed so little in exchange for so much.

"Moll," he prompted, the fingers on her chin tightening.

"Yes," she answered firmly, meeting his gaze unflinchingly. "Yes, I will marry you."

His eyes glittered for just a moment with what might have been satisfaction. Then he straightened away from her, his expression shuttered once more. "Come on," he said. "It's time I met my son."

Chapter 2

A couple of phone calls, a few final words to Harlan, and they were ready to leave. Charlie grabbed the duffel bag he'd packed and guided Molly out the rear exit of the music hall to where her car was parked in the lot that backed up to the river. He held out his hand for her keys and tried not to think about that little cove off to the left where 8th Street dead-ended at the water's edge. There, years ago, with the gentle lapping of the Ohio as background music, in the privacy afforded by the low, overhanging branches of willows and cottonwoods, he and Molly had introduced each other to all the delights that youth and love and hormones could offer.

At least *he'd* been introduced. Green as he was at the time, he'd never been too sure about her. He'd learned a thing or two since, and become even more convinced it hadn't been all that great for Molly.

He was surprised to see she still drove the little blue car she'd gotten as a high-school graduation present. In the glow from the parking-lot lights, he noted the rust around the lock when he opened the hatch to stow his bag. The whole shebang seemed to be patched together with chicken wire and duct tape.

He moved to the passenger side where Molly waited. "This door only opens from the inside," she said.

Walking around the front end, he opened the other door and folded himself into the car. With his knees bumping the dash, he eased the driver's seat back and reached across the console to get the door for Molly. He squinted at the odometer while she settled herself next to him. Fourteen thousand some odd miles. Obviously on its second time around.

"It's paid for," she said, staring straight ahead.

He turned the key in the ignition, glad to hear it catch on the first try. Clearly she wasn't the hotshot lawyer she'd figured on becoming, he thought as he backed the car out of its space and pulled onto Main. For the first time he wondered how she, as a single parent, supported herself and the boy. His son. She'd been nearly finished with college when they'd split, but her new responsibilities must have put a crimp in any future education plans.

In the brighter light of the Wheeling Tunnel, he stole a glance at her. Chin high, eyes level, back straight. Same old Molly. If she'd had a tough time of it, she'd be the last one to say so. That must have been a pretty scene with her momma, though, telling her she was carrying that no-good Cochrane boy's bastard. Of course by that time her mother wouldn't have been much help, anyway. From what he'd heard, they'd been living in genteel poverty since paying off the debts her daddy had left.

He checked his side mirror and merged on to the interstate, then slid another look her way. "I was sorry to hear about your momma." He saw her swallow and press her lips together before she turned away.

"I'll bet."

Okay. It was a lie. Not much of a lie. He'd felt bad for Molly when he'd heard. He was in Germany on that first European tour when word had reached him. It had been too late for flowers, so he'd sent a card, hoping it would reach her some way. It caught up with him when he got back to the States, marked Addressee Unknown. She'd done a good job of disappearing with his son. He shot another quick glance at her. He could play a little tit for tat.

"I was surprised when you didn't show up for Lucy's funeral. You two were thick once. But then," he said evenly, "you're full of surprises."

Molly closed her eyes and leaned her head back against the rest. *Lucy, Lucy,* she said to herself, *what have you done to us?* She and Lucy, Charlie's only sister, had been the same age. Attending different elementary schools, though, they hadn't really become close until sixth grade. From that point on, through middle and much of high school, they'd been inseparable. Lucy, the youngest child and only girl, had been spoiled and pampered as only a family with little money and lots of love can manage. Willful and adventuresome, she'd gotten herself—and Molly—into countless scrapes, but there always seemed to be an older brother, very often Charlie, around to bail them out. Later, as they got older, they'd drifted apart. Lucy grew interested in ever more risky pursuits. And Molly...well, Molly had grown ever more interested in Charlie.

Resentment had resulted, Molly knew. She'd taken Lucy's place as the number-one female in Charlie's affections. But Molly had never suspected how deep that well of resentment might run. When she'd discovered she was pregnant, Charlie was away on the tour his record company had arranged. After years of booking local honky-tonks, Charlie had gotten some nationwide airplay for his music, and he'd become the classic "overnight" success. Molly asked Lucy to intercede for her with him, never doubting her when she returned with his answer. It wasn't a convenient time for him, on the cusp of his career, to start a family. If she needed money to take care of things, that was no problem.

Within weeks, armed with her shiny-new Liberal Arts degree, a generous supply of soda crackers, and whatever belongings she could squeeze into her car, she'd left Wheeling forever. She'd read, along with the rest of the world, of the newest Country sensation's grief when his baby sister took that rain-slick curve a little too fast and plunged her Trans-Am off the edge of Chicken Neck Hill. Big with his child, Molly had shed her own tears in private.

"What did you tell him—" Charlie's words interrupted her reverie "—when he asked about his father?"

Molly opened her eyes and stared out the passenger window, getting her bearings. They had reached Washington, Pennsylvania, where they would catch Interstate 79, a straight shot into Pittsburgh. "I told him, if his father knew him, he would love him. He didn't ask any more than that."

That was true, as far as it went. How many questions had Tobie suppressed, afraid to hurt or, worse, anger her? Children could be exquisitely sensitive to the moods of their caretakers. Tobie had no one but her. His very silence said a lot.

She turned her head on the seat back to look at Charlie, wondering at what was going through his mind. Even being in his presence this short time, she recognized the familiar pattern of their quarrels from long ago. His tendency to act first and reflect later. His typical hotheadedness, followed by his more thoughtful, generous response. Now his face was a study in quiet concentration. She closed her eyes again, remembering the first time she had seen him wear that look...

"He's not really reading that."

"I don't think anybody *really* reads those magazines, Lucy." Molly peered through the porch-rail slats at the slick cover displaying a pouty-mouthed woman with truly amazing breasts. She hunched her shoulders, feeling her own thirteen-year-old chest more than a little inadequate.

"No. I mean he's not even looking at the pictures!" Lucy turned to Molly and said in her best conspiratorial whisper, "He's writing a poem." The way she said the word, it rhymed with "home." She giggled. "He hides 'em in his *Playboys* 'cause he thinks I won't look."

"You shouldn't look." But Molly continued to stare, fascinated in spite of herself. They were crouched in the bushes, their eyes level with the porch floor, and to her pubescent heart Charlie looked like a reclining god.

He sprawled lackadaisically on an old wooden swing that hung by creaking chains from the tongue and groove ceiling of the wraparound porch. One long, narrow, bare foot pushed at the floor occasionally, setting the swing in wobbly motion. Charlie's other leg was propped on the seat, its raised knee supporting the arm that held that raunchy magazine.

He'd bulked up nicely, Molly mused, since she'd last had a really good look at him. His shoulders weren't bony anymore, but a long, smooth, muscular line that looked to be a yard wide. He appeared to have a good start on some of those bodily changes Mrs. Richards was discussing in Health class, too. Tufts of curly dark hair sprouted around his nipples. They were still called nipples on a man, if she remembered correctly. They just didn't work. Coarse hair surrounded his belly button, too. *Navel* in polite company. *Umbilicus* if you're really being fancy-schmancy. Whatever. The hairs merged into a single thin line that arrowed down into his low-riding jeans.

She knew what lurked there, where that line ended. Not firsthand, mind, but intellectually speaking. She'd pored over the pictures in her Family Studies book, the ones showing the stair-step progression from little boy infant, to toddler, to adolescent, to man fully grown. Judging from the bulge in the soft, clingy denim, Charlie was rapidly closing in on full grown.

A warm flush washed over her, not wholly related to the steamy afternoon. Watching Charlie, she felt as lazy and languid as the fat bees playing bumper cars in the spirea that girdled the porch.

But this *was* Charlie, and she felt a little guilty thinking about him like this, gawking at him like this. She dragged her gaze up to his face and was just as enraptured by what she saw there.

He *wasn't* reading the magazine, she'd bet a month's allowance on that. His eyes were focused somewhere beyond it. His brows knit to a single black line with the effort of his concentration and he worried his upper lip with his teeth. He held a pencil in his right hand and scribbled intermittently on the magazine. Or something in it.

"C'mon."

Molly turned at Lucy's elbow jab and saw her companion rounding the corner post. She followed close as they crept low along the front of the porch to the stairs that came up behind Charlie. Swallowing her misgivings, she was right there when Lucy reached over her brother's shoulder and snatched the white loose-leaf paper out of his hand.

"Hey! Give that back!" He was out of the swing in a flash, whacking Lucy about the head and back with the magazine while she covered her head with her arms, laughing and shrieking. When the magazine disintegrated, finally, from the abuse, Lucy took off down the porch steps and across the yard, handing the paper off to Molly as she went.

Molly and Charlie faced each other, the swing between them, each weighing the other's determination.

"Give it to me, Molly," Charlie demanded, breathing hard.

Molly's own breathing quickened. She shook her head, eyes sparkling, clutching the paper to her chest.

He dove for her over the swing, taking her to the floor with him when the swing flipped. He twisted to avoid landing on her, and she took advantage of the chance his considerate move afforded her, shoving the paper up under her shirt. It didn't register immediately that his hand had followed, until she felt him go very still. Her laughter stopped and she sucked in sharply, as she stared into his dark, dark eyes, only inches from her own, and slowly became aware of his fingers curled over her naked breast.

He rolled away from her like a shot, but not before she detected the change in his lower body, where the firm ridge behind his zipper prodded her thigh. Trying to rise, he cracked his head against the swing and spat out a word she'd heard before, but not from him. He got to his feet, rubbing his head, and slammed into the house.

Confused and close to tears, Molly crumpled the paper until it was nothing but a damp wad in her palm. She looked about for Lucy, but her friend had disappeared. Her father should be coming by for her soon. She sat on the top step and leaned against the peeling white post to wait.

She heard a phone ring in some far corner of the house, and a few minutes later Mrs. Cochrane poked her head out the screen door.

"That was your momma, Molly. Your daddy's not going to be able to pick you up. I'll get one of the boys to drive you home." She disappeared back into the house.

Molly sensed the unspoken sympathy in the kindly woman's voice and heard what had been left unsaid. *Your daddy's passed out drunk in the middle of the day, again, Molly.* If she was lucky, he was at home this time. Not with one of his lady friends. Feeling things couldn't get much worse, she turned her forehead to the post and closed her eyes.

Moments later, she jumped as the screen door flew open and banged against the siding of the house. Charlie stormed out, hopping and stomping into his boots. "Why can't Cleeve go?" he yelled over his shoulder.

"Don't take that tone of voice with me, young man," Mrs. Cochrane hollered back. "You want to use the pickup to haul your gear Friday night, you can do me a favor now. And put a shirt on," she added as he reached the steps. "You're not escorting a young lady anywhere looking like that!"

The glare he threw her way told Molly exactly what he thought of this particular young lady, but he headed back into the house and returned, pulling on a blue chambray work shirt. Still defiant, he left it unbuttoned.

"Kick?" His mother's voice drifted through the screen once more.

"Yeah?"

"You clean up that mess on the porch. If you're gonna read magazines like that, you don't go leaving 'em around to offend the girls."

Molly rose and began gathering the scattered paper. "Leave it, brat," Charlie muttered, already loping down the stairs. "I'll get it later."

He stood next to the truck, cupping his hands around a cigarette, while she got in on the passenger side. Then he climbed in beside her, blowing smoke. Silent all the while, he pulled the visor down, narrowed his eyes against the low-hanging sun, and drove with an intensity out of all proportion to the sparse traffic on the quiet neighborhood streets.

Molly cowered in her seat, arms crossed in front of her chest, miserable beyond words. To add to her mortification, one fat tear slipped down her cheek and landed on her bare arm. Charlie chose that moment to slide her a glance.

He hissed a long breath out through his teeth, flicked his cigarette out the window, and turned his eyes back to the road. "Don't cry, Molly," he said at last. "It's not you....you're okay. I'm not mad at you. It's..."

He paused and she looked over at him, seeing his Adam's apple bob and his face redden. He's embarrassed, she realized.

"It's...dammit, Moll, we're not little kids anymore. We can't fool around like that." He downshifted, turning a corner.

Molly felt hot color flood her cheeks as his meaning came clear. She lowered her head and stared at her lap. A shuddering sob escaped, despite her furious efforts to hold it in.

"Aw, hell. Don't cry, Molly. It's not your fault." He threw her a panicky glance. "You wanna shift for me?"

Molly scrubbed at her cheeks and choked back another sob. "Huh?"

"You wanna shift for me? You know, handle the stick?"

"I don't know how—"

"It's easy. Pay attention. This here's first, second, third." He ran her through the positions on the gearshift knob. "Only when you see my foot go down on the pedal on the left, now." He gave her his crinkly-eyed smile. "Try to stay out of reverse."

Deep in concentration on her task, she forgot how humiliated she was. She kept her eyes on his legs, anticipating when he'd depress the clutch by the curves and dips in the road. Only a time or two, when she wasn't fast enough, he closed his hand over hers to assist. Just once, he winced at the ragged grinding of the gears. "No, Moll, only when I put the clutch in," he said.

Before she knew it, they were pulling into her drive. Char-

lie guided the pickup to a stop and idled it at the bottom of
her front steps. He looked past her to the house, then brought
his gentle gaze back to her. "You gonna be okay?"

She shrugged and nodded. She was used to her home life.
She knew what to expect when she got inside.

"Friends?"

She smiled a real smile and dipped her head. "Friends."

He reached over and stroked a long finger down her cheek.
"You're turning into a real pretty girl, Molly. I just noticed,
is all. I didn't mean to scare you."

She nodded again, smiled a farewell and scrambled from
the truck. Once inside, she made her way up the wide front
staircase to the second floor. She tiptoed past the closed door
of her mother's room and noted the closed door of the room
facing it. Daddy was home. Reaching her room in the turret
at the front of the house, she climbed on the window seat and
pushed the lace curtain aside. She spotted Charlie's truck as
it turned from her drive onto the main road and followed its
winding progress until it dipped out of sight. Only then did
she remember the wadded paper she had stuffed into the
pocket of her jeans.

She pulled it out and smoothed it flat on the windowsill.
Lucy was right. It looked like some kind of poem. Then she
saw the other markings. She had studied enough music to
recognize the chords for guitar. Charlie had written a song.

She read the words he had scrawled and they were like an
epiphany to her. All the vague, ephemeral yearnings of her
heart were there in black and white, expressed in Charlie's
spare lyrics. She saw him, then, no longer as a playmate, not
yet a lover, but as a soul mate.

Later, if she were asked to define the precise moment she
had fallen in love with him, she would say that one. She
recognized the change in her feelings, the slow segue from
the affection of a child to the first seeds of a woman's love
in her budding woman's heart.

She watched him with new eyes and new awareness over
the next weeks and months and years, as he grew into man-

hood. His mother still cleaned the Doyle house, and Charlie took over the yard work, so he came by often.

From the glider on the screened porch where she'd retreat with a book, she'd watch him peel off his T-shirt and use it to towel himself down in the blistering heat. She observed the play of muscles across his shoulders and back when he'd pull the cord to start that old gas mower.

He was the embodiment of temptation. The devil in blue denim. She was a churchgoing young lady and she believed in the devil. Her momma had warned her about him. But if it had ever occurred to momma that he might show up in tight jeans and Tony Lama boots, she'd neglected to mention it.

So Molly watched, and worshipped, and waited for the day when Charlie Cochrane would once again place his hand upon her naked breast.

"You need plugs somethin' awful. When was the last time you changed the oil?" Turning his gaze from the highway for a moment, Charlie watched her eyes flutter open. She must have fallen asleep. Probably hadn't been getting too much of that lately. "When's the last time you had the oil changed?" he repeated.

She pushed herself up straighter in the seat, blinked a few times, and sighed. "I've had other things on my mind."

He shook his head, exasperated. "Ballpark figure, Molly."

She pursed her lips and narrowed her eyes, thinking. "March, I believe. Last year. After that really rough winter."

Last March. A year and some. That didn't sound like the Molly he knew, no matter what else was on her mind. He considered the shabby—there really was no other word for it—condition of her car and her clothes and wondered again about her finances. "Is money a problem?"

She pokered up even more. "I have a reliable job."

Her *damn* pride. They were approaching the Fort Pitt Tunnel, which opened on the Pittsburgh skyline. He'd have to start thinking about a place to stay. "Which way now?"

"It's too late to go to the hospital, Charlie. Tobie'd be asleep. We wouldn't be able to see him."

"You don't stay with him nights?" It was just a question. He didn't mean any criticism by it, although he allowed it might be taken that way.

She shook her head. "I did at first. The nursing staff discourages it. They say we need a break from each other. Some separation." From what? she had thought. As preparation for that final separation? She would sleep better, they told her. But she hadn't. She hadn't slept since the day she learned she could be of no use to Tobie.

"Where do you want me to take you?"

His words interrupted her dreary thoughts. She directed him to her apartment. Suddenly it occurred to her that he hadn't made arrangements for the night. "Do you want to stay at my place? We could get an early start in the morning." She gave him a cautious look. "You can use Tobie's room."

What? Did she think he was gonna jump her? All he'd been interested in was a beer and a bed alone, hours ago. That hadn't changed. "I appreciate the hospitality," he said tightly.

He turned into a street of rambling old frame houses, many of which had been converted into apartments, judging by the number of mailboxes on the front porches. Shabby about summed up this neighborhood, too. Not *seedy,* exactly, just a little tired and run-down. The area seemed strangely familiar, until he realized he'd grown up on a street much like it.

Molly lived on the second floor of a three-flat. Charlie waited next to her while she gathered her mail. She ushered him into a common vestibule, casting her eyes about as they headed for the stairs leading to her floor. "I'm not in the habit of bringing men home with me in the middle of the night," she said by way of explanation.

"I'm happy to hear that. We'll be respectable real soon." He watched her stiff back precede him up the stairs. "What do the people here think of Tobie?"

She turned and looked down at him. "They love Tobie."

She gave him the silent treatment while she unlocked the apartment door and switched on some lights. The place looked pretty much like what he expected to see at this point. Pin-neat, but modest. Cheap, if you were of a mind to be unkind, which he wasn't. The main living space could be described as spacious or sparsely furnished, depending on your point of view. But he knew what Molly had been raised with, and this wasn't it.

She led him down a short hall, where two bedrooms were separated by the single bath they would share. She moved past him into the room on the left and turned on a lamp shaped like an airplane on a wobbly table next to the narrow bed. This was cozy, at least. Cluttered, like the rooms he remembered as a kid. He'd never had his own room, growing up. Molly had never had anything else.

"I'll change the sheets." She started out the door, but he grasped her arm.

"Leave 'em. I haven't slept with jungle cats in a while."

She shook his hand off and left the room. So much for his attempt at humor. He should have remembered Molly's sensitivity about females of the species. *Any* species. How many times had she accused him of catting around?

He found her on the phone in the kitchen. From her end of the conversation, he gathered she was talking to someone at the hospital. Probably the last thing she did every day.

She hung up and glanced at him, her face expressionless. "He had a good evening and he's asleep now. They're expecting us in the morning." She looked about to say more, then reconsidered. "Good night, Charlie," she said. Brushing past him, she went to her room and closed the door.

He'd been dismissed. Casual as you please. He felt like a fool standing there, so he moved about the apartment, shutting off lights. He wandered back to Tobie's room, tired but charged. He knew he wouldn't sleep now. He poked around, trying to acquaint himself with his son.

The closet didn't reveal much. Jeans, mostly, and some flannel shirts on hangers. One blue suit and a white shirt with the tie already under the collar. Molly took him to church. He smiled, remembering when he'd slicked back his hair and worn the same getup himself on Sundays. The boy was maybe a little tall for seven. That didn't surprise Charlie, given his height, and Molly's.

He pulled open the top drawer of the dresser and grinned wider. The junk drawer. Tobie had quite an accumulation for his tender years. Some handheld electronic games, action figures—these were Power Rangers, he thought. G.I. Joe must be passé. Rocks! Now there was an old favorite. A magnifying glass. He wondered if Tobie used it to burn holes in leaves like he had done.

He shoved the drawer shut, the bookcase under the window catching his eye. Tobie had a taste for the kiddie thrillers, but there was a decent sampling of the classics, too. Molly must read to him a good bit. They appeared to be beyond the reading level of the typical seven-year-old.

He squatted down and pulled a battered box from the bottom shelf. Magic tricks! He laughed to himself, sifting through the assortment of cards, strings, and rings. What gene had this particular interest been passed down on? He remembered amazing a freckle-faced Molly with his feats of prestidigitation. There'd been a time when Molly thought he could do anything.

With a heavy sigh, he replaced the box and sat on the edge of the bed. This room and what it represented were as familiar to him as his own hand. What else had his son inherited from the father he'd never met? He unsnapped his shirt pocket and slipped the photograph out. His prayers had become few and far between over the last hectic years, but he prayed now. He wasn't exactly sure what Tobie needed from him, but he hoped to God he had it.

He propped the picture against the airplane lamp and yanked off his boots. Drawing the comforter back a little, he pulled the pillow out and plumped it. Then he laid himself down among the jungle animals, locked his eyes with those in the picture and, after a time, he fell asleep.

Charlie was up at first light, as was his habit. If memory served him, it would be a while before Molly put in an appearance. He showered and shaved and rooted around the kitchen for something to eat. Slim pickings, he concluded, peeling a banana. Molly was a light eater and Tobie wasn't home for the present. He'd have to do something about that if he was going to be here for any length of time.

He prowled the apartment, trying to refamiliarize himself with the woman who resided there. His initial impression the night before had been on the money. Nondescript would best describe the place. They had the basic necessities and not much else. A couple more pictures of Tobie were all that personalized the space. He was a cute kid, even if it did seem the height of conceit to say so.

No evidence of another man's presence around anywhere. He was a little surprised that the possibility hadn't occurred to him before this. It had been eight years, after all. Molly was an attractive woman. A marriage or a solid relationship would have been the best thing for her in her situation. But Molly had been his, in his mind at least, as far back as he could remember. And he'd been hers. Not that he'd been a monk in the past years. But there had never been another Molly.

One corner of the room was noticeably bare, except for some shelving that housed her stereo system. He strode over and hunkered down to take a look at her CD collection. Music had been as important to her as it was to him, and he was glad to see she still managed this one extravagance. Let's see...she liked Garth. She liked Reba. She liked George Strait *a lot.* He pulled out about a dozen of his CDs, feeling maybe a tad jealous. Then he came to the Kick Cochranes. She had them all, every single one. Whatever it was about him she'd decided she couldn't stomach anymore, it hadn't been his voice.

He picked up the first one, *Bad For Each Other,* and half laughed, half winced as he regarded his image on the cover. God, if he didn't look full of himself. Hip cocked, jeans low-slung despite the tooled leather belt with the hammered silver buckle, big as a hubcap. Black hat, black hair, black eyes, affecting a lazy half grin that proposed to look both sexy and sweet as he peered out from under the wide brim of his Stetson. He'd never been able to take his public persona too seriously.

Remembering how he and Molly had laughed over the title song, a wave of nostalgia washed through him. It was everyone's opinion about them—"Bad For Each Other." He was from a hardscrabble background. Hardworking, hard-fighting, and hard-loving. Redneck and proud of it.

She was a daughter of privilege. Her daddy was the owner of the biggest furniture and appliance store in Wheeling and a councilman to boot. Of course, he had his hard-drinking and hard-loving side, too, but that was generally forgiven, considering the shrew he'd married. But he'd had no mind for business, was way too easy with the credit customers and died under a mountain of debt. Charlie did wince when he recalled that hellacious night.

He slipped the CD back into its slot. He'd always felt he owed her a big share of that album, and from the look of things, she could have used the money. He ran his fingers along the rest of her collection. She still liked Mozart and Chopin, too. Piano was her first love.

As that thought struck, he glanced quickly around the room. That's what was missing. As long as he'd known her, she'd always had a piano. Even in that ramshackle hole-in-the-wall they'd shared for a time, she'd brought her little spinet from home.

He stood, hands on his hips. That empty space along the adjacent wall now looked suspiciously bare. He moved to the spot. Indentations from the heavy piece of furniture remained in the carpet. A dull heaviness settled in his chest. He strongly suspected Molly had resorted to selling her possessions to care for their son.

Suddenly, he needed to get out, to be off to himself, to think. It was early yet. There wouldn't be many people about. And Molly was still asleep. He grabbed her keys from the counter where she had dropped them, and left the apartment.

Molly shrugged into her robe and belted it tightly. She put her ear to the door and listened for a few moments before opening it. This is stupid, she told herself. You're in your own home. But she wanted to meet Charlie on her terms, and before she'd showered and dressed wasn't her best time.

Cautiously, she stepped out into the hall. The door to Tobie's room stood wide and the bathroom was empty. He'd already been in there, she realized, seeing his shaving things on the shelf above the toilet tank. He was still an early riser. He'd never required much sleep. She remembered when his restlessness caused him problems in school, but it probably worked to his advantage now.

He still used a safety razor, too, she thought, lifting his and turning it in her hand. She recalled clearly the day when he had switched from the electric shaver he'd gotten as a present from someone. He had noticed the marks left on her breasts from his whiskers and decided an electric didn't get close enough. She replaced the razor, swamped with an overwhelming regret for those lost times. How had it come to this?

She disrobed and stepped into the shower, turning the water on as hot as she could stand it.

When she opened the bathroom door a little while later, the aroma of fresh-brewed coffee teased her nose. *Charlie.* She hurried to her room, quickly slipped into her clothes, and wove her wet hair into a thick braid.

As she rounded the corner from the hall, she saw him sitting at the counter where she and Tobie ate their meals. He had his nose in the morning paper, his hand curled around a mug of coffee, two fingers thrust through the handle hole, the way he always held it. There was something different about the picture he presented, but she couldn't put her finger on just what.

He eyed her over the top of the paper and indicated with a nod of his head the bag sitting on the counter next to the Swedish ivy. At the sight of the familiar white bag with pink-and-orange lettering running up the center, her stomach gave an audible growl and she saw Charlie grin. She reached for the bag and opened it. Two chocolate honey-dipped. Her favorite. "Is one of these for me?"

"They both are. I've had mine. I still can't abide chocolate."

Judging from the powdery residue at the corner of his mouth, he still preferred raspberry jelly-filled. As if he read her thoughts, his tongue came out to swipe away the sugar, and she had a sudden knee-weakening recollection of sweet-mouthed morning kisses.

In an effort to get a grip on her emotions, she walked over to the coffee maker and poured herself a cup. There was only one other stool at the counter. The one alongside Charlie. She hiked herself up on it and dug into the donut bag.

He put his paper down and turned on the stool to face her. Leaning back against the wall behind him, he eyed her lazily. "When did you start wearing your hair like that?"

She took a bite of donut and washed it down with a sip of coffee before she answered. "You don't like it?"

"I like that it's long."

Oh, yes. He had liked it long. It never seemed to matter to him that she couldn't do anything with the rowdy riot of red. "I don't have a lot of time to spend on my appearance these days. This style is easy."

He folded his arms across his chest and twisted slowly on the seat, knees spread, boot heels caught on the metal rung of the stool. Completely at his ease. "What else is keeping you busy these days? What kind of work do you do?"

"I'm a paralegal." Not the lawyer she'd planned on being. With little money and no help with Tobie, she'd had to put those dreams aside. It seemed another lifetime now, since she'd entertained that goal. It no longer seemed important.

"Do you like your work?"

Why all these questions? She sighed. "It's interesting. The firm I work for has been good to me since Tobie's been sick."

"Would you quit if you could, and stay home?"

She stared into her coffee cup. How many times had she wished for that choice when Tobie was very small? And now, when there might be so little time...

"I have to work. There's no way I can meet these medical bills without my health insurance."

He straightened away from the wall and leaned toward her. "That's not a consideration anymore, Molly. I'll write a check."

She swung her head around to look at him, mouth agape.

He'd write a check! Just like that. For the first time it really sank in, just what she was dealing with. Her family had been well-off, or at least she had thought so, when she was growing up. But nothing like this. For Charlie, money really was no object. "I couldn't—"

He gripped her chin, not to hurt, but firm all the same. "You're gonna be my wife. Not some fancy piece I keep on the side. *My wife.* You can work if you want to, but you won't have to."

"Charlie…"

"I'm not interested in some sham, either." He went on as if she hadn't spoken. "This'll be a real marriage. I'll have claims on you, and you'll have claims on me."

She licked her lips and pressed her fists to the edge of the counter, all appetite gone.

"You about finished there?" He nodded at her half-eaten donut and coffee. "I'd like to meet my son."

"Charlie." She looked at him, pleading. "Would you give me a few minutes with him…to explain?"

His gaze hardened. "You've had seven years to do your explaining. I'll be there this time." He rose, grabbing his hat and her keys. "Let's go."

Chapter 3

Except for the engine knock, there was silence in the car following Molly's terse directions to the hospital. Charlie felt more uneasy about the coming meeting than he cared to let on.

Despite Molly's claim that Tobie hadn't asked questions, he was bound to have some. How could he explain where he'd been for the last seven years? Without blaming Molly. And justified as he felt his anger was, he couldn't see any benefit from causing a rift between her and the boy. Everything he'd seen in the apartment pointed to Molly's excellence as a mother. The fact that she couldn't tolerate the presence of Tobie's father didn't change that.

He patted the pockets of his shirt before reaching into the side pocket of his jacket and pulling out a package of gum. He unwrapped a stick, folded it in half, and popped it in his mouth. Belatedly, he offered a piece to Molly.

He found her watching him with a bemused expression, the first hint of laughter in her eyes since she'd come back into his life.

"What?"

A smile tugged at her lips. "When did you quit smoking?" she asked, shaking her head at his offer of the gum.

He shifted her an uneasy glance. "Let's see…two years, three months, two weeks…" That was a big grin she was wearing now. Did the same thing to his insides it always had. "Four days, and—" he shoved his jacket sleeve up and looked at his watch "—nine hours." He gave her an abashed smile. "I'm not sure about the minutes. I didn't check the time when I finished that last puff, *but* I still miss it now and then." He shrugged. "It's hard on the throat."

So that was the change she hadn't been able to put her finger on, she realized with a quiet laugh. *Hard on the throat.* Probably not a good thing in his line of work. When had he become so responsible? Maybe other things about him had changed as well, but she didn't have high hopes. He was still devastatingly handsome, good-natured, with an easy grace. Just like her daddy. And now he had a confidence, a self-assuredness, he'd lacked before. The women would flock to him like ants to a picnic. How would she ever be able to live with that?

Charlie steered the car into the hospital parking garage, surveying the area as he did. So far, so good. No one but Harlan and his family knew where he had gone last night, and they wouldn't talk. But he knew his anonymity wouldn't last. It was too much to expect he could get through what had to be done at the hospital without being recognized. He just hoped this wouldn't turn into a circus. He guided the car into a space, switched off the ignition and turned to Molly. He saw his own trepidation mirrored in her face. "Let's go see Tobie," he said.

They entered through the main door of the hospital in the old section, where their footsteps echoed in the vaulted lobby. The visitors' desk, a huge mahogany piece that reminded Charlie of a bar, was off to one side. He held back a little while Molly got the passes. Two women worked behind the desk. The younger one, with the nose ring, gave him the once-over and went back to filing her nails. He'd almost started to breathe again, when the other lady, the one with blued hair and penciled brows, looked his way. Her eyes and mouth formed the perfect circles he'd come to recognize and sometimes dread.

"Aren't you Kick—"

He came closer, keeping his voice low, hoping she'd do the same. "Yes, ma'am, I am."

Nose Ring bestirred herself enough to give him another quick look-see but was apparently unimpressed. Blue Hair was another story. She rose from her chair behind the desk, her mouth working. "I admire your music so..." Her voice rebounded off the walls of the spacious lobby.

This had all the makings of a scene. In an effort to avoid it, he grasped her hand. "Thank you. I appreciate that. But I'm here to see a patient. I was hoping..."

"Oh! Of course." She collected herself nicely. "If you wouldn't mind..."

She slid a paper across the desk to him—room rates it looked like—and handed him a pen. "I don't mind," he smiled his answer, "as long as it's not a bill." He scrawled his name while Molly stood by, staring at the floor.

When he had finished, Molly led the way to the Transplant Unit. It was in the newer section of the hospital, where the ceilings were about ten feet lower and marble and mahogany gave way to Formica and Sheetrock. Along the way they passed people who talked behind their hands, heads swiveling. Charlie did his best to ignore it, noting that Molly kept her eyes focused straight ahead.

Though the wait had seemed endless since he'd learned he had a son, Charlie was unprepared when Molly turned into Tobie's room. He pulled in a long breath and followed.

She should have warned him. She realized it as soon as they stepped into the room. Thank God, Tobie was asleep. His first glimpse of his father's face wouldn't be of the dismay registered there before Charlie had a chance to cover it. She had lived with the gradual changes in her son for so long she no longer really saw them. But he bore little resemblance to the active, healthy boy in the picture she had given Charlie.

The stark black of his hair was the only swatch of color

against pale skin and white sheets, unless you counted the bruises. They covered his exposed skin.

Charlie looked shaken. Molly touched his arm. "We need to wash our hands. It's the most important thing in protecting him from infection. We don't have to wear masks or gloves."

They removed their jackets and she showed him the bathroom next to the entrance to Tobie's room and indicated the special scrub the nurses had told her to use. He said nothing while they washed side by side, but as he wiped his arms and hands down with paper towels he lifted his gaze to her. "He's real bad, isn't he?"

She couldn't give him hope she didn't have. "Yes," she said. "Some people live a long time with this, but his disease has progressed very rapidly."

"What if I'm not a match?"

"You come from a huge family, Charlie. Maybe one of them will match. We'll deal with it when the time comes." She sensed he needed this reassurance, faced with the loss of a child he hadn't yet come to know.

She turned to leave the bathroom, but he grabbed her arm.

"Did you tell him you were coming for me?"

She had debated with herself over that. Whether or not to prepare Tobie to meet his father. In the end she'd decided the chance Charlie would refuse to help posed too great a risk. "No," she said. "He has no idea. When I left here yesterday, he thought I was just going home."

A movement from the bed caught their attention. Tobie was waking. Molly moved to his side and kissed his brow. "I've brought someone to meet you, honey." She said the words in a rush, before he had time to question the presence of the man behind her.

Charlie stepped to the bed and put his hand on the rail. Dawning recognition washed across the youngster's face. His gaze flew to his mother, questioning.

"He's your father, Tobie."

Charlie watched the emotions flickering in the boy's eyes. Disbelief, wonder, puzzlement. A kind of wariness seemed to settle in for the long haul. Well, he couldn't begrudge him that. He'd be a little suspicious himself, given the same circumstances. He said nothing and waited for his son's first words to him.

"Where ya been?"

In three words Tobie had cut past awe, intimidation, anger, to the heart of the matter. The part that concerned him. It was funny in a way, but Charlie didn't feel like laughing. Molly bent, anxious to explain, but he stilled her with a hand on her shoulder. "I'm here now," he said firmly, "and I ain't leavin'."

Tobie's eyes again searched out Molly's. "But, Mom, he's—"

"Yes, he is, honey, but he's also your dad."

"I'd be happy if you'd call me that, too, Tobie."

At Charlie's words, Tobie gave him another quick appraisal, then slid a glance to his mother. She'd have some big-time explaining to do, Charlie guessed. When the boy's gaze returned to him once more, it was guarded, watchful. "I'll think about it," he said with a quiet reserve. Clearly, Charlie would have to earn his son's trust.

He reached across the bed to stroke Tobie's forehead, to touch for the first time this child of his seed, and Molly's. He was caught unawares by the force of his reaction. He came from a big, loving family. He knew the strength of those ties. But he'd never before experienced them from the parents' side. Never understood what made them put up with the guff, the whining, the bad behavior. Now he knew. There was nothing pretty or delicate about this bond. It was feral, untamed, frightening in its intensity. He would step in front of a train for his child, simple as that.

And he knew that he shared this bond with Molly. He understood, now, what had brought her to him, in spite of her fears. What he would never understand is what had kept her away.

At a sound behind him, he turned. A tall, middle-aged man with sad eyes walked in. He wore a white coat and had a stethoscope draped around his neck. A definite clue as to his line of work, Charlie thought. Molly introduced Dr. Morrissey. When Charlie shook his hand, he noted the recognition in the man's eyes. Country music fans came in all kinds of packages.

Morrissey did a brief examination of Tobie. Charlie caught sight of an ugly-looking tube protruding near Tobie's collarbone when the doctor raised the pajama top to listen to his chest. If nothing else, the tube served to deflect attention from Tobie's protruding ribs. Charlie turned away, wondering again if he would have what his son needed to survive.

As Morrissey straightened from the bedside, he directed his attention to Charlie. "I can take a sample of your blood now, for matching purposes," he said.

"You'll do it?" Charlie asked, a little surprised that he would bother himself with such a mundane task.

"I know how," he replied with a quiet smile.

After a few more words to Molly and Tobie, they left the room. As Morrissey guided him to a cluttered utility room on the unit, Charlie sensed the doctor had more than blood samples on his mind. He had the distinct impression the man was sizing him up. Fair enough, he supposed, since he was doing the same thing.

Morrissey gestured him toward a chair that had a side arm and reminded Charlie of a school desk. He took a seat and watched as the doctor rummaged in a drawer for some rubber-topped glass tubes and a syringe. When the older man seated himself in front of him, Charlie unbuttoned his cuff and rolled up his sleeve.

"We'll be testing your blood for other things, while we're at it, to make sure you're in general good health before we consider a transplant," Morrissey said.

Charlie thought he understood the implications of that. "A celebrity's life isn't always as colorful as the tabloids would have you believe. I don't have any diseases you need to worry about."

The man only grunted and laid out the tubes. Charlie glanced away. "What exactly are you looking for? For the transplant, I mean." He winced while the doctor cinched the rubber tourniquet around his biceps.

"Briefly, what we're after is called an HLA type. It's located on the sixth chromosome and inherited much the same way eye color and curly or straight hair is. Each parent has two of what we call haplotypes and gives one to a child. That makes four possible combinations for any one child, and that's why there's a one in four chance that any sibling will be a match." He paused and pulled on gloves. "Make a fist."

Charlie did as he was told and averted his eyes. He'd seen drinking straws that looked smaller than that needle. He decided to step gingerly around the minefield of siblings. Even if they were of a mind to try it, there wasn't time. "What are the odds of a parent being a match?" He felt a vigorous swabbing at his elbow bend.

"One in five thousand."

Charlie felt as if he'd been sucker-punched. He couldn't draw a breath. On the bright side, if you could call it that, he hadn't even felt the needle go in. Still, this gave him some sense of Molly's desperation to find him and his "huge" family. Anything to improve Tobie's chances. "That's better than the odds of finding a match in the population at large," he heard the man go on. *God,* what they were up against!

"I wouldn't bet on a horse with those odds," he said.

"We're in a different kind of race."

Charlie leaned his head back against the wall and stared at the ceiling while Morrissey applied a gauze patch and Band-Aid to his arm. After a few minutes he straightened to find the doctor writing on the tube labels. He pulled his shirtsleeve down and buttoned it.

When Morrissey finished, he addressed Charlie again. "We'll have the results in a few days. I'll call you into my office, privately, to discuss them with you."

There was something in his tone.... "Why the secrecy?" Charlie asked.

The other man rubbed his hands over his thighs. "A transplant—any transplant, but particularly one for bone marrow— is as hard on the donor as it is on the person receiving the tissue. You'll have to undergo anesthesia. There's going to be pain. You'll need to stay in the hospital overnight. You—"

"Are you saying I might not be willing...."

"I'm saying you have the right to decide, without any pressure from anyone else. If you don't want to do it, we'll just tell his mother you're not a good match. That's our usual procedure."

Charlie figured his confusion must have been apparent. The doctor continued in clipped, impersonal tones. "There's more to this matching process than identical tissue. There are psychological...emotional...issues to consider. We're required to fully inform you of your options, one of them being that you can choose not to do this."

Charlie kneaded the back of his neck, unable to believe what he was hearing. "I'd do this for a stranger," he said.

The doctor's mouth thinned and he shifted his gaze away.

Suddenly, Charlie went very cold. The man's meaning couldn't have been clearer. For all practical purposes, Tobie *was* a stranger.

"What did Molly tell you...about me?"

"Nothing. I had no idea who you were until I saw you in that room."

Charlie swiped a hand across his mouth and let out a long sigh. "I don't know what you think," he said at last, "but this was no one-night stand. Molly and me...we go way back." The guy didn't look convinced. "We're getting married."

The other man leaned on his elbows and clasped his hands between his knees. "Somehow I don't have the impression congratulations are in order."

Charlie had to give him credit. He didn't pull any punches. He had the feeling they were getting down to the lick-log now. "What are you really saying, Doc?"

"I'm saying the animosity between you two in that room was thick enough to spread on toast."

"And?"

"And..." Charlie sensed the man taking his measure. "Let me tell you a little bit about my job." He sat up straighter and drew a long breath. "If you're a match, we're going to take marrow from your hipbone, put it in an IV bag and transfuse it into Tobie through that tube on his chest *you* didn't want to look at.''

Charlie blinked. The man didn't miss much.

"By some miracle—and yes, it is a miracle. We don't understand how it happens—the marrow finds its way from his vein to where it's needed. That's the easy part. Tobie will be in the hospital for at least six weeks of daily blood tests and boring routine. That's where his state of mind becomes a factor.''

Ahhh. Now he knew where this was headed. He listened, every sense alert.

"We can't measure how much a patient's will to live affects his recovery. But anyone who's worked in medicine as long as I have knows it's crucial. I don't want any conflict in his life at this point if it can be avoided.''

"Meaning?"

The doctor eyed him levelly. "He loves his mother. If you can't get along with her, it would be better for him if you just donated your marrow and walked away.'' He rose and gathered up the specimen tubes. "I'll drop these off at the desk and finish my rounds. You can find your way back to Tobie's room?''

Charlie nodded absently and Morrissey left. He sat staring at nothing. He had the feeling he'd just been pretty soundly chewed out and he wasn't sure why. Of course, Morrissey didn't know the whole story, or even a big part of it. But the doctor wasn't concerned with that. He was only interested in what affected Tobie, and he was right.

It wouldn't be enough for him to marry Molly and only tolerate her in some cold relationship. She'd grown up with that. She couldn't help but communicate her misery to the boy.

No, he'd have to convince Tobie that he loved her. Like he used to. God! What a mess.

Molly and Charlie spent the rest of the day with Tobie. They covered each other for meals in the hospital cafeteria, so he was never alone. The boy was a little reserved, guarded, with Charlie at first, but he warmed up considerably when the conversation turned to his father's hat and boots. The hat especially seemed to catch his interest, and Charlie explained the system of *X*s used to grade a Stetson and the proper way to handle one. He borrowed a tape measure from the nurses' station to size Tobie, and promised he'd bring a hat for him on his next trip through.

That introduced a painful topic. Charlie pretty much earned his living on the road, and he'd have to get back to it. A lot of lives and families, from the other band members to his bus drivers, depended on his ability to perform. Summer was approaching, the height of the touring season. He'd see Tobie through the testing, however that worked out. He'd line up the other members of his family, if necessary. God willing, they'd find a match, there'd be a transplant, and he'd see Tobie stabilized. Then he'd have to go. Like it or not, he'd have to go.

They left when Tobie showed signs of tiring, promising to be back the next day. Charlie had seen enough sidelong glances cast his way to suspect what would be waiting for them at the hospital entrance, and he was right. Security personnel had kept them out of the hospital proper, but media types hovered on the grounds just outside the front door. Molly was startled, but Charlie seemed resigned to the situation.

He conferred for a few minutes with one of the guards, then came back to Molly.

"Here's the plan," he told her. "You get the car and bring it around the side entrance over by the lab. I'll wait inside until I see you and then make a dash for it."

It sounded good to her. They'd never expect Kick Cochrane to be making his escape in a bucket of rust like her old clunker.

"I'll make arrangements with the administration here to talk to the press tomorrow and maybe they'll leave us alone," he added.

Molly had no difficulty slipping through and retrieving the car, but a lookout spotted Charlie as soon as he stepped outside. He ran for the car, and Molly stretched over the console to push the door open for him. As soon as he was in, she hit the gas. They took the corner on two squealing wheels and headed down the street, more than a touch over the limit.

When she stopped for a light a couple blocks down, Molly hazarded a glance at Charlie. He was white, one hand stiff-armed against the dash and the other clinging to the door handle. "Who the hell taught you how to drive?" he yelled.

Maybe it was the strain of the past weeks and months. Maybe it was the hurt, knowing she'd been wronged and knowing she could do nothing about it. Maybe it was the simple pain and pleasure of seeing Charlie again. Whatever. Suddenly it all bubbled up inside her, demanding release. "You did," she said, and laughed.

God, he remembered so much, but he'd forgotten about her laugh. This was no delicate titter behind her hand, no high-pitched giggle. Molly's laugh was a throaty, full-bodied guffaw. He'd never been able to hear it without laughing himself. This time was no exception.

They laughed until they were limp and their sides hurt. The cars behind them were honking for them to go. Molly eased ahead at a more sedate pace.

"I never taught you that little maneuver back there," Charlie said, rubbing the moisture from his eyes.

"I've managed to learn a few things for myself," she replied with a sniff.

"Pull up here for a minute. I want to make a stop." Charlie indicated a strip mall they were approaching and Molly swung into a parking space. She frowned when Charlie reached over and grabbed the keys from the ignition, but she said nothing. He went into an automotive parts store and returned a few minutes later carrying a brown paper bag. Before Molly could get a glimpse of what was inside, he loaded it into the hatch. She was reaching to get the passenger door for him when she heard his knuckles rapping against the window on her side. She opened the door and he waved her over.

"I can wait to find out what other things you've managed to learn for yourself, if you don't mind."

She gave a hoot, but clambered over the console and gear-shift to the passenger seat. They had driven a short way when Charlie asked, "What are the laws about getting married in Pennsylvania?"

"I don't know. I've never been married in Pennsylvania." She caught him looking at her. "But I'll find out."

"I'd like Cleeve to come up."

She nodded.

Charlie slid her another glance. "Is there anyone you'd especially like to have there?"

Molly thought for a minute. "My landlady."

"Would that be a little lady about four foot by four foot, who favors pink curlers and furry slippers?"

Molly smiled. "You've met."

"This morning, when I went out."

"She's a fan."

Charlie gave a low chuckle. "I know. She's pleased we're getting married."

Molly turned to him. "I'd like Tobie to be there. Maybe we could arrange to have the wedding in his room."

Charlie nodded. "That'd be nice."

They drove in silence for a while, lost in their thoughts. When they pulled in front of Molly's apartment, Charlie turned to her again, his face shadowed in the dusk. He seemed to weigh his words before speaking.

"Did you write me, Molly? Did it get lost somewhere, and you thought I didn't answer?"

She closed her eyes against the temptation to put the blame where it belonged. She couldn't do it. As bad as he believed her behavior was, the truth was worse. She shook her head, heavy with regret. "I never wrote," she said.

They settled into a fragile routine of sorts over the next few days. Considerate of each other and polite, if distant.

Molly sensed that Charlie was making a special effort to get along, even going so far as to hold her hand when they entered Tobie's room. She wondered at his motives, but didn't question what she saw as her good fortune.

She became accustomed to waking to the smell of coffee brewing. The morning after their first visit to Tobie, she showered and poured herself a cup, settling down with another donut before she realized Charlie wasn't in the apartment. He came in, after a bit, covered with grease and she remembered their stop at the auto-parts store. She had new plugs and an oil change, he informed her on his way to the bathroom. His work on the old crate didn't come with any guarantees, though. They were going out to look for something more reliable that very afternoon.

For the second day in a row, Molly lost her appetite after half a donut.

Something more reliable turned out to be a Mercury Villager, fully-equipped, AM-FM, cassette, cruise control, power windows, passenger-area stereo and climate controls, internal and external thermometers, and a heater that you didn't need pliers to turn on. When she suggested that he might like to keep the car with him, he replied that he couldn't imagine why. He had transportation in Wheeling and a driver on the road.

His grease-covered clothes and the ones he was wearing were the only things he'd brought with him. He decided to take some time, while she stayed with Tobie, to go outfit himself. He gave Molly cash, saying he trusted her to find something suitable for a wedding and, if it wasn't asking too much, would she please wear her hair loose?

When he returned to the hospital room, he brought with him a simple flat-top guitar. He didn't always sleep nights, he explained, and he used the time to pick and compose. Molly figured it probably wasn't much more expensive, at least as far as he was concerned, just to buy another guitar rather than have one shipped from wherever he kept *however* many he had. She felt a little more charitable about the idea when she saw the pleasure Tobie took in learning the chords from his father.

At some point they found the time to visit the county building and fill out the necessary papers. Molly arranged with her pastor to marry them in Tobie's room late the following week.

And the reality began to sink in. She was going to marry the only man she had ever loved, under circumstances that filled her with dread.

Tobie wore out early the third day and they decided it would be best to let him sleep. They returned to the apartment and Molly made a macaroni-and-cheese casserole, one of Charlie's favorites from their scrimping days. Charlie had a beer and she unbent enough to have one, too.

The kitchen cleaned up, he uncapped two more long-necks and led the way into the living room. They sat on opposite ends of the sofa, a small lamp on the kitchen counter the only light in the room. Charlie watched her peel the label off the bottle with her chewed-up nails for a few minutes before he spoke.

"What happened to your piano?"

Her eyes went unerringly to the spot where he suspected it had been. She shrugged. "I didn't have much time to play anymore. It's hard in an apartment anyway, finding time when it won't bother the other residents."

He took a long pull on his beer. "If I remember correctly, your playing wouldn't have bothered anyone." He saw her sad smile. "Did you make some money on it?"

She shrugged again and nodded. "That, too." As if to avoid any further reason to talk, she took a ladylike sip of her beer and pursed her lips. When he made no effort to carry the conversation, she continued. "I gave lessons for a while, but between work and Tobie…" Her voice drifted off.

Charlie's hand tightened on his bottle. "Why, Molly? Even if you hated my guts, you were entitled—*Tobie* was entitled—to my support."

"I never hated you," she whispered.

He stared at her for some moments. "Was there another man?"

She looked up sharply and gave a short laugh. "I was working all the time and had a young child. Men weren't exactly beating down my door."

"A woman with a child doesn't scare a man off. I've kissed a few myself."

"How charming of you to say so." She took another drink and turned her gaze away.

Aw, hell. The same old needling. Same old accusations. How were they ever going to get past this? "Don't get sideways. They weren't bound to anyone then, and neither was I."

She straightened and lifted her chin. He saw her swallow. "I've decided to give notice at work...to stay home."

Maybe she was coming around, after all. "I think that's a good idea."

She toyed with the little pile of shredded label in her lap. "Tobie won't be able to go to school for a year after the transplant. It will be so much easier if I can stay with him." She angled a hesitant glance at him. "I know you'll be gone a lot."

Was that wishful thinking? he wondered. No matter. Whether he liked it or not, it was true.

She took a deep breath and went on. "We could talk to one of the lawyers in my office. About a prenuptial agreement, I mean. They're very ethical. They wouldn't...just because I worked for..."

Son of a bitch. She had this down to an art. Learned it at her mother's knee, no doubt. "You afraid I'm gonna run off with all your money, Moll?"

She had the grace to blush, and damn if it didn't make him feel like a heel.

"I was thinking of you," she said.

He watched the sweat drip down her bottle and settle like tears on her fingers. "I never cared about money when I didn't have any," he told her. "I still don't." He shook his head, disgusted. "If we're gonna get along at all, I don't want to hear any more about this."

Seeing her square her shoulders and nod, he felt a reluctant admiration for her. Suddenly, he was sick of this whole conversation. He stretched his arm across the back of the couch and tangled a finger in a silky tendril that had worked free of her braid. She went still but didn't draw away. His finger strayed to the soft, warm skin of her nape, where tiny hairs grew.

"I don't want to talk at all, Molly," he said in a husky whisper. She didn't move, didn't even breathe. He opened his hand, so that his thumb just grazed her collarbone above the neckline of her shirt. He felt her sharp intake of breath and the gentle quivering of her flesh. "I can make it good for you." His thumb slid back and forth. "I've learned some."

He lost her in that instant, he knew it. Any softening he had detected was gone. He could feel her stiffening, her withdrawal, under his hand. He could have cursed his brainless allusion to other women, other times.

"I'm sure you have."

He pulled his hand away and settled it behind her on the sofa. "Are you gonna make me wait?"

"Oh, please, Charlie." She turned her beautiful brown eyes, wide with undisguised hurt, to him.

He drained the last of his beer and looked at her again. "Will you be unwilling when we marry?"

She closed her eyes and shook her head. "No."

The ring of the phone broke into their painful impasse.

Charlie rose to answer, thinking as he did how completely, but superficially, he had moved into her life.

"That was Morrissey," he said when he hung up. Her eyes widened even more and she brought a hand up to cover her mouth. "He has the results. He wants to see me in his office first thing in the morning."

Chapter 4

Neither of them had any appetite for coffee or donuts in the morning. Molly assured Charlie that Dr. Morrissey all but lived at the hospital and seven-thirty wouldn't be too early. Shift report had not yet been completed when they made their way to the doctor's cramped office on the unit. Charlie took her hand outside the door.

"I don't care what he says, I want you with me when he gives me the results."

She couldn't quite identify the undertone she heard in Charlie's voice, but once Morrissey opened his office door, it didn't matter. She knew. This doctor had become the second most important person in her life over the past months, and she'd learned to read every shade in his expression. To gauge every nuance. She knew.

He motioned them to chairs, but her tears started to flow even before she reached hers. They seated themselves and Charlie gripped her fingers so tightly they went numb. He looked from her streaming face to Morrissey and swallowed.

"I'm not a match, am I?" His voice sounded tight, strangled.

"No, Charlie," she whispered on a shuddering breath. "You are."

Charlie shot a glance at the doctor.

"Yes," the man confirmed. He seemed to have some trouble getting the word out himself.

Charlie closed his eyes and leaned his head back, exhaling a long breath. His own eyes stung. "This is very rare," he heard the man go on. "I've read of cases at other centers, but we've never had one here. You and Ms. Doyle share an HLA type."

Yes. Bad for each other they might be, but they were the best possible combination for their son. He and Molly shared a haplotype. She had given Tobie that one, and Charlie had given him the other. He and Tobie were a perfect match.

The rest of what the doctor had to say scarcely registered, but they were given written instructions to take with them. Molly was still weepy when they left the office. Charlie hauled her into his arms and hugged her close. For the moment, their anger, hurt and distrust were forgotten, submerged in their mutual joy.

Tobie was just getting his breakfast tray when they entered his room. He greeted their earth-shattering news with all the equanimity of a seven-year-old who had no real conception of what was going on. He didn't like orange juice with pulp. Could they please get him some apple?

Charlie sent Molly for something to eat while he kept Tobie company. They dug a deck of cards out of the over-bed table. Go Fish was no more scintillating than it had been when Charlie was seven, so he offered to teach Tobie Five Card Stud. He'd played with his brothers for cigarettes and matches, neither of which was an option here. He'd also played with Molly for various articles of apparel. Vivid memories of those games flashed through his mind. They'd been fun. Molly had never had much of a poker face and he'd never considered cheating beneath him.

He chanced a peek at his son's innocent face. Better not plant any of those ideas. They'd crop up soon enough on their own. They settled on pennies, and Charlie had to stake Tobie some.

"How'd you get a name like that?"

The boy checked his hole card like an old hand. Maybe that was hereditary, too. "What? Charlie?"

"No." Tobie gave him a long-suffering look. "Kick."

Charlie started to answer, then caught himself. He wasn't sure just how much information Molly had provided on this topic. "I was an active child."

"When you were in your mom's tummy, you mean?"

"Yeah." That cleared that up. This parenting bit was going to take some getting used to.

"You're high card, Dad. You bet."

The kid was smooth. Slid that in real subtle-like. But it was the first time he'd called him "Dad" and Charlie noticed. He was afraid he'd go all teary, like some old lady. As a result he bet too much on a garbage hand.

When Molly strolled in a little while later, Charlie was about cleaned out. "You're not doing too well," she said.

"Beginner's luck."

She rolled her eyes. "He didn't lead you to believe he's never played before, did he?"

Charlie's startled gaze met hers. She laughed her throaty laugh. "I've got some beachfront property in Kansas you might be interested in."

At Charlie's disgruntled look, Tobie shrugged, unfazed. "You didn't ask."

Molly laughed again. "Like father, like son."

For Molly and Charlie the following days both dragged and flew by. The time spent with Tobie was easy, comfortable between them. They were united in their concern for his well-being.

Together they strove to keep him amused and cheerful when his strength and spirit waned. They coaxed him to take the medications that would prepare him for the transplant and did their best to support him through the side effects.

In an effort to remain free of colds or other infections, they both sharply curtailed their contacts with other people. Charlie, in particular, was careful to avoid anything that might jeopardize the transplant. And with the administration of drugs to completely eradicate his own bone marrow, Tobie's strength continued to ebb.

As a result, Molly and Charlie found they were spending more and more time alone together. That time was not so easy, not so comfortable. They had taken to retiring early to their separate rooms, separate thoughts.

Lying on her back, staring into the darkness, Molly heard Charlie leave his room and prowl the apartment again. The groan of the hallway floor, the thunk of the refrigerator door, the clink of a bottle being uncapped seeped through the thin walls. He would be up for a while. Again. He hadn't repeated his suggestion that they resume their sexual relationship. But he wanted to, she could tell. And so did she.

Molly couldn't explain, even to herself, exactly why she was reluctant to sleep with Charlie before the wedding. Certainly, she loved him. Knowing what she did now, she loved him more than she ever had. Maybe, in some perverse way, that was part of it. She knew if he had ever loved *her,* he didn't now.

She turned on her side and wrapped the pillow over her ears as strains from his guitar softly beckoned. Always, she had been unsure of her ability to hold him. She'd never considered herself pretty enough, vivacious enough, *fun* enough to keep his interest. Uncertain of her own attractiveness, she'd been excruciatingly aware of his. She remembered those early days, watching him perform in the clubs and bars. Sitting on the sidelines with her painted-on smile. In his line of work, there were always women. The women were bold, and he was gracious. She buried her face in the bedclothes, recalling with shame her accusations and his denials. Until, finally, the denials had ceased, and she feared she was becoming what she dreaded most, a pathetic creature like her mother, withering in the shadow of a charismatic man.

But now there was Tobie to consider. She loosened her grip on the pillow. Tobie was every bit as captivated by his father, in his own way, as the women were. And Charlie could provide for him in a manner beyond her imaginings. Money, glamour, his very body met Tobie's needs in ways she couldn't. In any tug-of-war for Tobie's affections, she feared she would come up short.

To his credit, Charlie didn't seem interested in a tug-of-war. Despite the questions she knew must plague him, the resentment he must harbor, he was going out of his way to be agreeable. She rolled to her back, arms spread, listening to the evocative notes drifting on the still night. They lured her, beguiled her, summoned her.

She shoved back the covers and slid her legs over the edge of the mattress, sitting up. The simple cotton sleep-shirt she wore was not the stuff of seduction, she decided ruefully. Then, Charlie had never been too particular about such things. He preferred to sleep skin-to-skin. She felt a flush warm her at the memory. Before her courage could desert her, she pushed from the bed and stepped into the hall.

Deep in concentration, he didn't even notice her presence. Barefoot, bare-chested, he appeared to have pulled on a pair of jeans and nothing else. She hadn't seen him like this in eight years, and he stole her breath. Nothing of the boy remained. His shoulders gleamed, a smooth burnished gold, in the lamplight. Muscles rippled and swelled with the movement of his hands on the guitar he cradled over his spread thighs. What she could see of his chest was shadowed with dark hair. And his hands—oh, his hands—touched the guitar strings as they had once caressed her. She remembered them on her, brown, long-fingered, calloused from his playing, gentle and caring. Would he ever touch her like that again?

His face drew her gaze and she was struck by the single-mindedness of his concentration. As he strummed, he crooned soft words into a little cassette player on the table next to him. Something displeased him. With a grimace, he punched the stop button on the player and plowed a hand through his hair, disgustedly. Reaching for the beer at his foot, he looked up and saw her.

She was a vision out of the past. In the dim light, eight

years disappeared. Coltish, he'd thought her then, and he saw her so now. Still with the slender, long arms and legs she would wrap around him, and he'd ride her to a mindless heaven. Chestier than any colt he'd ever seen, though. God help him, he liked a chesty woman and he wasn't going to apologize for it. He wondered if she had any idea how little that faded old shirt concealed.

Her hair was loose. He'd begun to think she slept with it in that damn braid. The tangled mop hung halfway down her back, longer than it looked when she had it all bound up. He ached to bury his face in the riotous curls, to inhale the fragrance that had tantalized him anew over the past week. The one he would associate with her till the day he died.

Jasmine.

Long ago he'd given up trying to determine what shampoo, what soap might be responsible for it. He'd decided it was some combination of whatever she wore and whatever her body chemistry did to it that made it uniquely her own.

He took a long pull on his beer, buying time. What did she want? There was a wariness, a vulnerability in her eyes. What had made her venture from her refuge?

"Did I wake you, Molly? I'm sorry."

She shook her head, her hair shimmering like new pennies. "I wasn't asleep." She crossed the short space between them hesitantly, giving him flashes of long thigh.

He watched her approach, scarcely able to breathe. He hoped she wasn't depending on his nobler instincts to make him behave. Living cheek by jowl with her for the past week had pretty well depleted them. God had only given him so much in the way of gallantry, and he was about out.

She parked herself on the footstool near his knee, hunched forward with her elbows on her thighs. Did a good job of hiding her chest, but he had a *lovely* view of her bottom. Unless he was mistaken, that was a panty line he spied, and it just about undid him.

She'd always been a modest young woman. Wore panties to bed every night. By the time he'd coaxed her out of them, he'd be as hot as a firecracker. He'd loved it. He had a sneaking suspicion she knew it, too. It was her ladylike way of being a tease. Was she teasing him now?

Nope. He didn't think so. That was skittishness in her eyes, and eagerness to please. Not desire. Hell, right now he'd settle for plain old lust, but he didn't see that, either. So why was she here?

"That was pretty." She nodded in the general direction of his guitar and tape player.

What was this all about? He loved music, but he didn't feel like discussing the finer points of composition at the moment. "That was crap, Moll." The light went out of her eyes as if he'd flicked a switch, and he felt like crud. He tried to soften his words. "I miss your piano."

That was true. He'd done some of his best work with her. Even when they were still kids, back when she'd discovered his writing. He'd get hung up on something with just the guitar. She'd tinkle out a two-fingered melody and the words would flow as though they were meant to be.

That was the real secret of his success. He'd always considered his voice only passable, but he could *write*. He didn't have to wait for decent material to come along. She'd had a lot to do with that. Her presence—and then her absence—had been his inspiration. She'd been the ache, the yearning in his songs.

She answered him with a nod and a tremulous smile, but he could tell his crude comment had pretty much destroyed whatever mood she'd been trying to set. "Was there something in particular you wanted?" he asked.

She didn't answer, just placed her open hand upon his thigh.

Ahhhh. This was coming clear now. He had to hand it to her. She could still surprise him.

"What is this, Molly? A reward? The man's proved himself useful, give him a tumble?"

"Charlie, don't."

"No. *You* don't. I don't know what I ever did to you that was so wrong. But I don't deserve—and I don't want—your charity."

With a stricken look she withdrew her hand and knotted it in her shirt.

He closed his eyes and exhaled a long, weary breath. "I'm in an ugly mood, Molly. Go to bed."

When he looked again, she was gone. But the jasmine lingered....

She was watching him again. She thought he couldn't see, but when you looked through that screen at just the right angle, it turned clear as window glass. She'd put her book aside on the glider seat awhile ago and sat with her chin resting in her hand, staring.

He resisted the temptation to strut. This was Molly, for crying out loud. But he knew he was looking good. He'd always be on the lean side, that ran in his family. Working out with the weights, though, had muscled his shoulders up real well.

He'd made the starting lineup for the Ironmen this coming year, his last at the high school. Well, he made it as kicker. He'd never have the weight to be a lineman. But he'd found his niche all the same. He was accurate, and he was fearless. He didn't care about getting sacked. The opposing team could unleash the whole Ohio Valley on him and he wouldn't rattle.

This would be his year with the ladies. They loved the football players. He unhitched the grass catcher and carried the load to the compost pile, feeling Molly's eyes burning right between his shoulder blades the whole time. That was one little lady he'd be happy to get out of his system.

He set the grass catcher on the ground, removed his hat, and stole a glance. Yep, she was looking all right. He pulled his T-shirt from his hip pocket and wiped down his face and chest. He shouldn't be having the kind of thoughts he was having about her. Hell, he *liked* her. She had a goofy sense of humor, and she'd turned out real sweet, considering the crap she put up with at home. She'd kept his secret about the composing, too. Didn't ride him about it like Lucy did.

He'd even showed her some of the stuff. She was good with words and he trusted her opinion. She'd looked at him like he was some kind of hero, some damn pagan god. Nobody else in the world ever looked at him like that. And him looking back like, when did her legs get that long? Where'd she get that *chest?*

He tamped his hat back on, disgustedly, and picked up the catcher. She's *too young,* Kick. She's not for you. Folks are right. Stick to your own kind. Don't go sniffin' around where you're nothing but the hired hand.

He walked back to the mower, ran it a few more swipes over the lawn, and pulled up again. Hell, it was hot. He squinted toward the house. Still watching. She'd gotten up from the glider and pressed her nose against the screen. He laughed to himself. Did she think he couldn't see? Her with that red head glinting like fire behind the screen where the sun caught it.

He'd heard she'd started dating. That jackass Jimmy Jordan, of all people. Well, her momma would be pleased. His family traveled in her circle. He was one person who'd never have to do a lick of work in his life. Classy guy, sitting back, taking everything that came his way, like he'd actually done something to earn it.

He had a real nasty mouth, though, discussing the girls in the locker room. Charlie had never heard Molly's name come up, or he might have felt obliged to bust his pretty nose, knock out a couple of those straight, white teeth his daddy had paid so much for. Although exactly what skin off *his* nose it might be, he couldn't say.

He needed something to drink. He looked for Molly again, to ask her, but she'd disappeared. No sense knocking on the door. Her old lady would only glare at him as if he'd stepped in something smelly and was trailing it through her house. He'd use the outdoor tap in that protected corner by the back porch, where the jasmine grew.

He strode over, turned on the faucet, and bent to take long gulps. The whap of a screen door sounded and bare feet with pink-painted nails appeared on the bottom porch step next to him. He followed the shapely line of slender legs up to find

Molly holding a droplet-covered glass of lemonade out to him.

"You looked hot," she said.

He licked his cold lips. "The water's fine, Molly."

"It's *poured,* Charlie." She extended her arm further toward him, insisting.

"You drink it."

She rolled her eyes. "We'll share." She took a sip and offered the glass to him again.

He accepted it from her, drinking his fill, draining it. His eyes drank their fill of her, too, over the edge of the glass. When he'd finished, he wiped his mouth on his forearm and pushed his hat back.

"Your momma know you cut your jeans off that short?"

"*Char*-leee."

"You're gonna give guys ideas."

She gave a desolate little sigh. "I don't think so."

"Like that ja...Jimmy Jordan."

"I'm not seeing him anymore."

"He'll get ideas real— What?"

"I'm not going out with him."

Had the creep tried something already? "Why not?"

She gave a one-shouldered shrug and he set the glass on the step to give his eyes somewhere else to look besides where they wanted to look. "He says I don't know how to kiss."

What a jerk. Probably never occurred to him that some things were worth a little effort. He watched her run her pink-tipped toes through the long grass near his boot. The sweet scent of jasmine hung heavy in the sultry air surrounding them.

"Would you teach me, Charlie?" she whispered.

"Huh?" He couldn't be hearing right.

"I don't know who else to ask," she rushed on. "I figured you've done it a time or two...."

"A time or two, yeah, but..."

"Lucy says..."

"You didn't discuss this with Lu—"

"No, but she says the girls talk about how you kiss." She stopped and bit her bottom lip. It looked puffy and real kissable when she went on. "I know I'm not pretty like them. I'm too tall and my hair's a mess. But you could pretend...."

She really thought she wasn't pretty. The dreams he was having about her at night had him flopping in his bed like a beached marlin, and she thought she wasn't pretty. What kind of a hellhole was she growing up in to have ideas like that about herself?

"Molly..."

"It's okay, Charlie." She touched his hand and he saw her fingernails, bitten down to the quick. "You don't have to. We'll still be friends."

His goose was cooked. "Just this one time, Moll."

Her big brown eyes widened with new hope. "I promise I won't ask again."

He had a feeling he would be doing the asking. Begging, probably. He stole a quick glance at the windows on the back of the house and steered her to lean against the brick wall. He braced his hands on either side of her head. Maybe if he kept a good twelve, fifteen inches between their bodies this would turn out all right.

She shot him an eager look, licked her lips and then wiped them with her palm.

Charlie gave a low chuckle. "It's okay if your lips are a little wet. The guys won't mind."

She ran her tongue over her lips again and closed her eyes, hands at her sides, patiently waiting.

Charlie lowered his own eyelids and pressed his mouth to hers.

He tried to keep it sweet, light, innocent. He did try. He kept his lips firmly closed against the warm cushion of her mouth. But when he lifted his head, her eyes fluttered open, and he read disappointment in them.

"That was nice, Charlie," she said with a polite smile.

Nice. A-w-w-w, he was a goner.

He sucked in a long, slow breath, never taking his gaze from her face. "Open your mouth for me, Molly," he whispered. Whether out of obedience or surprise he couldn't say, she did as she was told, her guileless eyes locked with his. "Trust me, honey. This is how it's done."

With one finger under her chin, he tilted her face to him and covered her open mouth with his. He tasted her sweet breath, lemon and sugar. His must be the same, he thought, while he could still think. He didn't know where his taste ended and hers began. He only knew he wanted more of the sweetness.

He moved his mouth on hers, increasing the pressure, gently nudging her lips apart. The first tentative probes of his tongue were teasing, tickling the corners of her mouth. He prodded playfully at her left front tooth—the one that had been capped ever since they'd taken that spill off his bike years ago—until he felt her smile. Then he pressed his advantage, sliding his tongue past the wall of her teeth.

He could feel the soft little whimper she gave under the hand that cradled her chin. Vaguely, in a dim corner of his mind, some rational voice cautioned him to stop, to hold up before this barreled out of control. He paid it no mind. His mouth wide and seeking, he thrust his tongue in and out, in and out of her clinging warmth. He felt her sag against the wall as if her legs would no longer hold her, and her hands crept up his chest to encircle his neck, seeming to need the support. Her fingers clutched in his hair, knocking his hat off. He felt it bump his shoulder as it tumbled.

Reaching for sanity, he pulled away. When her tongue followed his withdrawal, shyly touching his, he thought he would lose it.

Somehow the inches between them had disappeared. His bracing arm was flattened against the wall and her breasts— God, he never thought of *Molly* with breasts—were crushed to his chest. The fingers he'd tangled in her thick mane itched to cup those soft mounds, to discover if they were better protected under her shirt than they had been in the past. It was all he could do to plaster his hand against the brick and push off of her.

Her eyes, wide and dazed, held disappointment again, but of a different sort. "Oh, Charlie," she breathed.

He pressed his forehead to hers and nuzzled the soft tendrils near her sweaty brow. "We've gotta stop, Moll."

"I know." She gave a shuddery sigh, one hand sliding over his shoulder to rub against his chest.

He jerked when her fingertip found his nipple and it stiffened. That was a new one on him. He wouldn't have guessed his body would do that. She seemed to be fascinated, too, dragging her ragged nail across the little nub until he thought he would burst. If she'd drop her gaze a little bit more, she could see what else had stiffened.

Nope. Too innocent. She brought her doe eyes back to his. He licked lips that still carried her clean taste. "How old are you, Molly?"

Her eyes darted away and then back. "Sixteen."

He huffed in disbelief.

She sighed and chewed on her swollen lip. "I'm closer to sixteen than I am to fourteen," she said finally.

Fifteen. Holy Hannah. Her daddy'd shoot him. Hell, *his* daddy'd shoot him. "Don't go kissing Jimmy Jordan like that."

She gave him a dreamy-eyed smile. "I don't want to."

That was fine with him. The idea of her playing tongue tag with someone else had all the appeal of a hair on a gumdrop. "You're too young to be kissing anybody like that, Molly."

She lifted her hand from his chest and rubbed it across the jaw he had to shave a couple times a week now. "I know." Her thumb traced his lips. "Will you wait for me, Charlie?"

Oh my God. Did she know what she was asking? This was supposed to be his year with the ladies. They were gonna be hanging all over him. But he looked into her flushed, solemn face and he knew, however long the wait might be, he didn't want to come to her with the taste and scent of other women on him.

The screen door creaked and they jumped apart, looking as guilty as two five-year-olds playing I'll-show-you-mine-if-you-show-me-yours behind the huckleberry bush. Charlie

bent to pick up his hat and Molly grabbed the glass from the
step as her mother appeared at the top of the stairs.

"Mrs. Simon is here for your piano lesson, Margaret
Mary." She fixed Charlie with a fish-eyed glare.

He held his hat at belt level, but he didn't need its protection. The woman had a look that would shrivel stone.
"Molly," he heard himself say as he watched her long legs
carry her up the steps.

She turned at the top, her hand on the screen door, to look
at him.

"I'll wait."

And he had. Not that she'd ever believe it. But he'd come
to her a damn twenty-year-old virgin, too ignorant, too eager,
too raw with his need to make it good for her.

Now it had come to this. Despite her claims, he found it
hard to believe the Molly he'd known could have betrayed
him this way. But he couldn't fathom why, if she'd tried to
get in touch with him, she didn't just say so. Had it been her
plan to keep his son from him forever? She always knew what
family meant to him. Sometimes, he acknowledged, she en-
vied the closeness. Was that part of it? Was it misplaced jeal-
ousy? Or was she protecting somebody?

He drained his beer and stared at the empty bottle. He'd
drunk more of these in the last week than he had in the previous month, and now he asked himself why. He didn't need
them. And he knew how Molly felt about heavy drinking—
with good reason. Was this sheer cussedness on his part?
He'd have to learn to curb his cantankerous streak. Whether
he loved Molly or not, he'd committed himself to a real marriage. He didn't kid himself that it would be easy. It was time
he started working at it.

With a heavy sigh he put his guitar and recorder aside. No
easier in his mind, he went back to bed.

Chapter 5

"**Y**ou got a cigarette?" Charlie directed the question at his brother while he tried for the third time to stick a cuff link through the layers of fabric on the formal white shirt he wore. He muttered a curse when the little gold stud slipped from his clumsy fingers and rolled across the parquet floor to where the other man caught it under his foot.

"Hell no, Kick." Cleeve bent to pick up the errant cuff link, strode over to where Charlie stood with arm outstretched, and fastened it to the shirtsleeve. "Patsy's been on my case ever since you set us all such a sterling example." He took the second cuff link from Charlie's hand and fastened the other sleeve. "In the interest of conjugal harmony, I gave up the filthy weed."

Charlie let out an impatient breath and straightened the tie he'd needed help knotting.

"You're not nervous, are you?" Cleeve asked.

"No." Charlie's reply was curt. He shrugged into his suit jacket and stretched his arms until his cuffs poked through the sleeves. "What time is it?"

Cleeve checked his watch. "About three minutes later than

the last time you asked.'' He gave a low chuckle. ''You've still got time to back out.''

Charlie shot his brother what he hoped would be a silencing look. Born at opposite ends of the same year, they'd been taken for twins more than once and were as close as two people could be. Charlie tolerated abuse from this man that would earn anybody else a split lip. But there were times, like now, when Cleeve pushed his luck. ''I'm not backing out.''

The other man shrugged. ''I just hope you know what you're doing.''

So did Charlie. Pushing aside the heavy drapes on the single, wide window in the hotel room, he looked out on the day. It had started raining the night before, shortly after Cleeve had come in from Wheeling, and it hadn't let up since. The chill, gray weather suited his mood.

Due to Tobie's precarious health, and Molly's lack of any family whatsoever, Charlie had decided to sharply limit the number of his guests at the wedding. Only Cleeve would be there.

After his brother had driven in and given Molly a cool greeting, Charlie had taken him to the hospital to meet his nephew. Then Charlie had spent the night at the hotel with him, to give Molly some privacy for her wedding preparations. At least there would be that traditional start to this untraditional union.

Cleeve had used the time to try to undermine Charlie's resolve. He lit into him with every rational argument why this marriage was both unnecessary and unwise. Charlie's counterarguments had sounded increasingly lame even to his own ears. At last he was forced to admit, to himself at least, that he was marrying Molly for only one reason. He wanted to. All thoughts of control, of punishment, of getting even aside, he wanted Molly for his own.

It was a bitter admission, this acknowledgment of the hold she still had on him. It did nothing to improve his disposition. He turned from the window to face his brother again.

''You got the ring?''

"I got the ring." Cleeve patted one pocket. "I got the license." He patted another. "You sure about this?"

"Yeah, I'm sure."

"What reason did she give you…for not letting you know?"

Charlie's laugh was humorless. "Stiff-necked pride."

"Well, she's her mother's daughter."

"I guess," Charlie answered with a heavy sigh. "I never saw much of a resemblance before." He plowed a hand through his hair. "You never heard about Tobie, did you, Cleeve? She never came to you?"

Cleeve's gaze faltered. Some moments passed before he answered. "A few years ago…when her momma kicked?"

Charlie nodded, his black eyes riveted to Cleeve's.

"She came back for the funeral. Word got around that she had a kid. I might even have heard it was a boy." He ran a finger over his upper lip. "I didn't know his age. I never laid eyes on him, Kick. It was a long time after you two split."

Charlie sagged back against the window, curving his hands over the edge of the sill. "You never mentioned anything," he said, staring at his boots.

"Aw, hell. We all knew better than to bring *her* up."

Charlie fixed him with his steady gaze. "I got over her a long time ago."

"Oh, yeah. I can tell."

"You about done being a smart-ass?" Charlie countered, pushing away from the window. He reached for his hat and started for the door. "We've got a wedding to get to."

They were early. Charlie knew they would be, had half intended to be. It gave him a chance to scout things out, make sure they weren't walking into a media ambush. To be fair, the fanzines had been real good about the situation. After the news conference he'd arranged for them through the hospital public relations department, they'd left him alone to deal with the crisis in his life. Of course he hadn't said anything at the time about a marriage. Apparently that hadn't leaked.

The hospital staff had been unintrusive, too. Some folks

had brought in CD inserts for him to sign. Probably he'd have been disappointed if they hadn't. But on the whole, they'd gone about their work in a professional manner, providing information, care and support.

Tobie was awake, but subdued, when Charlie and Cleeve entered his room. He'd been eager to witness his parents' union and Morrissey had agreed, but warned that his doing so was not without risk. The transplant was scheduled for the next day, and Tobie's resistance was at its lowest ebb. The brief ceremony would take place at the doorway, and only Molly and Charlie would have any contact with Tobie at all.

A commotion just outside the room signaled the arrival of the rest of the wedding party. Charlie somehow made it through the introductions and small talk, but he only had eyes for Molly.

He had suspected she would forgo the typical white lace of a virginal bride. Well, Molly hated froufrou anyway, and she didn't look good in white. He had no quarrel with her choice. She wore a simple, elegant suit of some silky material in a pale yellow shade. The color seemed to change where the fabric clung to the curves and hollows of her body, appearing in the shadows almost like a blush on a pear. The outfit complemented her creamy skin and red hair. But nothing could disguise the purple smudges under her eyes.

Seeing them, Charlie was struck again at the toll the past weeks and months had taken on her. She must have spent another sleepless night. He had anticipated keeping her awake a good portion of the coming one, but he recognized with a pang of regret that if she showed reluctance, he didn't have it in him to insist.

Her smile seemed genuine, though, as she kissed Tobie, and the hands that carried a bouquet of flowers were steady. She appeared to have come to terms with what this relationship would entail.

The social niceties out of the way, Molly, Charlie and the others arranged themselves for the ceremony. The whole ritual was more than a little familiar to Charlie. Most of his brothers had married, and he'd served as Cleeve's best man three years before. Cleeve returned the favor now, handing Charlie the gold band he had chosen with Molly earlier in the week.

Gently he nudged the ring over Molly's knuckle, repeating the words that would bind him to her forever. He looked to the minister again, ready to continue, when Molly's single attendant, her landlady, stepped forward. Beaming, she un-curled her pudgy fingers and handed Molly the mate to the ring Charlie had placed on her finger.

With a start Charlie realized the cash he had given Molly hadn't all gone toward her wedding attire. Wordlessly, he focused on their joined hands while she made her vows in a breathless, almost inaudible voice.

The ring fit. How had she managed that? he wondered. Lucky guess? He looked at the matching bands gleaming on their fingers. Wide and gold. Plain and simple. Like their love had been. Once.

Charlie heard the minister say the words that made them one. Molly tilted her face for his kiss and, touching his lips to hers, he sank his fingers into the hair she had worn loose for him. For better or worse, it was done.

The rest of the afternoon and evening passed in a blur. Molly and Charlie had dinner with their guests while Tobie napped, and then they returned to spend the early evening with him. With a promise to stop in the next morning before Charlie was admitted for his part in the transplant, they kissed Tobie good-night and left.

They climbed the stairs to the apartment in silence. Charlie, a few steps behind Molly, saw her smile suddenly when she reached the top. Moments later he caught sight of what amused her.

He joined her at the door as she pulled a dripping bottle of champagne from a plastic pail serving as a makeshift ice bucket. On the floor alongside it stood two glasses, complete with white ribbons and fake lily of the valley twined around the stems.

Charlie stooped to pick up the pail and glasses and read the card nestled in the bowl of one. "Mrs. Kowalczyk."

Molly nodded. "My landlady believes in happy endings."

"And what about you, Molly?" Charlie straightened and regarded her steadily. "What do you believe in?"

Her smile faltered a little, but her chin lifted to compensate. "I believe in new beginnings, Charlie." She slid her key into the lock and led him into their home.

Taking a deep breath, she headed for the kitchen. A few sips of Mrs. Kowalczyk's thoughtful gift sounded good to her at that moment. All the pressures and tensions of the past week slammed up against the reality of what the next few hours would bring. She felt smothered, suffocated, with no-where to turn, no escape.

She set the bottle on the counter and opened the utensil drawer, rummaging through it. After a bit she felt Charlie come up behind her.

"What are you looking for, Moll?"

"A corkscrew."

"Honey, this is champagne. We don't need a corkscrew."

Her hand stilled at the endearment. It seemed to come so easily to his lips. Because it was meaningless? Not to her.

She shoved the drawer shut with her hip, embarrassed by her witless search. "Of course," she said. "I'd forgotten. It's been a long time since I had champagne." That was true, in its way. She'd never had champagne. Never *was* a long time. Turning to look at him, she was immediately unsettled by his nearness.

He'd shed his coat and tie, rolled his shirtsleeves up to his elbows. She watched his long fingers work at the seal on the bottle, his thumbs maneuver the cork. She jumped when the stopper gave and he aimed the fizz over the sink. He regarded her quizzically from beneath an arched black brow.

"Do you want to wait, Molly?" he asked, his voice tight, strained.

It took several moments for her to understand what he meant. She shook her head quickly, watching him fill the glasses. "No. I'm just nervous. Waiting won't help."

She took a glass from him, needing two hands to hold it steady, feeling his watchful eyes on her.

"I won't hurt you," he said in a husky whisper.

"I know." *How romantic.* She attempted a smile as he clinked his glass with hers. What did she expect? Sweet promises of undying devotion? Not likely.

"To new beginnings, Molly."

At his words her smile softened. Maybe they could salvage something from this mess, make something of this marriage. If he was willing. She took a sip of her champagne and rubbed a finger over her nose where the bubbles tickled it. He was watching her still, an uncertain look in his eyes.

"I don't think..." he began, took a quick sip, and continued. "I don't think we should take a chance on another baby at this point, do you? Not the way things stand with Tobie."

And with us, she finished to herself. She put a hand to her cheek, sensing hot color rise. Amid all the concerns of the past week, this one had never entered her mind. "No. Of course not. I'm sorry, Charlie. I didn't...I'm not..."

"I'll take care of it."

"I'll get a prescription for the pill as soon as I can."

He didn't answer right away. Molly saw him place his glass on the counter and fix his gaze on it. He inhaled deeply, his mouth tight, as if measuring his words.

"You were on the pill before, or so you told me."

She felt the color leach from her face at his implication. Surely he didn't think that she'd *deliberately*...that she'd wanted only a baby...not him. But he did believe that. She could see it.

"Oh, Charlie." She set her glass next to his on the counter and touched his hand resting there. His eyes slid to hers, their expression stark. "Do you remember," she whispered, "that trouble I had...with my wisdom teeth, before we broke up?"

His gaze moved over her face, gentling as he looked at her, and his mouth quirked into the half smile that twisted her heart.

"I remember you looking like a chipmunk."

She smiled in return, a sad smile. "The antibiotic I took

for it...interfered with the pill.'' She licked her lips. ''I didn't know. If the dentist or the pharmacist had said something, we could have used some other protection.'' She shrugged. ''No one did. And so there's Tobie. I didn't plan it that way.''

Under her hand she could feel the tension leave him. She saw him relax, muscle by muscle. He straightened and cupped her chin. ''I'm not sorry there's Tobie.''

He searched her eyes, seeming to wait for some response from her, some explanation she wouldn't, *couldn't* give. Finally he released her and reached for his glass again. He twisted his ring absently with his thumb.

''Does that fit?'' she asked, indicating his hand.

''Yeah.'' He glanced down and stopped his idle fidgeting. ''I'm just not used to jewelry.''

She nodded. ''I used your high-school ring...for sizing.''

That surprised him, she could tell. Maybe he didn't remember giving her the ring, didn't think she'd still have it. That hurt a little, because she treasured it.

Suddenly she didn't want to draw this out any longer. Didn't want to sip champagne and make small talk. She wanted to sink into the sweet oblivion she knew his touch could bring her. To lie with him in the darkness where no words were necessary, and she couldn't read what was in his eyes. To go willingly with him simply because, although he didn't love her, he'd promised not to hurt her. And that would have to be enough.

She lifted her hand and brushed the backs of her fingers along his cheek. ''I'm going to bed,'' she whispered. ''Give me a few minutes?''

''Moll...''

Turning her hand, she pressed her fingertips to his lips. ''Just a few minutes, Charlie.'' Her mouth replaced her fingers in the briefest touch and she was gone.

His head whirling in the cloud of jasmine she'd left in her wake, he watched her go. Damn. She bewitched him now with her artless seductiveness, just as she had the raw, lanky, wet-behind-the-ears punk he'd been.

When he'd insisted that she marry him, he'd never really

thought ahead, never gotten to quite this point. He'd never considered what it would mean to bed her in what seemed no more than a business arrangement, with no sweet words, no tender phrases between them. He knew if she showed the slightest reluctance, he wouldn't be able to do it.

But she didn't. In some crazy way she appeared determined to make this as easy as possible. For him.

He capped what remained of the champagne and put it in the refrigerator. Rinsing the glasses they had used, he heard the bathroom door open and close. After a while he heard Molly leave the bathroom and open her bedroom door. For the first time since he had come to share the apartment with her, that door didn't close.

He wiped down the counter and hung the dish towel over the stove handle. He knew he was stalling. Then he remembered Molly's words. *Waiting won't help*. Rubbing a hand over his jaw, he headed for the bathroom. He used to shave at night, when he and Molly had been together. Maybe it would be a good idea now. Another stall, he admitted to himself, but one that could have some advantages.

When he entered Molly's bedroom a short time later, he half expected to find her huddled in bed with the covers up to her chin. He should have known better. Molly was no coward. She stood at the front window of the darkened room gazing through the lace curtain, the picture she presented all in shades of gray except where the moonlight touched her hair and caught fire.

She wore a simple short gown that could have been a slip. Probably *was* a slip, as a matter of fact. Molly liked clothes that did double duty. She'd commandeered his undershirts for sleeping when they'd lived together. They weren't much longer on her than they were on him. He felt his body stir at just the memory. This particular garment she had on now made the most of her assets which, to his way of thinking, were considerable.

She turned when he came in, noted the white shirt he had bunched in his hand and gestured toward the clothes hamper near the closet. She watched him as he stuffed the shirt in the hamper and pulled his billfold from his pants pocket. He saw her start and look away when he removed the small square packets and placed them on the nightstand. He unbuckled the leather strap on his wristwatch and set it and his wallet on the pine dresser next to her earrings and the small bouquet she had carried. The sight of their everyday objects mingled that way seemed more intimate somehow than what they were about to do.

She was staring out the window again. Only her fingers picking at the delicate curtain gave away her agitation. Charlie sat down in the chintz-covered chair next to her and bent to pull off his boots and socks.

"I don't have any penchant for skittish females, Molly," he said quietly, tucking the socks into his boots. "That doesn't turn me on. If you don't want to do this, just say so."

He felt her fingers settle on his naked shoulder, stroking gently.

"I'm only nervous, I told you," she said in an even voice. "I'm not unwilling."

Her palm was warm where it touched him, her fingers trailing down over his collarbone to where his chest hairs started. Her hand slid lower, the middle finger seeking and finding his nipple and dallying there. He sucked in a breath, open-mouthed. It was a little unsettling, just how quickly he was ready. He'd been with more experienced women than Molly, but they hadn't known to do that. He doubted his reaction would have been the same even if they had.

He rose and stood facing her. His eyes had adjusted to the dimness, and colors were clearer now. Sepia tones, instead of gray. Warm, brown eyes, a pearly luster to her skin, her hair dark shades of red, deep and shadowed, like secrets. *Molly by moonlight.*

He didn't realize he'd said the words aloud until he saw her smile, her gaze soft and unfocused. "'I'll come to thee by moonlight....'" she whispered.

"'Though hell should bar the way,'" he finished.

Her smile widened and she touched her forehead to his chin. His lips burrowed their way into her fragrant hair.

"I'm embarrassed to admit," she said in a muffled tone, "how long it was before I learned you didn't make that up." She lifted her head and looked at him. "It sounded like something you'd say," she added in her own defense. "Except for the 'thee' part," she acknowledged with a shrug. "I thought you were trying to impress me."

"I was." He gave her a smile that reached the corners of his eyes and crinkled them. "A good line's a good line. I only steal from the best."

He'd looked like a highwayman that night, she thought, riding, riding to her out of the blackness. His steed a battered Harley. Cowboy boots instead of Wellingtons. She'd known he would come for her, would know where to find her. She'd waited for him on the tree stump, chilled by the grim reality of death despite the sultry night.

If he'd been born in an earlier time, she knew, he'd have been a troubadour, traveling the countryside on horseback with his mandolin and his songs, breaking hearts. As it was, he had ridden his motorcycle, his guitar strapped to the carrier. The soul of a poet in the body of a steelworker. Breaking hearts.

But he'd come to comfort her that night. The memory of his kindness warmed her, reminded her of why she loved him even if he didn't love her.

She threaded her fingers into the thick black silk of his hair, pulled his mouth down to hers, whispered against it, "It's okay if you don't love me, Charlie. Just pretend."

She'd caught him by surprise again. He hadn't anticipated her bold move, and he pressed hard against her before he had a moment to think. Then there was no room for thought. His hands came up to grip her shoulders and crush her to him as his mouth opened over hers. His fingers grasped the thin straps of her slip, sliding them down her arms and baring her breasts.

He pulled away a little to look at them cradled in the hammock made by her slip suspended between her arms. They

were just as he remembered, pale, firm and generous, the
nipples a little darker, or maybe they only appeared so in the
dim light.

He weighed one in his palm almost reverently and Molly
arched her neck to him in silent invitation. Dragging in air,
his hands unsteady, he cupped her face to make her look at
him.

"It's been a long time for me, Molly. I'll go as easy as I
can."

Finally, it seemed he had said something that pleased her.
She smiled up at him, stepping back. Straightening her arms
at her sides, she let her slip glide to the floor. Years ago he
had thought she was the most perfectly formed woman he'd
ever seen. This, when he hadn't seen any others naked and
close up. He had more experience now, but it hadn't changed
his opinion.

His gaze drifted slowly over the body she revealed to him.
The slender rib cage beneath her lush breasts, the gentle swell
of her belly—a little rounder than he remembered—the legs
that went on forever. His eyes settled on the lacy scrap of her
panties, the ones that were guaranteed to drive him straight
up a wall, the ones that barely covered the springy triangle
of hair, darker than the hair on her head, he knew, but still
red.

He glanced up when she moved closer to help him with
his pants. He needed help. He could manage the belt and the
button all right, but she applied a gentle, kneading pressure
to hold him out of harm's way while he eased the zipper over
the bulge of his erection and down. Then her hands went
around him to shove his pants and underwear down his backside. The slide of her warm hands over his buttocks, nudging
him nearer, started a wildfire in his vitals that had him breaking a sweat and puffing like a steam locomotive. With the
weight of his belt, his clothes settled to the floor and he
stepped out of them, leaving them where they lay.

With the witchy-eyed look he remembered, part knowing
and part shy, she brought her hand around and cupped him.
This had always seemed easier for her when his hand covered

hers, guided her, showed her what he liked, so he did that now. But he liked it too much. He wasn't going to last until they made it to the bed if she kept that up.

He brought her hands up to rest on his shoulders and eased her close until their skin made contact, head to toe. It was like coming home after a long absence. He sensed the welcome in her body whether she willed it or not, and it took the edge off his urgency. Helped him to go slow.

He wanted to kiss her. A real kiss, not one of those proper pecks they'd been giving each other for public display. A hot kiss, long and languorous, wet and deep. That was unusual for him because, generally speaking, kissing was his least favorite part of this whole business.

Not with Molly, though. There had been a time when they'd elevated kissing to an art form. Bringing each other right to the edge with just their mouths and his hands *outside* her clothes. That was how he wanted to kiss her now, with all the tenderness only she brought out in him.

He turned his head and opened his mouth on her neck, touching her with his tongue and, gently, with his teeth. He felt her breath come in hot pants, ruffling the hair near his ear. Her fingers gripped his shoulders hard enough to leave marks even with her skimpy nails. His mouth went searching for hers, their tongues mating, their moans mingling.

He brought his hands to her hips and rolled her panties under his palms till they slid down her legs to pool at her feet. Her knees bumped his shins as she stepped out of them and kicked them away.

Then she did something he couldn't recall her ever doing before. She raised herself up on her toes, lifting one leg and wrapping her inner thigh around the outside of his, placing her foot on his calf. That opened her to him completely, settled his rampant erection against her moist cleft. He heard her whisper his name, just the breathy catch of her voice at his ear. Then she moved upon him and he saw the red haze of her hair even with his eyes closed.

There would be no going slow now. He lifted her and eased her backward onto the bed she had already prepared. His mouth never leaving hers, he got himself sheathed. He did manage that. Then he got himself inside her. And there was only the blood beating in his ears, the frantic thrusts, the rush of pleasure, and the guttural cry of his release.

He hadn't learned as much as he'd thought.

Charlie pushed himself up higher in the bed, sitting next to Molly's sleeping form. He'd awakened from the best sleep he'd had in months just as dawn light sifted through the curtains. Molly slumbered on, her arms wrapped around the pile made by *both* pillows, her nose buried in the crook of an elbow. She was still a bed hog.

Of course she was used to having this one to herself. He knew that for certain now. Between his hands on her this time and eight years ago, there had been no others.

For which he was grateful.

She wouldn't feel compelled to give him a critique of that performance of his. Unlike other women he had known. "Slow down, Kick," they would say. "You're not done yet," they would tell him, and he'd learned. What the hell had come over him this time? Man his age prided himself on having a little finesse, a little technique, some control. And that hooey he'd handed her about going easy. What a laugh.

He tunneled his fingers into her tousled hair, resting the tips on her warm scalp. Somehow just that contact with her soothed him.

It hadn't been awful for her, he knew that. She'd been ready, slick. His entry had been tight, but easy. It just hadn't been *mind-blowing* for her, the way it was for him. "That was *nice,* Charlie," is what she'd say. Good God.

He stared down at her, letting his fingers wander through her hair to her nape and the shallow indentation there. She snuffled a little, burrowing deeper into the bedclothes, and he stilled his hand.

Maybe he should wake her up. It was possible he could go a little slower this time, give her some idea of what it could be like. He rubbed his hand on her silky, bare shoulder, and she heaved a contented sigh and settled her palm on his thigh.

But she didn't waken. Seeing her sleeping so deeply, he had second thoughts. She was in for a hell of a day. She really needed this sleep. And seeing those smudges under her eyes disappear would be better than sex. For her anyway, he laughed to himself. That was damn straight.

She squeezed his thigh and he nearly shot off the bed. He'd better put a stop to that or any good intentions he had would go up in smoke. He laid his hand on top of hers and their rings clinked, drawing his attention.

She still had his high-school ring. Not only *had* it, she'd known where to find it. He hadn't thought of it in years, wouldn't have been able to say what happened to it. But he remembered now....

He crossed the bridge after leaving the mill in Mingo Junction on the Ohio side of the river and headed his Harley south along Route 2 toward Wheeling. He'd heard the news at change of shift when he got off the evening turn at eleven. He hadn't even bothered with a shower. Just changed his steel-toed boots for Tony Lamas, his hard hat for a motorcycle helmet. Probably still had raccoon eyes from the goggles he wore near the blast furnace. Didn't matter. He had to get to Molly.

Brendan Doyle had pulled some prime stunts in his forty-six years, but tonight he'd outdone himself. Which was only fitting, Charlie figured, since this stunt would prove to be his last. He'd had the bad form to drop dead on top of one of his lady friends. This would be big talk in a small town. Molly was going to need help holding her head up, mourning the man she was ashamed to love.

He slowed his bike as he made the turn on the road leading to her house. The place was already dark. Her momma had probably retired for the night with a cold compress over her eyes. He wished he could feel some sympathy for her, but she'd always treated him like something she'd scrape off her shoes. That had only gotten worse since he'd really started seeing her daughter. Anyway, he hadn't come for her. And he knew where he'd find Molly.

She was sitting on the tree stump at the end of the drive. Poker-straight, knees clamped together, hands knotted in her lap. He cut the engine before he got to her so he could glide up without raising any dust or gravel. He brought the bike to a stop in front of her and straddled it.

Molly didn't look at him. She turned her attention to something off in the distance. "You've heard, I suppose," she said airily.

Oh, boy. She was going to act like she didn't give a damn. This was gonna be hell on a hickory stick. "I heard."

She brought her gaze to the hands in her lap, spreading her fingers, examining her nails. "This came as a total surprise. We never knew he had any trouble with his heart." She said this as if she were trying to decide between the Misty Lilac polish and the Mango Frappe.

Charlie yanked off his gloves, unhitched his chin strap and pushed his visor up. "Happens like that sometimes."

"Miz Willetts must have been *very* surprised."

Her voice keyed up a notch on that comment. She was losing it. "Moll…"

"She isn't even *pretty!* How could he, Charlie?"

She clamped a hand over her mouth, and for a minute he was afraid she was going to be sick. He saw her swallow hard.

"Honey…"

She bit down on her bottom lip and shook her head firmly, side to side. Charlie pursed his lips and blew out a slow breath, allowing her time to compose herself.

"So," he said. "You want to go for a ride on my bike?"

She looked at him, licked her lips, sniffed once, but her voice was steady when she answered. "I've got a false tooth from the last time I went for a ride on your bike."

He lifted his helmet off, shook out the hair he wore too long just because it drove her momma nuts, and gestured Molly over. When she came, he adjusted the helmet on her head and fastened it.

"What about you?" she said.

"I've got a hard head." She still looked skeptical. "We

won't go far." He helped her to mount behind him. "Hold on tight."

He could have saved his breath on that score. She grabbed bunches of the front of his shirt with a fierceness that had him cursing chest hair. He could feel her forearms trembling where they gripped his sides. She was ready to fly apart.

He didn't take her far. Just to that little cove where Eighth Street dead-ended at the river's edge. He came here sometimes to think and dream. He never brought anybody else. Didn't trust himself to bring Molly. But tonight was different.

It was peaceful here, quiet. Just the gentle lapping of the water and the occasional low growl of the barges as they made their way up the river.

He pulled a blanket from the carrier and spread it on the stubbly grass under a willow. Molly toed off her shoes and sat cross-legged. Charlie stretched out beside her, resting back on his elbows. They were silent for a while, but Charlie sensed her tension.

"You wanna talk?"

She brought her knees together and up, wrapped her arms around them, rested her forehead against them. "No."

Charlie leaned his head back and looked up. He could hear the wind whispering through the leaves on the droopy branches a few feet above his head, but it was too dark to see them. He could barely make out Molly except for the pale glow of her white T-shirt.

"Do you wanna cry?"

He heard the hiss of her breath through tight lips. "I'm not going to the university in the fall."

He gritted his teeth. "Sure you are. What would you want to stay around here for?"

"I'm not going to run away. Just because I'm a laughing-stock…" Her voice quavered.

He pushed up to a sitting position. "C'mon, Moll. You've never let the talk get to you before. It's what small people do. Talk about other people." He'd wondered how much of the gossip she was aware of. She was well-liked. Hell, so was her daddy. That didn't stop the winks and the snickers.

"You're gonna go be my college girl. Forget about all this. Make me proud."

"Will you hold me, Charlie? I'm cold."

He didn't think that was a good idea. But her request was so plaintive, and he saw her shiver in spite of the steamy night. He pulled her into his arms and settled her against him, tucking her head under his chin. "I didn't clean up before I came. If it bothers you, just give me a shove."

In answer she hugged him close, nuzzling her lips on his neck just above his T-shirt. He was instantly aware of how good she smelled, how soft she was, of her breasts pressed against his chest.

His body started crowding his jeans. He shifted, bringing a knee up in an effort to get more comfortable. She lifted her head questioningly, then she slid her hand down his chest and placed it over his zipper just below his belt. There was no hiding that bulge, no disguising the thrust of his hips into her palm before he could catch himself.

He groaned and shifted her hand to his thigh. "That's just bein' a hound, honey. It's okay. Don't pay it no mind."

She pulled her hand away from his. He saw her reach behind her back under her shirt, her elbows angled like wings. She'd freed her breasts before he realized what she was about, shoving her bra and T-shirt up above them.

He'd touched her breasts before, his hands sneaking under her shirt, long fingers stealing into her bra to tease the nipples till they puckered and peaked. But he'd never seen them. She displayed them proudly to him now, the pale globes gleaming, the perfect dusky circles at their center beckoning.

"Honey, you don't want to do this. Someone might see us."

"I don't care," she whispered fiercely. "I'm cold and numb, Charlie. Make me feel."

She raised up on her knees in front of him, grasping the bottom of his shirt and tugging it out of his jeans and over his head. She pressed herself against him, rubbing her breasts on his chest, and he gripped her upper arms, pulling her more tightly to him when he knew he should push her away.

"Molly, don't do this," he pleaded into her hair. "I'm a mess, honey, I need a shower. I just wanted to make sure you're all right."

"I'm not all right," she cried, nipping at his ear with her teeth. "What are you going to do about it?"

"Ah, Moll, I want you so damn much." He brought his hands around to cup her breasts, circling them until the nipples pebbled into the centers of his palms. "Tell me to get lost, honey. Make me stop."

But she wasn't listening to him. She kissed him open-mouthed, with her tongue. The way he liked. The way he'd taught her. She locked her arms around his neck and leaned backward, pulling him down with her onto the blanket. He helped her wriggle out of her jeans and underpants, kissing her breasts as she arched to him. She pushed his jeans over his hips while he was still digging in the pocket for the protection he'd started carrying a couple months before. He managed to get it on pretty smoothly because, to tell the truth, he hadn't wanted to look like a fool when the time came, so he'd practiced once or twice by himself.

Then everything was a haze of heat and need and friction. She was wet where he touched her. She rose to him when he slid a finger in to test her, like he'd heard to do. But he was too much for her. He knew he was hurting her, could hear her sharp intake, feel her tense when he pushed. She wouldn't let him pull out and finish on top of her. She wrapped those long legs and arms around him and held him deep while he took that sweet, wild plunge into ecstasy.

Her fingers were toying idly in his hair when he came back to himself. His first reaction was one of self-disgust. He was crushing Molly. She winced when he withdrew from her and rolled away. She was tender, he guessed, and he felt even worse.

He didn't know what to do about the damn condom. He bet the cool guys didn't worry about that after. Well, no way was he one of the cool guys. He found a tissue in the pocket of Molly's jeans and used that. Then he straightened his clothes and helped Molly with hers.

He couldn't believe what he'd done. This was the girl who meant heaven and earth to him, and he'd taken her on a threadbare blanket over lumpy ground on a hot, sticky, buggy night. Judging from the streaks on her face, he'd made her cry, too. But then, she needed to cry, so maybe it was a release of sorts. He lay beside her without a clue as to what to do or say.

"I remember, Charlie," her voice came to him on the quiet night, wistful and strangely calm, "it wasn't always bad between them."

He turned on his side to look at her as she spoke. Gently, he smoothed back the hair that clung to her face, wet with sweat and tears.

"I remember when I was real small, he would touch her sometimes…like he cared. And she would touch him back. Then all that stopped. I don't know why. Maybe he had other women even then."

With one finger he softly traced her cheekbone, her nose, her lips, her chin.

"For a long time I thought it was my fault."

"No, Molly, it wasn't your fault."

"I'm very much like him. It's why my mother can't love me." Her lower lip began to quiver and she pulled it between her teeth.

"Shhh, honey. She loves you."

She shook her head side to side on the blanket. "I can't live in that house anymore."

"You'll be leaving for school in a couple of weeks, Molly. You won't have to stay there then."

"There'll still be summers. I can't go back there."

He shrugged. "Then stay with me. It's time I got my own place, anyway. It won't be much, but you'll be welcome."

She rolled her head on the blanket, her eyes seeking his. She rubbed her hand over his jaw and he heard the rasp of his beard against her palm. He hadn't even shaved before he'd come to her. Her delicate skin would be raw from him.

"Will that happen to us, Charlie? Will we end up like them?"

He shook his head in denial. "I swear I'll never hurt you like that." He could read the doubt in her eyes even in the darkness. He pulled his class ring—the only thing he had besides his heart that was his to give her—from his finger and pressed it into her palm, closed her hand around it. "You're mine now, Molly, and I'm yours. For as long as you want me. I'll never hurt you that way."

She still had that ring.

They'd given up any pretense of being just friends after that night. Despite the noses in both families that might have been pushed out of joint, the redneck ruffian dreamer and his classy "college girl" were officially a couple. Molly continued to look at him as if he were some kind of pagan god, when she wasn't worried about how the other women were looking at him. And for his part, he was true to her, although he allowed as how she might have heard differently from some who liked to meddle.

In the end, love wasn't enough, where there was no trust. She'd listened to the stories he'd quit denying and she threw him out of her life. There had been other women since.

But when he'd told her it had been a long time for him, that was the truth. Because the simple fact was, he didn't much care for cold-blooded sex. It seemed somehow joyless as well as loveless. All a matter of technique and timing. When the itch got intolerable, he could always find a woman willing to scratch it, but lately he'd felt emptier, diminished afterward. He'd come to the conclusion that his old man had been right all those years ago. Sex was better with someone you loved.

That was the real kick in the teeth.

He didn't want to love Molly. He remembered too well the depths of his despair when he realized she'd meant what she'd said back then. She didn't want him. He'd come back looking for her, cocky with his newly earned money and his fame. He couldn't find her. His early success was tainted by that loss. He'd thrown himself into his work because he didn't care about anything else. That time had been the most productive of his career, but he remembered it as a black pit.

He looked down at the woman sleeping peacefully beside him. The thought of giving Molly that kind of power over him again scared him witless. Nope, he didn't want to love Molly.

But he did.

Chapter 6

"Mrs. Cochrane?"

Molly jumped when she realized the nurse was talking to her. Had called her name more than once, in fact. She felt a flush heat her face as she answered, but the woman only smiled.

"You're not used to the name yet. I understand. Your husband's out of recovery now," the nurse continued. "Everything went very well. He's been taken to his room on the unit if you'd like to go see him."

Molly glanced at a sleeping Tobie, undecided.

"I'll let him know where you went if he awakens. The bone marrow takes some preparation, so Tobie won't be getting it for a while yet. I'll call you in plenty of time."

Reassured, Molly bent to kiss her son's brow and left his bedside.

Charlie's room was on another floor in a different wing of the hospital. She was a little out of breath when she reached it and what she found there didn't make her breathe any easier. They'd been told that receiving blood after a marrow donation was not unusual, but seeing the fluid dripping into his arm was unnerving all the same. And he looked so pale. The stubble of his beard stood out starkly against his cheeks like short, black brush bristles. There was a faint sheen on his forehead that might have been perspiration, but his hand was warm when she clasped it. At her touch he dragged one eye open.

"How are you feeling?" she asked.

His other eyelid fluttered up and he turned his head slightly to look at her. "You can tell that guy on my behind…with the jackhammer?…he can quit anytime now."

"Are you hurting, Charlie? Do you need some—"

"I'm just kiddin', Moll."

Something about the set of his jaw told her he wasn't just kidding. "Are you sure? Can I get you anything?"

He could still manage that sexy half smile. "Right now I'd sell my tongue for a cigarette."

"This is a hospital, Charlie!" Appalled as she was, she couldn't contain her laughter at his outrageous suggestion.

"You're no fun." His grin widened. "That's not true. You were fun last night."

She caught her breath. His brain must still be addled from the anesthesia, she thought. Neither of them had made any reference to the previous night, though this morning she had caught him watching her more than once with a look she couldn't read.

Before Molly could respond, a nurse came into the room and punched some buttons on the pump regulating the blood flowing into Charlie's arm. Then she claimed his attention while she took his vital signs and checked the bandage covering his hip. Molly noticed the effect of Charlie's potent charm on the woman, even under the weather as he was. How he managed to look roguish in a paisley-patterned hospital gown was beyond her. When the nurse left, she tried to disguise her reaction, but Charlie wasn't fooled.

"She's just doing her job, Molly. And I'm just doing mine." His shoulders lifted under the ugly gown. "If I'm not pleasant to fans, after a while I won't have any fans."

"I know," she answered lightly, looking away.

He was silent long enough for her to feel uncomfortable about it. When she forced her eyes back to him, his were grim. "You're going to have to trust me," he said.

"I know," she repeated, but not lightly. Trust was a quality definitely *not* learned at her mother's knee.

He let the subject drop. "How's Tobie?"

She smiled weakly. "Sleeping. They said they would call me before they start the transfusion."

"He sleeps a lot. Was he always like that?"

"No!" That surprised a laugh out of her. "Not usually. More like you, as a matter of fact." She came closer to his bed and gripped the side rail. "I want to thank you, Charlie...for what you've done for him."

Somehow she'd picked exactly the wrong thing to say. She could tell by the way his expression closed off from her, the glitter in his eyes.

"He's my *son*, Molly. This wasn't some favor I did for an acquaintance." His next words carried a bitter bite. "Do you expect me to thank you for feeding him, for looking after him these past years?"

"No, of course not."

"Then don't insult *me*, Molly."

"I only meant..." But she wasn't sure what she had meant. Before she could continue, they were interrupted. The unit secretary spoke from the doorway. "The transplant unit called, Mrs. Cochrane. They're ready."

Molly turned back to Charlie. "Stay with him," he said.

Not knowing what to say, she touched her lips to his cheek. Last night might have been a new beginning, but their marriage had a long way to go.

"I don't feel any better yet."

Molly held the place in *Old Yeller* with her thumb and glanced up at her son. "It took a long time for you to get this bad, Tobie. Dr. Morrissey says it will be a while before you feel like your old self again."

Her gaze shifted from Tobie to the IV bag connected to the tube in his chest. The marrow was almost all in. It didn't

look much different from blood, actually. More precious than
diamonds. Utterly beyond price. It seemed odd to her that the
administration of this life-giving gift could appear so un-
eventful.

"He didn't know about me, did he, Mom?"

Her head whirled at Tobie's question. The one she dreaded.
The one she knew would come, but still didn't have an answer
for. "No, he didn't know."

Tobie digested this information for some moments. "Was
he famous when you had me?"

She sighed. "You know how long it takes to have a baby,
Tobie. He was famous when you were born, but not..."

"When I got started," he finished for her.

"That's right."

"And you thought he wouldn't want me."

She felt as if an animal were gnawing at her heart. "Not
exactly, honey. It's complicated. But...whatever I thought...I
was wrong."

"Did you love him, Mom?"

Ah. At last a question she could answer honestly, without
evasion. "I've loved him since I was younger than you are
now. I'll love him all my life."

Tobie moved restlessly in the bed, twisting the sheets.
"That's a sad book, Mom. Did you bring any *Curious
George?*"

Molly left the hospital when regular visiting hours ended.
Both of her men were tired and so was she. She fixed herself
a cup of tea and placed the two phone calls she had promised
Charlie she would make.

His mother, still kind if more reserved with Molly than she
had been in the past, was happy to hear everything had gone
smoothly. Her own uncertain health and advancing age pre-
vented her coming up to meet her grandson just yet, but she
hoped to be able to soon. Molly let out a sigh of relief when
she hung up. That conversation had gone better than she had
hoped.

Harlan Atkins she had glimpsed only briefly the night she

had gone to find Charlie. Her call to him was a little more troublesome. An older member of the band, he was apparently Charlie's right-hand man. He was handling things in Charlie's absence, and they had consulted each other several times over the past week and a half. Most of the band members—Charlie's brother, Beau, Jase, the keyboardist, and Dale, who played fiddle—were old-timers and familiar to Molly. The man Harlan referred to as Shooter she didn't know, and he appeared to be trouble. Harlan was anxious for Charlie to get back and Shooter, it seemed, was not the least of the reasons.

Her phone calls out of the way, Molly sipped the tea and glanced around the room. It was too silent in Charlie's absence, but everywhere she saw signs of his presence.

His guitar stood against the wall where her piano had been. He would leave it behind, he told her, when he went back on the road. She remembered enough of what he had taught her to continue Tobie's lessons and it would help pass the time for him.

A pile of his papers lay on the end table near her saucer. More of his scribblings, as he called them. She was tempted to read them, but didn't. He always showed her his stuff when he was ready.

The dining counter between the kitchen and living room held the pile of change he emptied from his jeans pockets every night. And a package of gum.

She missed him.

He'd been back in her life less than two weeks and he'd become as essential to her as the air she breathed. She rose, took her cup and saucer to the sink and went to her bedroom, to lie naked in the sheets that still smelled of him.

"I've gotta go back, Moll."

She nodded, unable to speak past the lump in her throat. He had already said his goodbyes to Tobie the night before and made arrangements for a cab to take him to the airport. Only two days out of the hospital, and walking with the slight limp that indicated his hip still pained him, he was determined to get back to work. He was stuffing the few things he would take with him into his duffel bag.

"I'll be talking to you and Tobie every day. Any problems and you know I'll be here in a New York minute. But a lot of people are hurting when I can't perform. I've gotta get back."

"I understand." She did. It had just never occurred to her that he would have to leave so soon. But the transplant had gone like clockwork, Tobie's condition was stable, and the next few weeks would be wait and see. Charlie didn't need to be here for that.

"Molly."

She looked up to see him watching her across the expanse of their bed. He was wearing what he'd slept in, the black sweatpants that had been the only thing he could put on over his bandage with any degree of comfort. Loosely tied, they rode low on his lean hips. His discomfort had precluded any lovemaking since his surgery, but at this moment he looked every inch the virile male animal. With an effort she raised her gaze to his face.

"These guys, most of them, stuck with me when my future was no more substantial than the bubbles in my beer. I owe them."

He gathered his shaving things from the bathroom and returned, stowing them in the bag on the bed. "They've got two million dollars worth of mortgages," he continued, eyeing her, "and I've cosigned every one."

She was familiar with this side of him. The man who took his responsibilities, his commitments, seriously. There were those who thought the "good time" Charlie was the sum of the man. His easy manner and lazy smile were deceptive. They sometimes made his success look like an accident, a fluke. But she'd seen how hard he worked for it. There was steel inside him, and she knew it.

"I *do* understand, Charlie. It's just…"

"It's just that you think I'm gonna jump on every pair of spread legs between here and Amarillo."

The harsh rasp of the zipper on his duffel was loud in the silence that followed his remark.

"You haven't lost your colorful way of expressing yourself," Molly said as calmly as she could manage.

"I'm vulgar, you mean."

She thought that went without saying, so she said nothing.

"You're right. I'm a vulgar man. Earthy. It's part of my appeal." He grabbed the shirt, jeans and underwear he would change into. "Makes me seem…unpredictable…dangerous." He gave a short, self-deprecating laugh. "We both know I'm not."

The look he gave her belied his claim. She thought him very dangerous to the well-being of her heart.

"You gonna help me with this?" Indicating the dressing on his hip, he headed for the bathroom and she followed. The bandage was hard for him to reach and would be tricky to get off. He leaned against the sink, resting on the balls of his hands, and she knelt beside him. Gently she eased the sweatpants down, exposing his hip and buttock and the thick pad that covered it. The outer layer looked like an Ace bandage, only with some adhesive substance on it that made it cling to his skin. She picked at the edges, but she could tell by the way it stretched over his groin area and upper thigh that it wouldn't come off without considerable discomfort.

He seemed to read her mind. "It's gonna hurt like a sonofabitch no matter what you do, Moll. Just give it a yank."

She gave a few quick tugs and heard him inhale sharply. He glanced over his shoulder at her. She'd succeeded in uncovering only a couple of inches. He tightened his grip on the edge of the sink. "You remember all those times I pulled your pigtails, Molly? Now's your chance."

Biting down hard on her upper lip, she yanked firmly and the dressing tore away in her hand. Charlie grunted and muttered something unintelligible.

"You okay?" She was almost afraid to ask.

He blew out a long breath. "You got even."

"I'm sorry, Char—"

"I'm just teasing, honey." His voice was a little shaky. "How does it look?"

It looked like he'd been beaten with a stick. Purple bruises surrounded the puncture marks, though they were fewer than she had anticipated. She didn't see anything that appeared infected and the gauze held only a couple small dots of dried blood. "It looks pretty good, Charlie," she lied. "I'll see if I can get some of this adhesive off."

She stood and reached into the medicine cabinet for her nail-polish remover.

"You gonna make me smell like a flower garden?" He sounded like his ornery old self again.

"This is lemon-scented. It'll make you smell fresh. Which you are," she said pointedly.

"Nah, not me. I'm reformed." He sucked in a breath as she knelt again and dabbed a saturated cotton ball against his skin. "I've got two left hands." He used one of them to brush a long red curl as it trailed behind her ear and down her neck.

She shivered slightly. "To go with your two right hands, as I recall." She noticed his buttock tense under her stroking fingers and wondered if she was hurting him. Then she noticed the unmistakable evidence of his arousal and she glanced quickly up at him.

He watched her with hot eyes, his desire palpable. He must have sensed her responding heat. His next words implied as much. "I want you, honey. But right now I'd only disappoint both of us and embarrass myself. You almost done there?"

She scrubbed at the adhesive a little more, her knuckles brushing his arousal when she cleaned the area in front that had been covered by the bandage. The action was intimate, familiar and erotic all at the same time. He held his body tense, every muscle rigid until she had finished. Her own breathing was erratic, she realized, as she rose to put away the things she had used.

To her surprise he peeled his pants the rest of the way off and dropped them on the floor. "I'm gonna get a real shower for a change," he told her. He'd been limited the past few days by the need to keep his dressing dry. "Want to join me?'' His suggestion seemed made in jest, but she heard the challenge behind it, saw the dare lurking in his dark eyes. He was totally unconcerned with his nudity while she was aware of nothing else. She felt her face coloring and wrapped her robe more tightly around herself, wishing she had the nerve to call his bluff.

He only grinned and tipped her chin up. "Maybe next time," he said. "You blush real pretty for a redhead, Molly. You'd better git, before I haul you in there with me."

She left the door ajar slightly so she could hear him if he needed her and stood hugging herself outside it. His comment had caught her off guard but it also caused her to reflect.

They had never done anything like he'd suggested—never shared a bath or a shower.

She wasn't naive. She knew lovers did that. She'd lived in a dorm. Some of the girls there had shared a shower with a different partner every other week. But that reminded her too much of the kind of woman her father had favored. She had avoided any likeness to them at all costs.

And, to be honest, she sometimes wondered if that wasn't part of the reason she had feared that Charlie strayed. Their physical relationship had always been tender. Certainly he had wanted her often enough and he'd seemed satisfied. But she had listened to the talk of the women she'd worked with and, by comparison, what she'd shared with Charlie had sounded tame, conventional, unadventuresome. That wasn't entirely true, she amended mentally. Those poker games they had played were certainly...adventuresome. Yes, they'd had their moments.

But they'd been only moments. Bold, multihued splashes in a rather pale watercolor past. And he was her *husband* now. The thought of him going to another woman for what he couldn't get from her ate like acid on her soul.

Still, she'd heard the sly comments others made. No one was married on the road. How could she trust him, when she didn't know how to hold him?

Behind her, the water shut off abruptly and she hurried to the bedroom to dress.

When Charlie emerged a short time later, searching for his boots, she realized a part of him had left her already. He'd traded the casual button-downs he'd been wearing for a western-cut shirt complete with pearlized snaps. Not flashy, exactly, but not down-home. The black boots he eased into were some fancy leather she couldn't identify, stitched and tooled. The jeans were tight, the better to define what some fans had deemed the best legs in country music. He might only be a rhinestone cowboy, but he glittered when he walked.

He was Kick Cochrane again, the celebrity, the commodity, the product. She watched him standing at the counter, sipping coffee and scribbling something on a small piece of paper. Despite his appearance the eyes he lifted to her were still Charlie's, warm and concerned. He motioned her over to him.

"This is the hotel where I'll be staying tonight," he said pointing to a number on the paper. "I'll let you know day by day where I'll be." He grasped her chin and looked directly into her eyes. "You need me any other time—if I'm on the bus, performing, anytime—you call this number. Give whoever answers this name." He flicked his pencil against the paper. "You'll get me. If you need me, I'll come. You understand?"

She nodded. Glancing out the window that overlooked the street, he released her. Molly followed his gaze and saw a cab roll to a stop in front of their building. He turned to her with a torn expression. "I've got to go."

He reached for his hat and his duffel, dipped his head and touched his lips to hers. She couldn't watch him leave. Her back to him, she heard his steps across the floor, heard him open the door and pause, heard his bag hit the floor and his palm slap the jamb.

In moments he was back with her, turning her into his arms, the expression in his eyes savage. With his hand tangled in her hair gripping hard enough to hurt, he crushed his mouth to hers. There was nothing gentle or coaxing in his kiss. This was primal. A claim. A brand. And her response was the same. He plunged his tongue into her mouth and she welcomed it, stroked it, pulled him in until he groaned. She wrapped her arms around his neck and clung, eight years of longing in her embrace.

When he lifted his head, at last, she didn't open her eyes so he wouldn't see the plea in them. She heard his ragged breathing, but she would not look at him.

"Molly."

She shook her head, eyes squeezed shut. "Just go, Charlie."

He pressed a kiss to her forehead, his breath hot against her skin. "I'll come back to you as soon as I can."

"Please, Charlie, just go."

She felt his mouth on hers in a last, hard kiss and then his heat was gone. When she opened her eyes, finally, so was he.

She was in that fragile state between waking and sleeping when a shrill sound shattered the calm of the darkness. Her eyes shot open, her heart pounding like some wild thing struggling to be free of her chest.

The brittle ring cut the night again, recognizable this time. The phone! *Oh please, God, no!*

She pushed herself up in the bed, her trembling hand groping for the receiver. The clock tumbled to the carpeted floor where it landed facedown with a heavy thud. The phone slipped and clattered against the night table as she tried to bring it to her ear. *Please, God, not Tobie. Not when he's come so far.*

She slid her legs over the side of the bed, holding the receiver in two sweaty palms so she could speak into it. Her voice, when she answered, was thick with suppressed sobs.

"Molly?"

A sob escaped then, one of relief. "Charlie." Her suddenly boneless legs gave out and she sagged to the floor next to the bed.

"Are you all right, honey? What's wrong?"

"Just give me a minute," she gasped, trying to catch her breath. She laid her head back against the mattress and clutched the phone to her chest, sure he must hear the runaway gallop of her heartbeat. Some semblance of coordination returning to her limbs, she felt for the clock near her thigh and turned it so that she could read the flickering red numbers. Eleven forty-seven. She must have just drifted off.

She brought the receiver up again and spoke into it. "I'm sorry, Charlie. I thought you were the hospital."

"Aw, Molly." She heard the remorse in his voice. "I didn't think. We finished the show a little while ago and I was finally able to get away."

"It's okay."

"I won't call late again."

"No! Call." She swallowed and wiped the perspiration from her upper lip. Her breathing had regained some similarity to a normal pattern. "It'll give me something to look forward to…instead of something to dread."

"Are you sure? It's just that…I know I talked to you earlier today but… Well, you can't speak freely with Tobie sitting right there."

She realized then that his concern was as great as her own. He was hounded by the same fears, needed the same reassurances. As caring and helpful as the doctors and staff had been, she had never felt this kind of connection with them.

"I know, Charlie. Call." She sighed heavily. "He was the same today. There was no change."

"No worse, but no better."

"Dr. Morrissey said any improvement would be very gradual for the first several weeks. At least there are no signs of any problems." She would have the easier time of this, she understood now. She could see for herself Tobie's progress, day by day. "How did the show go?"

"Good. Folks have been great. Supportive. We're rescheduling like crazy. I can't see a break for the next month."

A *month*. With their relationship so shaky. How could they strengthen it this way? She missed him, and she didn't even feel comfortable with telling him so.

"Who's Shooter?" she asked for want of something to say.

Charlie's answer was a muffled groan. "Harlan mentioned him, did he?" He paused as if considering his words. "He's fairly new. Been with us maybe…six months. Plays pedal steel mostly. *Good* musician.''

"What's the problem with him?''

He paused again and she sensed his reluctance to discuss the man.

"The problem is with his drinking. When he gets to slammin' 'em back, he hits on fans. Young ones. Nothing illegal, I don't think. Just…real poor judgment.'' His agitation came over the line in a quick burst of expelled breath. "He'd be hard to replace. Last fellow we talked to wouldn't know a Dobro from a capo, had the nerve to call himself a musician. I hope Shooter can clean himself up. The band doesn't need a reputation for that kind of trouble.''

"Kick Cochrane, protector of fans. Is that how you see yourself?'' It was small of her, she knew, even as she said it. But she'd seen him in action. He knew his way around fans.

He was silent for so long she thought he wouldn't respond. When he did his tone was careful, measured. "There's something real unappealing about a thirty-year-old man coming on to sixteen-year-old girls. I wouldn't think even *you* would accuse me of that.''

"Charlie…''

"We've had this fight before, Molly. We both lost.''

"You're right.'' She had nothing to gain from antagonizing him. She had to learn to take him at his word, to bite her tart tongue, to keep her doubts and her misgivings to herself. It would help immensely if she couldn't hear the raucous laughter, the loud voices, the twangy music behind him even as they spoke. She could practically smell the smoke and the beer. "I'm sorry,'' she managed to get out.

"I'll call tomorrow.''

"Yes.'' She hung up, wide awake now with her memories and her fears.…

She steered her bicycle toward her daddy's store, dodging pedestrians on the wide sidewalks of the plaza on Market Street. She was proud of her skill on the bike. Since spring she'd been allowed to ride it to school in good weather.

Of course, she'd had to argue with Momma about that, but Daddy had taken her side and, eventually, he'd won out. Daddy and Momma argued all the time anyway, so it didn't bother her much. She was in third grade, after all. *Fourth* grade, she corrected herself. She'd just been promoted. With straight *A*s. She released one of the handlebar grips and patted the brown report-card envelope she had tucked into the front waistband of her shorts.

Daddy would be pleased with that. She couldn't wait to show him. He'd smile a mile. She grinned herself at the thought, feeling her lips stick to her teeth as the wind dried them. The breeze felt good against her skin as she pedaled the bike. It was a stinky hot day. She had her hair hiked up in pigtails to keep it off her neck.

She'd better stay away from Charlie. Sashaying past him with her pigtails was like waving a red flag in front of a bull. He could never resist a quick yank.

Not that he was ever mean about it. He was the best friend a kid could have. He'd taught her to ride this snazzy bike, running along beside her, his hands gripping the seat, while her daddy was too tied up with business and her momma kept to her room. She didn't mind his good-natured ribbing about the pink fenders and the purple plastic tassels streaming from her handlebars, either. Although, to be honest, she secretly admired the banana seat on his bike and the fact that it had no fenders at all.

She slowed as she neared the corner where her daddy's building stood. Hauling her bike around the side, she squinted up at the sun. The seat would be hotter than blazes by the time she got out, but Daddy had chided her often enough about leaving her bicycle in front where it might get in the way of customers. She sighed, nudged the kickstand down with her toe and parked the bike. Careful to avoid the drips from the air-conditioning unit that rattled a few feet above her head, she skipped into the building by the service door.

The corridor was cool and dim. And quiet. Daddy was in his office, most likely. These midafternoon hours were the slowest for the store. The early-bird shoppers had come and gone and the late-afternoon crowd, heading home from their offices, hadn't yet put in an appearance. She stopped at the water fountain for a quick drink and slipped her report card out of her shorts so she wouldn't get splashes on it.

She headed down the hallway, past the deserted stockroom and the door marked Authorized Personnel Only that she knew was just the employee restroom, to the third door on the right. Her daddy's office.

The outer room where Miss Bonnie held sway appeared empty.

Miss Bonnie had been her daddy's secretary since she graduated high school five years before. During that period she had married, had a baby, and divorced, but she had always been *Miss* Bonnie to Molly. None of those events had affected her sunny disposition or her awful typing, but her position at Doyle's Furniture and Appliance, at least, seemed secure.

Molly eased up to the corner of the desk where the secretary kept a cut-glass dish filled with cellophane-wrapped mints and snitched a couple. Evidently her daddy helped himself to these, too, she thought, unwrapping one and popping it into her mouth. He came home smelling of mints pretty often.

There didn't seem to be anybody around, Molly decided, glancing about the office. Sometimes when things were slow, her daddy relieved the salesmen while they had a cup of coffee and a smoke at the lunch counter across the street. Maybe Miss Bonnie had joined them.

She turned to go look out front in the store proper when a sound stopped her. A strange, animal-like sound. Not a whimper, not a groan. Something in between. It seemed to come from Daddy's private, inner office on the right. Molly looked that way, saw the door slightly ajar, and crept over. The door made no sound over the carpeted floor as she pushed it further open, peered around it, and froze in place.

The smell hit her first. A sharp, strong, slightly sweet odor. She'd smelled it sometimes on her daddy's breath when he'd stumble into her room late at night to listen to her prayers and kiss her good-night. It wasn't an unpleasant odor, but she didn't like it.

Her eyes registered a number of images all at once. The bottle and two glasses on the cluttered desk, each partly filled with a liquid the color of weak tea without milk. The brassy blond hair of Miss Bonnie, come loose from the combs that usually scraped it into a frizzy cascade at the back of her head, now tumbling in wild disarray. The splashy, flower-patterned dress hiked high on Miss Bonnie's thighs. And those thighs spread wide astride a man's lap.

Her daddy's lap.

Molly knew it, though she couldn't see his face. From their position, it appeared his face was buried somewhere in the front of Miss Bonnie's dress.

But that was her daddy. Those were his arms wrapped around his secretary's backside, white shirtsleeves rolled up to reveal the dusting of red hair on his freckled skin. Those were his hands cradling the woman's bottom, clenching in the fabric of her dress as he guided her hips in a rhythmic push and pull. Those were his fingers, one of them circled by a ring of white gold that was a match to Momma's, sliding beneath the hem of the skirt, revealing to anyone who cared to look that Miss Bonnie was wearing nothing at all underneath her dress.

Of course, they didn't expect anybody to be looking. That much was obvious, even to Molly. Whatever faint noise she might have made was covered by the drone of the air conditioner, the radio turned on low with Tammy Wynette warbling about no-good, cheatin'-hearted men and the foolish women who loved them anyway, and the disgusting sounds made by the couple grappling on the creaky chair behind the desk.

Suddenly Molly's stomach cramped and churned. Afraid she would be sick, she wheeled and ran through the office, down the corridor and out the door she had come in.

She'd almost made it to her bike before she had to stop and brace herself against the baking brick. She spit out what remained of the mint and upchucked the lemonade she'd sipped after school at Grover's drugstore. With shaking hands she pulled the hem of her T-shirt free of her shorts and wiped her streaming eyes.

Only then did she remember the report card still clutched in her hand. She slipped the stiff white paper from its envelope and opened it to look at the grades she'd earned with such pride. They meant nothing to her now. Her fingers trembling, she ripped the paper into tiny shreds and threw them to the breeze that scattered them across the asphalt parking lot. Then she sagged against the brick wall of the store and crumpled to a heap at its base. Knees drawn up, she wrapped her arms around them and cried until there were no tears left.

She never told a living soul what she had seen. Not Momma, not Lucy, not Charlie. Especially not Charlie.

When her daddy asked her later that evening, with mint on his breath, what had happened to her report card, she shrugged and looked vague. If he could lie without saying a word, so could she. Days later they got a copy of the report from the school and her daddy was pleased, as she knew he would be. But when he suggested an ice-cream sundae to celebrate, she recalled his hands where they'd had no business being and she said, "No, thank you." If he ever wondered about her withdrawal over the next weeks, he never betrayed it by word or deed. And, gradually, she adjusted to the sham that passed for her family life.

But her innocence had died that day. She'd learned her lesson well. Never trust an easy smile and a glib promise. And when she grew from girl to woman and found it was her destiny, or her misfortune, or maybe only the capricious whim of fate that she loved a man who was so much like her father, she remembered that lesson. She remembered that a man you adored, even one who claimed to love you, could cheat and scheme and lie right through his smiling teeth.

Chapter 7

Charlie came awake when Harlan rapped lightly and entered his bedroom at the back of the bus. He slept better on the bus than just about anywhere else. The steady rumble of the engine was mind-numbing enough to knock him out.

He knuckled his eyes, rolled to the side of the bed and stood, hauling a pair of jeans up over his briefs. Still only half awake, he shambled to the sink, splashed water on his face and brushed his teeth. Scratching his fingers over his scalp and ruffling up his sleep-matted hair, he turned to Harlan.

"What time is it?"

"A little after seven." Harlan sank into the barrel chair next to the bed and tapped the rolled paper in his hand against his knee. "I thought you'd be awake."

Charlie blinked a few times and rubbed his chest. "What day is it?"

"Friday," the other man answered with a short laugh.

Charlie stretched to adjust the window blind and squinted out at the telephone poles whizzing by. "Then this must be Tulsa." They'd been in Memphis last night. He'd actually slept in his own bed at his place just outside of Nashville the night before that. *Big* bed. He'd wished Molly had been in it with him.

"We should be pulling into town in about half an hour." Harlan paused for a moment and fingered the paper. "We've got a problem with tonight's show."

Charlie gave his friend a long glance over his shoulder. "So what's new?" This road trip was turning into the usual chaos, compounded by the fact that they were squeezing in dates to make up for the ones they had missed. He'd been back less than two weeks and already it felt like a month. He'd had a few free hours in Nashville to get a little shopping in and that had been the extent of his time off.

At least Tobie had sounded cheerful when they'd talked the last few times, and Molly had been pleasant. More than pleasant. There had been no repeat of the comments she'd made when he'd called that first night. He sensed a genuine longing in her to have things right between them. An answer to his own hunger.

"This isn't just a couple blown amps."

He stopped in the process of smearing shaving cream on his jaw to glance again at Harlan. "What's the problem?" He took a swipe over his cheek with the blade.

Harlan watched him in dismay. "I'll never understand how you can shave with a razor on a moving bus. I'd be afraid I'd slit my throat." He shook his head and continued. "They had a fire at the arena last night. Just a small one. Nobody hurt. But the fire marshal put in an appearance. Padlocked the doors until they bring the wiring up to code. We're locked out."

Charlie thought for a minute, rinsing his blade under the tap. "What else is available?"

"It's a Friday night, Kick. Everything big enough is already booked." Charlie turned full around, leaning his hip against the sink, to look at Harlan. "We're gonna have to cancel," his friend informed him.

He felt his heartbeat kick up into overdrive. He tried for

all he was worth to keep the elation out of his voice. "St. Louis tomorrow night, right?"

Harlan nodded.

"What's the latest I can show up?"

"Sound check's at six."

Charlie let out a low whistle. "I'll do the radio station interviews here as long as they're early. Tell Nada to get on the phone and see about getting me a flight to Pittsburgh. Private plane is fine. I don't give a damn about the cost." He toweled the rest of the foam from his face. "I'm goin' home."

Harlan rose, his eyes glinting and his mustache curving upward over his smile. "I'll see to it."

Charlie waited for the door to close behind the other man before he fisted his hand and punched the air. Hot *damn!* He had a day and a *night* off.

"He's lost all his hair."

"What?"

"He's lost all his hair, Charlie. The doctor warned us this would happen from the medication, remember?"

He remembered, all right. It was one of those bits of information he'd shoved aside under the heading "things to worry about later." Well, it was later. He'd let Molly know what time to expect him and she'd intercepted him before he reached Tobie's room. Now he knew why.

"When?" he asked, slowing his stride to match hers as they made their way down the hallway. Had this happened days ago and she was keeping it from him? He didn't want that. He wanted to know what was going on with his son, the good and the bad.

"This morning. Most of it was spread over his pillow when I walked in." She lifted her palms in a helpless gesture. "The rest just came out in clumps when I rubbed my hand on his head." She shrugged. "All at once. Just like that."

"How's he doing with this?" They stopped outside Tobie's room.

"He's a little down." Charlie detected the quaver in her

voice. Her lips tightened and her eyes filled but, with an effort, she regained her composure. "He's happy you're here, Charlie." She gripped his arm and looked directly into his eyes. "And so am I." Raising her face to him, she pressed her mouth to his.

Encumbered as he was with a big white box under one arm and his bag held in the other, he couldn't embrace her. But he wouldn't ignore her invitation. Instead he deepened the kiss, leaning into her until her head rested against the corridor wall behind her. He slipped his tongue along the seam of her lips, coaxing her to open to him. When she did, he dipped into her, sipping and stroking. He felt her hands creep up his shirtfront to frame his face gently and hold him to her as, oblivious to the activity in the hallway around them, she kissed him back. His tongue took one last, long, slow sweep of her mouth and he lifted his head.

She'd pinked up nicely, and he was pleased to feel her breath coming in choppy pants. Her lips were puffy, wet, and still parted. That had been no wifely peck of greeting. She'd forgotten herself in that kiss.

Of course, so had he. Bringing them both back to the present, he said, "Let's go see Tobie."

Moments later he appreciated Molly's warning. They'd been told forthrightly that Tobie would lose his hair. They'd even been prepared for the lag time between the administration of the medication and the loss. But he wouldn't have wanted to walk into this cold.

His boy looked like a little old man. The few remaining tufts of his hair stood like chicken down on his head. Even his eyebrows were patchy and sparse. Charlie told himself this didn't make Tobie any sicker, though it surely made him appear that way.

He used the few minutes he spent washing his hands to collect himself before he went to greet his son. Then he hugged him hard, trying to determine if it was only wishful thinking that made him believe the child in his arms was a little more sturdy, a pound or two heavier.

If Tobie was upset by his hair falling out, he did a good

job of covering it. He greeted his father eagerly and seemed especially anxious to find out what was in the white box.

"I believe I promised you a present, didn't I?" Charlie set the box, which resembled a bakery-cake box, only bigger, on the bed and dug in his jeans for his pocketknife. He cut the strings that held it closed and nodded to Tobie to lift the lid.

The round-eyed expression on his son's face as he regarded his gift was all the reward Charlie could ask for. Carefully, he lifted the black Stetson from the box and handed it to Tobie.

"It's been steamed to curve just like mine, and you can leave the feather in the band or take it out, whichever you like."

Tobie shot a quick glance at the featherless hat his father had set on the bedside table and took the feather out of his. Charlie grinned at Molly over their son's head, and she smiled back, but there was a concern in her eyes he couldn't comprehend. Only a moment later, he understood.

Tobie placed the hat on his head and it settled low, nearly covering his eyes and flopping his ears down like the handles on a jug. The kid looked like one of those seven dwarfs, Charlie thought. Bashful maybe, or Dopey. Aw, God. Tobie'd had a thick head of hair when he'd measured him, and he hadn't taken this into consideration.

Molly recovered first. She plucked the hat from his head. "You'll need to wear a scarf with this, honey, till your hair grows back. You know, like a pirate."

"I've got just the thing," Charlie said, following Molly's lead. He rummaged through his duffel bag, coming up with one of the big patterned bandannas he sometimes tossed to fans during a show. Quickly he tied it on Tobie's head, knotting it over one ear. When Tobie adjusted the hat this time, it was a good fit.

"Real cowboys wear it like that sometimes," Charlie offered, "to keep their sweat from staining the hat too much. Course, I wouldn't know firsthand," he continued. "I haven't been on a horse since I was a kid taking pony rides at the fairgrounds."

They seemed to have kidded Tobie through the difficult situation and Charlie looked at Molly with new admiration. How many situations like this had she coped with? She dealt with Tobie's fatigue, his disappointments, his boredom, his crankiness hour by hour, day by day, week by week, with no relief, no letup. Meanwhile she maintained her own cheerfulness and concealed her fear. For the short while he'd be here, he could give her some support.

He noted the empty dishes on the over-bed table that indicated Tobie had finished lunch. He'd bet Molly hadn't. "Why don't you go get something to eat?" he suggested. "Tobie and I will have some guy-talk."

Molly looked a little uncertain about the idea, but tempted all the same. "What about you?"

"I ate on the plane." He removed the tray from the table to a pass-through near the door. Returning to the bedside, he hooked the toe of his boot around the wooden leg of a chair, dragging the chair up close and taking a seat. Tobie was already digging in the over-bed table for the deck of cards and pile of pennies he'd won the last time, while Molly still hesitated.

"Go on," Charlie urged. "Take your time. We'll be fine." He was emptying his pockets of his own stake when Molly headed out the door. He noted that in his absence Tobie had perfected the shuffle he'd taught him. "Dealer calls the game. Name your poison."

"Five Card Draw," Tobie answered, leveling a glance at him from under the hat brim. Kid was a natural. "Deuces, fives, tens, and one-eyed jacks are wild."

Charlie huffed. "You've been playing with your mother again, I can tell." He shook his head. "I hate to burst your bubble, but when you play with the fellas, they're never gonna let you call every other card wild, and there is *no* such hand as seven aces."

"She said you taught her how to play," Tobie commented, putting four cards aside and drawing four more from the deck.

Charlie hoped that was all she said. He discarded one loser and Tobie gave him a replacement. "Sometimes you have to have special rules for females. Your momma's not much of a poker player.''

Tobie did a dead-on imitation of Molly rolling her eyes. Maybe there was more of her in the boy than he'd first suspected, Charlie thought.

"She's awful, Dad," he said with a laugh. He made a big show of placing his bet, and Charlie saw it.

Tobie laid out his hand with a flourish. "Full house, aces on top."

Charlie glanced at the cards on the table and saw junk, ace high, but he looked at his son's laughing face, folded his own two pair, natural, and conceded.

They continued their good-natured play for a while. Charlie noted his son appeared to have a flair for the game, even disregarding the bent rules. But after a time, Tobie began to tire.

"Would you like to stop for a while? Take a nap?" Charlie suggested.

"Okay, I guess." Tobie seemed reluctant, but resigned. "Will you still be here when I wake up?"

Charlie looked into his son's uncertain eyes. "I'll be here. I'm not gonna disappear on you. And I'm not just talking about right now." He pushed the table out of the way, leaned forward and rested his elbows on his knees. "Tobie, performing is what I do for a living. Some kids' daddies drive trucks and some fix leaky toilets. I write songs, and I'm lucky enough that people pay me to sing 'em. So sometimes I have to be gone."

Tobie was quiet but he didn't take his eyes from his father's face. Charlie pushed on.

"I'll be here tonight and tomorrow morning. Then I have to go back. It doesn't matter where I am, I'm still your daddy. I think about you all the time. If you need me, I'll be here."

Tobie nodded, seemingly reassured. He removed his Stetson and lay back against the pillow, settling the hat on his chest. Charlie reached to take it and put it aside, but Tobie stopped him. "Leave it where I can touch it, Dad."

Charlie leaned back in his chair, propped his elbows on its

arms and folded his hands on his abdomen, watching his son's eyes grow heavier. Still fighting sleep, Tobie murmured, "I love you, Dad, and not just because you're...you know...famous."

Charlie's breath caught. How easily the words seemed to slip over his boy's tongue. At what point did they become so difficult to say? And why? He could think of a dozen, an easy dozen, people he loved deeply and he couldn't recall ever saying those words as an adult. Not even to Molly. And God knew how much and how long he'd loved her.

He licked his lips. "Well, let me tell you something," he began. Already he could feel his pulse quicken and his palms grow damp. "I love you, too." There, that wasn't so hard. "And not just because you're...you know...bald."

Tobie seemed to reflect on that for some moments. Then a scowl knitted what was left of his eyebrows below the red bandanna. "What's *that* got to do with anything?" he groused.

Charlie gave a low chuckle. "Exactly," he said.

He watched as his son lost his battle to stay awake. Tobie drifted off with his fingers still curled around the curved brim of his hat. Charlie leaned forward, stretched his arm across the bed rail and settled his hand there, too.

They ate dinner at the hospital cafeteria before heading home that night. Charlie didn't want to have to deal with public recognition in a restaurant and Molly, not anticipating his visit, had nothing special to fix at home.

Not that she needed to worry. All his money and high living hadn't affected his tastes much. He seemed perfectly happy to scarf down the Swiss steak smothered in gravy that the hospital dished up.

"He's going to need more room, Molly."

Charlie's voice broke the silence in the van as he steered it down the city streets toward their apartment. She had known this was coming, that it was only a matter of time before he pointed out that the flat was too small to be suitable for Tobie when he came home to recuperate. The fact that she agreed with him didn't alter the fact that she found herself forced to accept more of his generosity. "I know," she said.

He slid a glance her way. Her pride was nipping at her, but she was doing her best to be gracious. He'd try to make this easy for her. "He's not gonna be able to go to school, or a public pool, a ball game, the zoo, for the next year. He's gonna need some space to roam around, keep from going stir crazy."

She turned her head slightly to look at him and softened somewhat as she read in his face his effort to be accommodating. "It sounds like you've had some feelers out."

He nodded his assent and stole another quick glance. "I've been in touch with a local agent. I figured you're too busy with Tobie to waste a lot of time hunting around. Anyway, she found a place outside of town, part of an estate the heirs are squabbling over. The place is up for rent until everything is settled." He stopped at a traffic light and rested a hand on the seat behind her head while they waited. "It's on a good piece of land, with a little woods and a pond where he could fish, have a playmate over now and then. The house itself is not real fancy, I've been told, but I think you'd like it."

It sounded like a palace. She said nothing, only looked down at her hands.

He gave a heavy sigh and eased the car forward as the light changed. "We'd have first option to buy when everything's straightened out, if you're happy with it."

Her head came up sharply then. "Would you want to relocate around here?"

He shrugged. "I like this area. Hell, I've been a Pirates' fan all my life. And it's close to my folks, but not too close. I love 'em, but I wouldn't want to live in their pockets. Besides, you and Tobie have put down roots here."

"I thought you had a home," she said, staring at his profile, shifting in and out of view as they passed the streetlights.

"Outside of Nashville, yeah." He gave a short laugh. "I'm there maybe four weeks out of the year. Need it mainly when I'm recording. We can spend some time there, if you like, when Tobie's stabilized." He glanced at her. "Hell, I'm not fussy, Molly. I live on a bus."

She bit her bottom lip, shook her head, and laughed a little to herself. She could just imagine that bus.

"So, what do you say? We can take a look tomorrow morning before we go to the hospital."

What was the point in being petty? He didn't flaunt his wealth. It was just there, at his disposal. He could be happy in a two-room hole-in-the-wall. She knew. She'd been there with him. "That'll be fine," she said, and smiled at him.

He didn't really need to unpack. Just his shaving things and the gift he'd brought for Molly. He figured the way she reacted to his present would pretty well determine how things would go for the rest of the evening. She'd changed into jeans and a T-shirt, locking herself in the bathroom to do so. That wasn't a good sign. He didn't remember her being all *that* modest.

When he walked into the living room, feeling like a supplicant with his gift in his hand, she was setting two mugs on the counter. Tea for her and coffee for him. She'd never make a tea drinker out of him.

She glanced up, eyes wide and mouth agape when he set the package on the counter. The lady at the lingerie store had wrapped it with their trademark paper, all the while making coy remarks about him being newly married. Meantime he'd just wanted to crawl in a hole. He would never get used to the type of female who could talk about uplift and cleavage and French cut with any yo-yo who happened to walk in.

He didn't think Molly recognized the wrap. Probably she didn't buy her underthings at boutiques. "This is for me?" she said.

"Well, yeah. I hope you like it." He hoped they'd get over this stiffness that seemed to have insinuated itself between them since they'd been home, too.

She opened the present the way she always did, carefully, without tearing the paper even a little bit, folding it neatly and putting it aside, while he sat on his hands. He heard her inhale through pursed lips as she spread the tissue paper and lifted the teddy out of the box. "It's lovely, Charlie," she breathed.

Yes, it was. Just the right color for her skin, too. Champagne, not white. And not much froufrou at all. Only an edging of lace to encircle each thigh and a little patch there toward the center to show off her...cleavage. "I was kind of hoping you'd wear it to bed tonight."

Oh, yes, he was. He was still trying to decide if he'd undo the snaps first, taking his sweet time about it, his fingers lingering there between her thighs and lifting the teddy up. Or should he slide those skimpy straps off her shoulders, taking his sweet time about it, his mouth lingering over her breasts, while he skimmed the teddy down and off. Maybe they'd try it both ways, taking their sweet time about it, just to see which way they liked best.

"Maybe," he heard her say, but her smile was brittle and she was folding the garment into the box again. She put the gift aside and regarded him with an uneasy look.

Uneasy. What the hell was this? He wasn't the world's greatest lover, but he'd never been anything but tender, considerate with her. She had no call to be skittish with him.

He got off the stool, trying to swallow his disappointment.

With more conviction in his voice than he felt, he said, "Let's have some music, Molly. What would you like?" He strode over to her CD player, fingering the discs.

"Play something of yours," she suggested, perking up a little.

"Ugh. I can hardly stand to listen to some of them anymore." He pulled a disc from the rack. "How about George? He's got a nice way with a ballad. You like him, I can tell."

He started the player and the mellow tenor flowed around the room like warm syrup over hotcakes. Both arms braced on the shelves, Charlie eyed Molly over his shoulder. "Come dance with me, honey."

She hesitated just a moment before she rose and walked toward him. He stood facing her and smiled to himself as she wiped her palms down the front of her jeans. A characteristic gesture, one he recalled her making every single time they'd danced together. Unless things had changed considerably in the last eight years, and he'd venture to guess they hadn't, Molly was still no dancer.

She laid one hand on his shoulder and the other in his palm. Very proper. Her momma would approve. They hadn't completed a turn around the room, though, when they banged knees pretty good. Molly lifted her head to apologize and bumped his chin.

"I'm sorry, Charlie," she murmured, catching her lip between her teeth.

"It's all right. Just relax." He felt her stiffen even more in his arms and he grinned into her hair. Couple more awkward turns, and she came down real hard on his instep. He laughed out loud, then, and she looked up at him, her face a flustered shade of red.

"Did you forget everything I ever taught you?" he said when he could. "I will never understand how a woman with your musical ability can have absolutely no sense of rhythm."

"It's all in my hands, Charlie," she said, laughing with him. "It's a long way from my hands to my feet."

He stared down into her face, the smile leaving his, and a smoldering expression replacing it. "Kick off your shoes, Molly."

She'd known how this would end the moment he'd asked her to dance. And if she were honest with herself, she would admit that this was what she wanted. She backed away from him a little, pushed her shoes off and nudged them to the side of the room. Then she stepped back into his arms, placing her stockinged feet over the tops of his boots. The old way. The way he'd taught her.

He slid his thumbs into the back pockets of her jeans, spreading his fingers over the curves of her bottom and pulling her close. Just the way he always had. The position threw her off balance slightly, so that she had to wrap her arms around his neck to keep from tipping backward. She rested her forehead against his cheek, and thigh to thigh, belly to belly, chest to chest, his body communicating its every desire to hers, they danced.

Past and present merged in her mind, and the years slipped away.

She remembered the first time they had danced like this. Charlie had been performing at the old Blue Moon Lounge in Wheeling, and she'd gone with Lucy to see him. Lucy'd had her eye on the band's drummer at the time and disappeared with him when the group took a break. Molly had been left with Charlie.

He'd been leery of her, careful not to be alone with her, since that kiss they'd shared the previous summer. But the hour was late, the lights were dim, and the jukebox was chugging out slow ones. So he'd asked her to dance, taught her to dance.

That was the first time she'd truly experienced exactly what desire did to a man's body. Nestled against him, absorbing his heat, she was aware of his every breath, every pulse beat. And against her belly, she could feel him rise and swell.

She'd been embarrassed when she realized what was happening, and, to his credit, he'd seemed embarrassed, too. Charlie'd never been one to impose himself on a woman. He'd apologized when he noticed her confusion and guided her to a small, secluded table where she had a soda and he smoked. But whenever she'd lifted her gaze from the glass to steal a glance at him, she'd found his black eyes watching her.

At last he'd stubbed out his cigarette and leaned toward her. "I'm sorry," he'd told her, "if I offended you. I didn't mean to, and I don't expect anything. But you're beautiful—" those were his exact words; he thought she was beautiful "—and sometimes just thinking about you does that to me."

It was another year before he held her that way again. In between she'd seen him with a different girl every week, two-steppin' his way across hearts. And she'd done her share of dating, too, slapping the young men's hands away from her bra and out from under her skirt. They didn't seem to have nearly the consideration for her person that Charlie did.

The next time they'd danced had been at a party at the Cochranes'. His family gave the best parties. They didn't have much money, so everyone brought drinks and food. But music and laughter and good times rocked the house. Molly had finagled an invitation from Lucy, though they weren't as close as they once had been.

The house had gotten hot and loud. Molly escaped to the yard where the night air was cool and filled with the high-pitched buzz of crickets rubbing their wings together in eager anticipation of whatever it is that crickets eagerly anticipate. She saw Charlie sitting in the darkness on the bottom back porch stair, smoking and sipping a long-neck. He must have had the same idea.

She eased down beside him and, with her hand on his, guided his bottle to her mouth.

He jerked it back. "No, dammit, you're too young."

"Lucy has one."

"Not if I catch her." He glanced over at her mutinous face. "You can get into all kinds of trouble that way, Molly."

She turned her head to look away. "You think I'm a little girl."

He took a long drag on his cigarette and blew a cloud of smoke high into the air. "No, Molly," he said with more vehemence than she expected. "I don't think you're a little girl." He took a slow pull on his bottle and licked his lips. "You're a lovely young woman. Smart. With a future." His gaze settled on her, gentle as the moonlight. "I'm not what your momma has planned for you, honey."

"Look at me, Charlie," she answered with a laugh. "I'm the image of my father. I faced the truth a long time ago." She shook her wild red head sadly. "I'm not what my momma planned, period. I'll do what I want with my life."

A slow tune, all throbbing guitars and moaning fiddles, drifted through the screens on the back of the house. Molly's heart ached in answer. "Dance with me, Charlie," she whispered.

He looked at her with his teasing half smile, more in self-defense than anything, but she couldn't know that. "You've learned how, then?"

That cut. She stood abruptly and turned to go back inside, but he grabbed her wrist. He set his bottle on the step and ground his cigarette out on the heel of his boot, then rose to face her, all teasing gone from his expression. "Be careful what you ask for, honey. Sometimes you just might get it." He slid his hands around her, hooking his thumbs in the pockets of her jeans, spreading his fingers over her bottom. "Kick your shoes off, Molly."

He never took his eyes from hers as she did what she was told. She doubled her arms around his neck and balanced herself on the tops of his boots, her toes gripping. Unafraid and unembarrassed, she didn't pull away this time when he settled himself in the notch at the top of her thighs. Instead, she rocked to him, eliciting a deep-throated groan that vibrated from his chest into hers. Their position raised her enough so that he only needed to tilt his head a little to dip his tongue into her mouth, open and waiting for him.

She lost herself in the taste and scent and feel of him. The lean, hard muscles shifting under her hands and against the softness of her breasts. The masculine flavors of tobacco and beer mingling with the salty tang that was distinctly Charlie. The sultry, arousing smell of sweat on hot skin. In his arms she lost all sense of time and place and propriety.

As if from far away, she became aware of his hand working its way under her shirt, fumbling with her bra, sliding around to her breast. His fingers, calloused and stealthy as a whisper, stroked her nipple. She twisted one hand in the neckline of his T-shirt, combed the fingers of the other through the long, thick hair at his nape and thrust herself against him. Barely moving, they swayed in time to the music and made love with their mouths, Molly telling him as clearly as her young heart could, just what she would do for him, with him, if only he would ask.

But he didn't. Not that night.

And slowly Molly drifted back to the present to find his hands under her shirt, her bra hanging loose, useless, his palms cradling her breasts, his thumbs teasing her nipples to pouting, begging peaks. His tongue trailed a hot path along her neck, teeth nibbling, lips suckling their way to her swollen, exquisitely sensitive mouth.

He nudged himself against her, his thick, hard shaft clearly delineated through the soft denim of his jeans, and she realized that hers were already undone, the zipper parting even more as he pushed his hand into them, slipping his fingers into her panties.

She slammed back to reality with a vengeance. "Oh, no, Charlie! We *can't!*" She pushed at him frantically, trying to dislodge the hands that seemed to be everywhere.

He was too far gone to heed her. "It's okay, honey," he muttered into her ear, his breath hot against her skin. "Shhh. I can make it good for you, I swear."

"Charlie! We can't!" She shoved him hard and he released her, standing back, his breathing labored and deep.

He stared into her distraught face and her words registered at last. Not "Charlie, I don't want to." Not "Charlie, I don't feel like it." But "Charlie, we *can't!*" And he thought somewhere, for certain, the gods must be laughing at him.

All the tumblers to this lock clicked into place. Her heightened concern with privacy while she changed her clothes. Her lack of enthusiasm for his gift. Her uneasiness when he suggested she wear it to bed. And her words, "Charlie, we *can't.*" He looked at her stricken expression and saw his plans for this one damn night going up in the smoke that surely must be coming out his ears.

"Margaret Mary," he was barely able to get out. "Are you on the rag?"

She paled, then reddened and focused her gaze in the vicinity of his Adam's apple. "Charlie, that is so vulgar."

He raised imploring eyes heavenward. God, that was it. He's dying here, and she's worried about vulgar? "*Are* you?"

She ran her tongue over her lips and spoke to his throat. "I have my—" she swallowed hard "—period, yes."

He raked his fingers through his hair and tried to get a grip on himself. He wasn't some kind of raving animal. He was a faithful husband. A *frustrated* faithful husband.

"I'm sorry, Charlie."

She looked so distressed. He wanted to take her in his arms, to soothe her. That wouldn't be a good idea. He wished she'd get her clothes back together, but he wasn't goi g to h lp her with that, either.

As if she read his thoughts, she worked at the zipper on her jeans and made that awkward-armed move women did when they tried to hook up their bras. He had to look away.

"I don't know what came over me, Charlie," he heard her say, and glanced back to see her shaking the curls that tumbled in beguiling disarray. "I just forgot." She shrugged and he had to look away again.

Maybe the situation wasn't as hopeless as he thought. If she'd been aroused enough to forget herself for a minute there. Maybe… "What are we talking about, here, honey? Is this just the beginning? Or…or, maybe…you know." He made a vague gesture with his hand. "The…uh…the end?" He'd almost said *tail* end, but caught himself. For sure, that'd be vulgar.

Didn't matter. She was looking at him like he'd suggested eating rattlesnake. "Are you saying it wouldn't make any difference?" she asked in a disbelieving tone.

It was hopeless. He'd never been able to coax a woman past this particular hang-up. To tell the truth, he'd never really put much effort into it before. But she had her hand spread over her chest like she did when she was greatly appalled about something. He'd just try to get out of this with as much dignity as he could muster.

He settled his hands on her shoulders and inhaled deeply. "I'm gonna take a shower, Molly. A cold one. And you're not invited this time." He gave her shoulders a firm squeeze and released her, then added with a wink and a forced smile as he moved away, "I'd appreciate it if you *didn't* wear that teddy to bed tonight."

Molly rummaged through the bottom drawer of her dresser and dug out the gown she'd sworn she'd never wear. The women at the office had been kind to give it to her and she appreciated their thoughtfulness, but something like this would never have called her name.

She shook out the voluminous folds and laid the nightgown on the bed. White and ruffled about summed it up. Deeply ruffled around the neckline, ruffled long sleeves, a huge flounce—that was the only word to describe it—at the hem. It was ghastly. Perfect for tonight.

She quickly shed her clothes and pulled the garment over her head, almost suffocating in the yards of fabric before she got her face and hands through the openings. She glanced at her image in the mirror above the dresser. Better, but the hair was still a problem. She scraped it back with a comb and wove it into a braid tight enough to make her eyes slant.

Just in time. She heard Charlie emerging from the bathroom. He stood gape-jawed as she moved to go past him and take her turn. From the corner of her eye she stole a glimpse of the clothing he held ready to stash in the hamper. His underwear and the T-shirt he'd worn. Evidently he'd just slipped his jeans back on to rejoin her before shucking them entirely and getting into bed.

Oh, my. He was going to sleep in nothing tonight. Like he always had. The thought left her strangely breathless.

Her own nighttime preparations took just a few minutes. When she returned to the bedroom, Charlie was stretched out on the unmade bed, bare feet crossed at the ankles, hands folded behind his head. He still wore the jeans.

"Where'd you get that?" He asked the question as if her gown were the only thing on his mind since she'd left the room. Probably, it had been.

She smoothed her hands over the copious folds. "The ladies I worked with gave it to me as a wedding present."

"Did they think you were Scarlett O'Hara?"

She laughed. "It's not my taste exactly, but they meant well." She fingered the fabric. "I guess it's supposed to be bridal."

Charlie's heated gaze met hers. "What's under it is plenty bridal enough for me."

She felt herself coloring under his scrutiny. "I'm so sorry, Charlie. I didn't know how to bring—"

"Hey, I'm cool. Everything's settled down, now. Don't fret." He gave her another long perusal, his eyes lighting on her face this time. "You're not wearing your hair that way to bed."

Her hand went to the braid hanging down her back. "It's all—"

He let out a disgusted breath and shook his head. "C'mere, Molly." He sat up and patted the center of the mattress, inviting her to sit next to him.

She floated over to the bed and climbed in. He gripped her shoulders and turned her so her back was to him. She sat cross-legged, the gown puffing around her like a cloud. As he released the band holding the braid, she felt a tug and then his long fingers threading through her hair, gently combing out the snags. She placed a hand on each knee and tipped her head forward a little, enjoying the sensation.

All at once he stopped and she waited, not breathing, for what he would do next.

"You look like a marshmallow, honey," he murmured. "Do you taste just as sweet?"

She felt the warm flat of his hand against her nape as he pushed her hair up out of the way and exposed that vulnerable spot. His mouth pressed to her, hot and wet. Then he systematically kissed and bit and licked each bony prominence of her spine down to the neckline of her gown and back up again while she sat perfectly still, swamped by the most overwhelmingly intense wave of desire she'd ever experienced. He touched her only with his mouth, his hand having left her to help support him on the bed. But she responded with her whole body, feeling a heavy languor engulf her. Her breasts swelled and tingled. Her womb clenched. Her toes curled.

She had read somewhere that a woman didn't reach the peak of her sexual responsiveness until her early thirties, but that information had held no meaning for her. Until now.

Now, when every nerve ending seemed to howl her need. A need that must go unfulfilled, unsated, tonight.

Charlie's mouth had ceased its sensual plunder and his forehead rested in the curve of her shoulder. Through his stillness she could tell he was struggling again for control. He raised his head, finally, kissed the spot where it had rested and turned to switch off the light on the table next to him. "Good night, Molly," he said into the darkness that enclosed them.

She lifted the sheet and settled herself in alongside him. She heard the bed creak as he sat up, heard the rasp of his zipper, the swoosh of his jeans from his body, and the muffled sound they made as they landed in a heap on the floor. Then he, too, got under the sheet. Once again on his back, she thought. Again with his hands stacked behind his head.

In moments she felt his heat lure her, the pull of his magnetism. She wanted to touch him, to stroke him, but she didn't dare.

"Do you have cramps?" His disembodied voice came to her, softly on the night.

"No," she whispered in return. "I've never been bothered much with them." Lying on her side, facing though not seeing him, she slid her hand over the mattress till two fingers gently bumped his hip. Naked, just as she suspected. She heard his breath catch in the middle of an inhalation, then resume its even rhythm.

With her middle finger, she drew circles, round and round, ever larger, on his hip.

"Are you still as regular as you used to be?" His voice sounded tight, choked.

She smiled to herself. "I was regular because I was on the pill, Charlie." Then she stopped, stilled her hand, remembering what she'd told him. "I haven't seen anyone yet about a prescription, but I will."

"That's all right. Don't bother." His voice was lazy again, easy. He brought a hand from behind his head and smoothed her hair, delineated her features for himself with his thumb.

"I don't like to think of you taking a pill every day when I'm only here off and on. I'll take care of it for a while."

Her fingers resumed their stroking. "Actually, I've been pretty regular since I had Tobie."

"I'll have to get me a calendar." She heard the smile in his tone. "Keep a record on the road."

Her courage mounting, she slid a finger into the fold of his groin, where the coarse hairs started. She could give him some release, she supposed, though they'd never done anything like that. She knew how he liked her to move her hand on him.

Maybe he'd taken care of it himself in the shower, she thought, and then was glad he couldn't read her thoughts. She moved her fingers a little further along into the thicket and heard him mutter something on an expelled breath. Was it her imagination or did his hip relax? Or tense? Did his thighs shift, subtly, further apart? His hand tightened in her hair. That wasn't her imagination.

She opened her palm low on his belly and felt him rise, thick and firm against the backs of her fingers.

"What are you doing, Moll?" he gasped, sounding as if he'd run a long way.

She thought it was perfectly obvious what she was doing. She turned her hand to close it around him, but he grabbed it and pulled it up his chest. "Did you change your mind...about making love?"

When she didn't answer, he stretched to switch on the light. She squeezed her eyes shut against the brightness and to avoid meeting his. "You didn't, did you?"

He gave a short laugh and released her hand. "Look at me, Molly."

Reluctantly, she did so.

"Were you thinking, you know, just me?"

She bit her lip and focused her gaze on the wall past his shoulder.

"You were, weren't you?" He sounded perplexed, befuddled. On the periphery of her vision she saw him plow a hand through his hair. "Honey, we never did anything like that when we were...together...before."

"People *do*."

"Well, I know that. But *we* didn't."

He was silent for a long while. She sidled a glance at him and found him watching her with a still expression. "What did you think, Moll? If we didn't...make it, I'd avail myself of the first willing female to cross my path?"

That idea had never occurred to her. Her hurt and confusion must have shown in her face. His regret showed in his. He brushed her hair back from her brow and nuzzled her. "You just wanted to do it...for me."

Her nod was barely perceptible. He took a deep breath and let it out slowly. "Honey, I appreciate the thought. But we're still kind of...new to each other. I'd like to do things...you know...*regular* a few more times...before we try anything...fancy."

She released a shuddery sigh. She should let the whole subject go, but somehow she just couldn't. "You took care of it already, didn't you? In the show—"

"What?"

She'd really shocked him this time, she could tell. He gave a hoot of laughter. "What are you askin'?"

"Nothing."

"Yes, you are." He laughed again, flopping back against the pillow. She supposed she should be glad he was so amused. "We're gonna have to come to an agreement, Molly," he said when he could catch his breath. "You're allowed to be private this time of the month, and so am I." He reached to switch off the light again. "I forgot how entertaining living with you could be," he said, still chuckling.

"Never mind."

"You'll make me blush right down to the root of my—"

"Oh, *hush!*"

He seemed to have laughed himself out. She heard him settle in and, even in the darkness, she sensed his eyes trained on her.

"Molly?" His voice was quiet again. Serious.

"Hmm?"

"I didn't."

She buried her burning face in the pillow and heard him chuckle.

"C'mon. Roll over here." He grabbed bunches of her gown and pulled her flush against him. "This is going to be a helluva night. We may as well get as comfortable as we can." He nestled her head on his shoulder and she turned her face into the bulge of his muscle, inhaling his scent.

For as long as she could remember, as far back as that crash on his bike, the smell of Charlie's skin had meant comfort, acceptance, warmth. It was that way now. Feeling the peace flow through her, she absently trailed her fingers over his chest. He wasn't an exceptionally hairy man, she thought lazily. She didn't care much for that. His chest hair covered his breastbone and fanned out over his pectorals. One thin line bisected his abdomen down to where the hair flared out again, low, where her hand wasn't supposed to venture. The rest of his skin was smooth. She sighed and combed her fingers through the silky mat, encountering a nipple in her foray. It immediately stood at attention. His nipples seemed to be as sensitive as hers. She wondered if all men were like that, and walked her fingers back to the taut little peak.

Charlie made a noise like a drop of water hitting a hot skillet. "God almighty! You're enough to tempt a eunuch, woman!" He flipped her unceremoniously to her other side, tangling her legs in her gown and hauling her tight against him. His arms wrapped around her, he folded his hands on top of hers. "Now, keep your hands to yourself and go to sleep."

She lay quiet for a while, but one more question nagged.

"Charlie?"

"What?" He sounded at the limit of his patience.

"Do other women...you know....when they have their...?"

He hissed a beleaguered breath out, ruffling her hair. "I don't know."

She thought that over and realized it was the most satisfactory answer he could possibly have given. She eased a little deeper into his embrace, though it was a long, long time before she fell asleep. Even then, her last thought was that the boardlike form behind her hadn't relaxed at all.

Chapter 8

Molly scuffed her toe along the wooden porch floor, surveying the grounds. The lawn, dotted here and there with pockets of shrubs and stands of maple and aspen, sloped away from the house in all directions. She could see only a small portion of the treed, gravel drive that wound from the front yard over and around gentle hills to a gated entrance about a half mile away. Off to the left lay the woods Charlie had mentioned, not so small, and apparently allowed to remain wild, though it was difficult to tell from this distance. At the very edge of the woods she glimpsed the glint of sunshine on water—the pond, stocked with game fish, or so the agent had informed them.

The house itself was not pretentious, or maybe it only seemed dwarfed by its surroundings. With fifteen rooms, it certainly would provide enough space for Tobie to roam. Built just before the turn of the century, it was a warm, red-brick Victorian structure. A little gingerbread, but not too much, graced the wooden porches front and back. A turret, its stained-glass transom windows spangled with sunlight, fronted two stories of the house on the right, and a small-paned, glass-enclosed room that in another age would have been called a conservatory provided balance off to the left. The roofline was broken by a domed cupola and four chimneys that serviced eight, yes *eight,* working fireplaces.

Pots of geraniums flanked the porch stairs and hanging baskets of brilliantly hued impatiens swayed at intervals above the railing, adding a homey touch. That, Molly concluded, was her strongest impression of the dwelling. She'd been wrong in her initial estimation. It wasn't a palace. It was a home. They could be a family here.

She glanced over to where Charlie was gamely signing pictures of himself at the agent's request, for her two children, several of their friends, the other agents in her office—and her postman, from the sound of it. Molly smiled to herself. He was doing his best to be gracious, but this wasn't a good day for him.

He'd been up before her, but not by much. She could only sleep through so much of his banging around the apartment. The better part of her morning had been spent listening to the litany of his complaints. The coffee was weak, the cereal stale, his boots were too tight. He couldn't find his blue-striped button-down, and Molly had had the bald-faced effrontery to set a bracelet on top of his hat. When she'd suggested to him that she might drive to this showing, he'd given her a look that would curdle milk. To say the man was testy was putting too fine a point on it. He hadn't slept at all last night.

Charlie appeared to be finished. He handed the woman the pictures and her pen with a smile Molly knew was forced only because she was so familiar with his natural ones. Then he folded his third stick of gum for that morning into his mouth and gestured for Molly to join him while the agent got the keys from the lockbox and led them into the house.

The sense of warmth and welcome lingered inside, intensifying the impression of homeyness. Though the rooms weren't overly large, they were airy and bright, unlike those in many Victorian homes, including the one she'd grown up in. High ceilings, white-painted woodwork and long, lace-curtained windows combined to lend an aura of spaciousness.

They paused for a few moments in the marble-floored foyer while the Realtor catalogued the home's amenities and handed Charlie the listing. Craning her neck, Molly caught a glimpse of the monthly rental figure. More than twice what she had grossed in a month as a paralegal. Charlie didn't bat an eye.

"There's a full bedroom and bath on this floor toward the back," the woman pointed out. "It's private, nice for in-laws or elderly visitors. Five more bedrooms are on the second floor. The two bedrooms and bath on the top floor were used for live-in help when the former owners occupied the place." She hesitated a bit, then continued. "There's been a woman coming a couple of times a week to keep things up, and a gardener. Will you be wanting live-in help?"

Molly shook her head before Charlie had a chance to respond.

"Just day help, then," he said firmly, addressing Molly.

She was about to object even to that when the hard glint in his eyes stopped her. Charlie had never given any indication that his money meant much to him, but the lift of his chin told her this was important. That he furnish for his wife the services his mother had provided for hers. If Mrs. Cochrane's role as a servant in her home when she was growing up had ever eaten at him, Molly hadn't known. But she realized now that it must have rankled. She wouldn't begrudge him this.

She nodded. "Just day help."

He turned back to the agent, rolling up the paper she had given him and stuffing it in his jeans pocket. "We'll keep the gardener, too."

The Realtor remarked on a few more of the home's features and left them to explore on their own. As they wandered the downstairs rooms, Molly noticed that the furnishings exuded a quiet comfort despite their elegance. On many pieces there were signs of wear and use. She paused in the dining room and ran her hand along the smooth surface of a rosewood sideboard, fascinated by the play of rainbow colors refracted through the crystal prisms of the chandelier.

"The place rents furnished," Charlie commented, watching her.

She might have guessed. The flat she was living in now had come furnished, and Charlie knew it. She would be bringing little to this house. Just as she brought little to the marriage. Except for Tobie, of course. And to Charlie, Tobie was all that mattered.

She pulled her hand from the chest and strode, her back poker-straight, toward the wide French doors at the far end of the room. They opened onto the conservatory, which ran the whole length of the house on this side. Stepping across the threshold, she caught her breath.

The room had once been a summer porch, she presumed, though it was obviously used year-round now. The original outside wall where the room was attached had been left as exposed brick. The remaining walls were white-painted wainscoting to about waist height and glittering small-paned glass above that. The effect was almost like walking out of doors, with views of tall trees, lawn and sky on all sides.

Still, it wasn't the pretty scenery that stopped her breath. In a corner where harsh sunlight was filtered to harmlessness through the trees stood a concert grand, its wood case gleaming black.

She approached the piano slowly and raised the keyboard cover, though she knew what she would find. There it was, Steinway and Sons inscribed in gold lettering on the inside of the cover. She felt her fingers twitch with eagerness to glide over the keys, but she restrained herself.

The slight yellowing of the ivory gave away its age. This piece was from the early part of the century, the peak of the company's quality. She had never seen one, touched one, much less had one at her disposal.

She looked up to see Charlie, a shoulder lazily propped against the brick, arms and ankles crossed, eyeing her.

"You knew this was here," she murmured.

He shrugged offhandedly, removing his Stetson and rubbing his forearm across his brow. "Said something on the listing."

"Charlie, I can't—"

He made an impatient sound and pushed away from the wall, striding toward her. "What the hell is this, Molly? You 'can't.'" He tossed his hat on the piano. "You'll be cooped up here, same as Tobie, for months. What's the harm?"

She raised her chin, stiffening as he neared. "I can't keep *taking* from you, Charlie. I have some—"

"Pride?" He laughed, the sound erupting from him without humor. "Oh, you have that in spades."

"I know what I've brought to this marriage," she said, her voice tight.

"Ah. Are we keeping score? I wasn't aware of that." He bent forward, resting his folded arms on the piano lid, looking to where her traitorous fingers stroked the keys despite her determination to resist. "Seems to me this ought to rack up some points in my favor, not that sour expression you're wearin'."

She pulled her hand away from the keyboard, knotting her fingers behind her back. He sighed and shook his head.

"I'm rich, Molly. I've got more money than I could spend in a dozen lifetimes." His shoulders lifted in a bemused gesture. "Sometimes all that money still doesn't make any sense to me. I know what ten dollars is. I can hold it in my hand. It'll buy me a couple six-packs—a case, if I don't mind drinkin' dishwater. The rest is—" he spread his hands "—just a bunch of zeros."

He looked at her, his eyes pensive. "So. Am I supposed to be afraid you'll try to make off with my fortune? I'm having a devil of a time getting you to accept what you're entitled to."

She inhaled sharply. "I'm not—"

"You're my wife," he said firmly. "You're Tobie's mother. Everything I have is yours." When she would have challenged his statement, he stopped her with a glance.

"My folks didn't have much when I was growing up," he continued. "They never had a savings account when I was a kid. As far as I know, to this day they don't have a checking account. They're simple people, but what little they had, they shared.'' He straightened and pressed his hands flat against the dark wood. ''I don't want *my* money and *your* money, *my* property and *your* property. I'm a simple man. I want what my folks had.''

She stood still, chewing on her lip, avoiding his eyes.

''I don't intend to walk away from this marriage, Molly. Do you have plans along those lines you're not telling me?''

Her eyes, wide with surprise, flew to his. ''No,'' she whispered.

He seemed to relax a little, stretching his arms against the piano and arching his back like a panther preening in sunlight. ''I like to hear you play that highbrow stuff, honey. Humor me.''

She still appeared unconvinced. He tried another approach. ''I've been with women who wanted me for what I could buy them. I know the difference.''

That got a rise. ''I don't want to hear about your other women,'' she snapped, pruning up like she'd sucked a lemon.

He gave a bewildered laugh and shook his head. ''There weren't as many as you think.'' He shrugged disarmingly. ''This may come as a total surprise to you, but not every woman in the world finds me irresistible.''

She threw him a disbelieving glance and he laughed again, with genuine amusement this time. ''I don't know how you can manage to flatter and insult me with the same look, but you just did.''

He watched her close the keyboard cover, run her hand over the piano a final time and turn her back to it. She wouldn't bend one iota. He'd have to bring up the subject that lay like an abyss between them. He came around the edge of the piano to stand in front of her. ''Do you still think I'd try to take him from you?'' he probed.

Her head jerked up. She met his eyes, and he read the unspoken fear at the back of hers.

''He's a fine boy, Molly. Any man would be proud. I know

you're responsible for that. You've done without to care for him."

"It was never a sacrifice," she replied, reddening slightly.

"I know that, too." He searched her face for what was in her mind. "Are you afraid I'll take him from you? Is that what you think," he whispered, his voice urgent, "when you touch me? 'If I don't, he'll take Tobie'?"

Her gaze darted over his shoulder and through the adjoining room to the one beyond where the agent paced, in sight but out of earshot.

Charlie didn't even turn his head. "She's not gonna intrude here, Molly. She wants to ice this deal." He moved closer, crowding her. "Answer me. Is that what you're thinking...when I put my hands on you?"

As if to underscore his words, he grasped her waist and pulled her to him, then settled his palms over the soft curves of her bottom. "Tell me, Molly. Is that what you think when I touch you here?" He nudged against her. "And here?" One hand slid to her breast and kneaded gently, possessively. "'If I don't let him, he'll take Tobie.'"

Her hands went to his chest to push him away, but he pressed his forehead to hers, rocking against her as he had so many times in the past, and her will fled. She felt the moist warmth of his breath on her cheek, inhaled the spicy cinnamon scent of his gum, the citrus tang of his after-shave. Beneath her palms his heart beat out a steady rhythm as insistent as his words.

"Tell me, Moll. Is that why you let me? Is that what you think...when I touch you?"

She turned her face into the open collar of his shirt and pressed her mouth to his thudding pulse. Molded tight against him, she could sense her nipples stiffen until they were as hard as pushpins. And, even through their clothing, she was certain he was aware of them, too. Feeling as exposed as if she were naked, she answered as honestly as she could.

"Charlie, when you touch me, I can't think at all."

The tension ebbed from him slowly. His hands moved from the more sensitive areas of her body to her shoulders, where his thumbs made caressing circles as he put her a little away from him. Hesitantly she lifted her head and met his gaze.

It appeared her words had pleased him. "Good," was all he said in reply, but his smile was easy and his eyes mischief-filled.

He swooped his hat from the piano and tamped it back on his head. "What d'ya say we go take a look at the bedrooms?"

Moments later, his eyes on the gentle sway of Molly's hips as he followed her up the stairs, he was questioning his sanity. They turned into the first room, light and airy like the others, but he only saw the bed. Or rather, the bed with visions of Molly sprawled upon it in reclining splendor.

It went pretty much like that from room to room, each bed seeming more inviting than the last. Small beds, actually, he realized as he took another look around. The staircases and doorways in these old houses weren't built to accommodate the big mattresses and box springs.

Well, that was all right. They wouldn't need an Olympic-sized bed for what he had in mind. They'd had some fun times in that little twin he'd cadged from home when Molly had spent summers off from college with him. *He'd* had fun, anyway, he thought, remembering.

She'd gotten awful quiet. He watched her stroll into the last room, the only one with a bath attached, according to what he'd seen on the listing. This chamber was larger than the others, allowing space for a sitting area in front of the fireplace. He followed her into the room and came up behind her just as she entered the bathroom.

He let out a low whistle. The bath had obviously been another bedroom, maybe a nursery, when the house was built, and converted at a later date. They could have held a dance in it, although he intended to keep any parties held here strictly private.

The walls were covered in some flocked paper of a deep red shade. Bordello red, he'd call it, but not to Molly. An honest-to-God chandelier hung from the ceiling over the tub, provoking thoughts of the interesting light patterns it might cast on wet skin. Above the gold-veined marble sink, a huge gilt-framed mirror hung at an angle from the wall, reflecting what appeared to be a spectacular view of the tub. For the first time Charlie found himself wondering about the elderly couple who had owned the home.

Directing his gaze to the tub, he swallowed hard. It was a monstrous thing, big as a boat, with the copper plumbing for it coming right up through the floor. What appeared to be a copper boiler for hot water was attached to the pipes, though he wasn't sure it was in working order. The tub sat on clawed feet and was rimmed with polished wood. Charlie had never seen the like.

He slid his gaze to Molly, who was standing silently, open-mouthed. As if she felt his attention, she turned to face him. "I believe I could float in that tub," she said weakly.

He glanced from her to the tub and back, a wicked smile curving his lips. "I believe we both could. We'll have to try it sometime."

Molly pulled herself together with a little shake and walked past him through the bedroom and out to the hall. "Would you like to see the third floor?" she asked when he joined her.

He shook his head. "If you're happy with the place, let's just skip it. I don't think I could stand to look at another bed."

She laughed her throaty laugh and headed down the stairs.

Life was definitely looking up, he thought as he followed her.

The mood in the car on the way to the hospital was light. They had initiated the necessary paperwork to rent the house. Charlie had instructed Molly to redecorate as she saw fit and not to be chintzy about it. Molly understood him well enough by this time not to argue the point.

"What will you be doing when you leave this afternoon?" she asked.

"We've got a show in St. Louis tonight. Tomorrow all of

country music will be converging in Nashville to rehearse for the awards show Monday.''

"Oh, yes. I remember.'' She'd already arranged to have Tobie stay up late to watch. "You're nominated for an award yourself, aren't you?''

He nodded, not taking his eyes from the road. "Couple of 'em. I don't expect we'll win this year. We've had our share. The new talent needs the recognition.''

How like him to downplay his own achievements. He'd been named Top Male Vocalist last year, and the year before that if she remembered correctly. A dart of guilt pricked her as she was reminded of an incident she'd noted watching last year's program. She'd given short shrift to the possibility that her presence in his life might have caused an upheaval in another relationship. "The woman who kissed you... last year when you won... did she mean a lot to you?''

He turned to look at her this time, a slight frown puckering his brow. "Who? Dolly? Honey, Dolly kisses everybody. It doesn't mean anything.''

She had to laugh. "No, not Dolly,'' she said, feeling just a little presumptuous referring to an icon by her first name. "The woman who was sitting next to you.''

She had him there. He couldn't remember attending that show with anybody special. As near as he could recollect the female on his left had been his seven-year-old niece, and the one on his right had been... "You don't mean Janine?''

"Well, I don't know her name!''

He chuckled to himself. This was gonna be fun. "Describe her for me.''

"She had big hair.'' From the corner of his eye he could see her hands fluttering around her head. "Blond. And big...'' She made a cupping gesture, chest high.

"Boobs,'' he supplied helpfully.

She threw him a disgruntled look, ready to jump on his vulgarism, but he beat her to the punch. "That's Beau's wife.''

Her head whirled. "Beau's married?''

"Beau's married." He grinned and nodded firmly. "Fell a ton. It was fun to watch, him being such a lady's man."

Molly stared out the windshield, momentarily speechless. Robert "Beau" Cochrane had been a lady's man, all right. Playboy of the Western World…or Wheeling, West Virginia, anyway. Seven years older than Charlie and handsome as sin, he'd been light-years beyond her experience. He'd been having his way with the ladies while she was still shinnying up trees with his skinny little brother, so she knew him only by reputation, but that had been the stuff of legends.

Still, if Beau had the looks, Charlie had the presence. Put him in a roomful of females and he seemed to suck out all the oxygen, leaving them panting. She shifted a quick glance at the air-guzzler. "I hadn't heard."

"Oh, yeah." He favored her with a charming smile. "Janine was real happy we won that award. She dropped twins not two weeks later."

"Do tell." He was teasing her now. She was in for it. Ignore him, her momma would say, and he'll stop. Momma never did have a handle on Charlie.

"Mmm-hmm. If the camera had panned below those honeydews—" he imitated her cupping gesture and she rolled her eyes "—you'd have seen the watermelon underneath." He very generously demonstrated that contour with his hands, too.

She told him with a look to keep his hands on the wheel and he just laughed. She sensed he wasn't finished riding her yet.

"I had absolutely nothing to do with that, Moll. I ain't sayin' I've been a saint the past few years, but I never plowed that field."

Her hands came up to contain the laugh that erupted despite her better judgment. Charlie grinned widely.

"So, Beau's got two little girls," he went on, "cute as june bugs. In about a dozen years he's gonna be frantic, trying to keep them away from the guys like him."

"Is he a good husband?"

"Yeah." He glanced her way again. "Most of the men in

my family have been dragged kickin' and screamin' to the altar. We do all right once we get there." He turned the car into the hospital parking garage and stopped at the gate to get a ticket.

"The girls were traveling with us for a few weeks this spring."

Molly couldn't hide her surprise. "On the road?"

"Oh, yeah." He nodded, his eyes roaming the garage for a space to park. "These long spells apart are no good for family life. Most of the guys bring their wives and kids when they can. Even if it's just for a weekend. Come summer, when schools let out, it gets to be a regular circus."

She had never imagined that. It sounded like fun.

"I'd be bringing you along, if Tobie was able." He slowed and maneuvered the car into a slot. "Maybe next summer."

She mulled the idea over while he cut the engine and set the brake. "Isn't it kind of hard to find any privacy?" she asked.

"Honey." He gave her that devil-eyed grin again. "I'm the boss. Rank does have its privileges. We have our own bus."

He pulled the keys from the ignition and handed them to her, a silent reminder that he wouldn't be with her when she left that evening. She bent to tuck them into her purse, then lifted her head to see him disposing of his gum in the little piece of wrapper he'd dug out of his jeans. She smiled at the pang of recognition that pierced her. He'd always been fastidious about some things.

Catching her eye, he removed his Stetson and balanced it over the space between the dashboard and the steering wheel. Then he unhitched his seat belt and turned to her. "I'm going to kiss you goodbye right now," he said. "Because we won't get another chance to be private...and we don't want to shock Tobie."

A slight shiver coursed up her spine and she braced herself for his possession, but he surprised her. With a gentle hand he released her seat belt and grazed his knuckles across her breast as he pushed the strap from her. He slid to the edge of his seat and coaxed her to come to him with his hands and his smile and his eyes.

His eyes. Gazing deeply into them, she was struck anew. They weren't dark brown as were those of so many people whose eyes appeared black. Charlie's were a deep midnight blue and they glittered now with tiny lights like the rhythmic pulsings of faraway stars.

They beckoned her and she slipped into his arms. He dipped his head low over her, but still he didn't kiss her. He cradled her jaw in his warm palm, brushing his thumb along her bottom lip and firmly pulling it down as his own lips parted above hers. So close. So close she could see each spiky lash, each pore, the flare of his nostrils with each breath. And still he didn't kiss her.

She gripped his shoulder, cupped a hand to the back of his neck and dragged him to her, closing the final distance between them. She heard the feral sound of satisfaction that rumbled from deep in his throat when her tongue sought his. He was generous in his victory, his tongue plunging deep, seeking the sweet hidden recesses of her mouth, eliciting her soft whimpers of response.

His cunning fingers stroked her throat until she arched to him, showing him wordlessly where she needed his hands to be. And for long minutes they kissed, and suckled, and petted, until both knew they had to stop or go too far.

Charlie raised his head first, then lowered it once more to curl his tongue one final time around the nipple that lay exposed, glistening between the parted edges of Molly's blouse and the bra that had been shoved out of the way. When he lifted his head again, they were both panting.

"Honey, don't look at me like that," he muttered, "or it's not gonna matter that we're in a car in a public facility, or *what* time of the month it is."

In answer she closed her eyes and turned her head into the arm that supported her, opening her mouth and nipping his biceps through his shirtsleeve.

He sucked in a deep gulp of air. "Oh, that's a big help, Moll. C'mon, honey, we've gotta stop."

She twisted around to look at him. "You started this." She was talking to the top of his head. His gaze was centered on her breast again. She watched in fascination as a single blunt fingertip circled the areola and her nipple stiffened at his touch.

He raised his head, smiling into her eyes. "You have beautiful breasts. Did I ever tell you that?"

Her head rocked slowly against his arm.

"You do. You have the most beautiful breasts I've ever seen." He winced slightly. *What a stupid remark, Kick. She doesn't want to hear about other breasts you've happened to see.* He wanted to touch her again, but she started to sit up and pull her clothes together.

"Turn around, honey," he said. "Let me hook you up."

She did as he told her, her stomach fluttering wildly when his hands slid around to help her adjust herself into the cups of the bra. She buttoned her blouse as he connected the hooks.

"You know you can get these to fasten in the front," he offered.

She looked daggers at him over her shoulder.

"It's *just* a suggestion! You can go without, too. That's fine with me. At least around the house," he amended. "Not when you're getting groceries at the A & P."

Her laughter came out in a huff. "Charlie, what a sexist thing to say. I thought you were a real nineties man."

He wasn't about to be dissuaded. "Molly, you're endowed. I'm a guy, okay? I know how they think. And when it comes to that, the nineties man is no different than the guy from the Stone Age."

She twisted around to face front again, tucking her blouse into her skirt and he gave her the once-over. She looked thoroughly kissed and her hair was all over the place, but that was the style now. He finger-combed his own hair, glad he could just stuff most of it under his hat. His jeans still felt a little snug, but he thought he could pass muster.

He blew out a deep breath. "Let's get inside. While I can still walk."

* * *

Molly leaned her head against the wall of the elevator and closed her eyes. Charlie'd been gone only a few hours and she wondered listlessly if this was to be the pattern of their life together. A short, vibrant spurt of days when Charlie was present and every cell in her body was on red alert. Then the long, slow, weighty stretches of his absence when she seemed to hover in suspended animation. She opened her eyes and glanced at the flashing numbers. Even this elevator trip down three floors to the cafeteria level seemed to take place in slow motion.

Pressing her lips together, she was reminded by their tenderness of that impassioned kiss. What had come over her? Thank God for the modicum of privacy provided by the dim garage and the tinted windows of the car. She'd never been so wanton. She knew if he had urged her further she would have succumbed, no matter the public circumstances or the time of month.

It was almost as if she were in some kind of thrall to him.

She had loved the boy, and she had loved the youth, but neither had prepared her for the man. The man was such an enigmatic combination. The friend and confidant of her childhood, her first and only lover, and the celebrity whose present way of life was beyond her comprehension.

She was startled when the elevator bumped to a stop and the doors opened. Exiting, she turned left down the corridor toward the hospital dining room, her mind still occupied with Charlie.

She had teased him about not being a nineties male, but she realized it was true. Oh, he was amenable to her working if she wanted to and she knew he respected her judgment. Major decisions would be joint ones.

But in other ways he was a throwback to an earlier time. A time when a man meant the vows he made. When his word was his bond, and the bond of blood was the strongest of all. When the greatest sin a man could commit was not to be there for his child.

At twenty, pregnant with his child, she had not understood that about him. Chances were, at twenty, Lucy hadn't either.

More than anything, she wished she knew where she stood with him. He found her body pleasing, of that much she was certain, though he'd never expressed his appreciation so directly before. His words had both embarrassed and inflamed her, and she hadn't known how to respond. Yes, he found her body pleasing.

But if he felt more than that, he'd never said. For a man who made his living through words, he was stingy with them. Was she a fool to want to believe him when he told her she should trust him?

Men lie, Molly, she heard her mother say. *It's what they do best.* Was she a fool to try to blot out the memory of the way she had seen her father? And the memory of the way she had seen Charlie?

Charlie stomped into the dressing room, slamming the door behind him. He jerked open the refrigerator, saw *cans*, and slammed that door, too. He threw himself into the only comfortable chair in the room, thrust his booted feet up on the dresser and crossed his ankles. Resting his head against the chair back, he brought his hat down to cover his face.

He ignored the light tap on the door, hoping whoever was there would get the message. No such luck. He heard the door open and close and the heavy clunk of boot heels across the linoleum floor, then the muffled whump of the seal breaking when the refrigerator opened again.

"You want a beer, Kick?" Harlan asked.

"Not from a can," he answered through the hat.

"You can't taste the difference. Where'd you ever get such a crazy idea?"

"I can taste the difference." He could hear the metallic pop of Harlan's beer and the scrape of chair legs on the floor as the other man took a seat. Hell. He was going to stay and chat.

"The show went pretty well," Harlan said after a long swallow and an "Ahhhh."

Charlie recrossed his ankles, shifting in the chair and lacing his fingers over his belly. He still wasn't used to the feel of the ring on his hand. "It stunk."

"Aw, anybody can break a guitar string, Kick. It only took a couple minutes to fix. The way you kept up the yammering, the audience didn't even notice." Harlan beat out a tattoo on the seat of the chair. "The crowd seemed to like the new material."

Charlie nudged his hat up with his thumb. "That's another thing. Are we all going our own way up there, or what? Jase was late coming in on the bridge, and I don't know what the hell you were doing back there on the drums."

Harlan looked at him quietly for some moments, then cleared his throat. "We talked about that, remember? Before you left for Pittsburgh. We were gonna try it this way."

Charlie looked away sharply and blew out a disgusted breath. "I forgot."

The older man shrugged, taking another swig of his beer. "I don't think the crowd noticed that, either." He grinned down at the can in his hand. "Judging from the intimate apparel all over the stage, the ladies were happy with the performance."

"Ladies, my eye." Charlie dropped his feet to the floor and leaned forward in his chair, elbows on his knees. "When do you s'pose that's gonna stop? I'm a married man," he said, thumping his fingers against his chest. "Shooter's the only bachelor left in the band and he doesn't need any encouragement."

"Well, I don't—"

"Hell, Harlan, we've got little kids in the audience, we've got older people. How does that look?"

Harlan put his can aside, rubbing his hands together and looking at Charlie through narrowed eyes. "Your boy doing all right?"

Charlie sighed. "He's lost his hair." He closed his eyes and pinched the bridge of his nose. "The doc says it'll grow back." He removed his hat and scratched his fingers through his own hair. "He's cheerful. Not showing any signs of complications."

Harlan took a deep breath and seemed to relax a little. "Well, that's good. We've noticed you're a little edgy, is all." He shot another furtive glance at Charlie. "Sometimes these trips home aren't all we hope they'll be. The wives or girlfriends are—" he cleared his throat again "—unavailable."

Charlie lifted his head to gaze at Harlan, unable to believe the ears he felt burning. What a dandy topic of conversation among the fellas this was. Tread lightly around the boss. He's a little bit cranky 'cause he didn't get laid.

He leaned back in his chair, stuck his feet up on the dresser and plopped his hat over his face. "Stuff a sock in it, Harlan," he said.

Chapter 9

Molly headed to the waiting room for a cup of coffee while Tobie's nurse helped him with his bath and did his assessment. The morning was still gray, she noted, peering out a rain-streaked window as she fed quarters into the machine. It didn't look like it was going to clear up.

Gingerly, she lifted the plastic door and slipped the steaming coffee out. Glancing around the lounge for someone familiar to while away the next few minutes with, she spotted Gail Ramsey sitting in a corner by herself. The thin, dark-haired woman was hunched over, elbows on her knees, a tissue clutched in a fist against her mouth.

Gail's four-year-old son, Jeff, had undergone a transplant several weeks before Tobie, and Molly thought he was due to be discharged soon. Had something gone wrong? Fighting the natural resistance she felt at the prospect of hearing bad news, she steeled herself to offer what comfort she could. She walked over to Gail and took a seat beside her on the couch, shoving aside magazines to make room for her coffee on the table in front of it.

"What's the matter, Gail? Is Jeff having problems?"

The woman turned tear-reddened eyes to Molly and smiled weakly. "No. He's doing well, as a matter of fact. Dr. Morrissey says he can leave the hospital tomorrow."

Molly felt her shoulders sag with relief and only then realized she'd been holding them rigid. She put her hand on Gail's arm, ready to mouth congratulations, but hesitated. Her friend's manner and appearance didn't jibe with her words. Something was wrong.

"What is it, then? Can I help?"

Gail straightened, twisting the tissue in her hands. "Oh, Molly. He's doing so well I almost feel guilty getting down like this." A sigh shuddered out of her. "It's everything else."

Molly slid her hand down the woman's arm to her hand and squeezed. "Tell me."

"Jeffy will be discharged tomorrow, but we won't be going home. We'll have a little three-room suite in that apartment building the hospital makes available to families from out of town."

At her words Molly recalled the unit's stipulation that the patients remain in the area three months post-discharge for follow-ups. That hadn't been a concern for her with Tobie, since they lived locally. Gail, if she remembered correctly, was from some small town in eastern Pennsylvania.

Gail's voice quavered as she continued. "I miss Michael and the girls. But he has to work and they're still in school. And even with the hospital subsidizing the housing, the cost is..." She shrugged and bit her lip, unable to go on.

Molly was reminded starkly of how heavily that same concern had weighed upon her a few short weeks before. With Charlie's arrival, money had ceased to be a consideration at all.

"I don't want to seem ungrateful. I thank God every day that Susan was a match for Jeffy and he's getting better."

"I understand, Gail." She did. She remembered vividly how guilty she had felt worrying about mundane things when her child's life hung in the balance. But the world didn't go away.

Gail blotted her eyes. "You're so lucky, Molly. I'm glad for you and jealous at the same time. We have insurance, but the bills are still staggering. My parents have taken out a second mortgage on their home to help us. Even so—" she shook her head "—I don't see how we'll ever come out from under."

Molly had been aware of this situation repeated in family after family, but for the past few weeks she'd been blinded to it. Now the uneasy mix of hope and helplessness she'd felt returned with stunning clarity. She remembered the talk of bake sales, church events and fund-raisers—anything to raise the money to help a child. There had to be a better way.

Even as she had the thought, a plan was forming in her mind. Before marital unhappiness had turned her into a recluse, Molly's mother had been a hostess of some renown in Wheeling society. Organization was her forte. Not for nothing was she her mother's daughter, Molly thought.

She picked up her coffee and blew on it before taking a cautious sip. Then she faced Gail again. "We'll keep in touch when Jeffy is released," she said. "I think there may be a way to help you."

Charlie stared at his reflection in the dressing-room mirror. Less than an hour till showtime, and he had some thinking to do. He smoothed shaving cream over his jaw and reached for his razor.

He'd been honest with Molly when he'd said he didn't expect to win tonight. Counting the awards he'd gotten for songwriting, Best Video, Best Album, he had enough of those little statuettes to put one on every single mantel in that big old house they were renting.

He'd been glad to win them. It was gratifying to have his hard work and talent acknowledged and appreciated. And in his mind he recognized that, in all fairness, it was someone else's turn. But in his gut, he wanted to win tonight.

This one was personal.

He had some words he wanted to say to a little boy. In public right out over the airwaves, he wanted to let Tobie know that he missed him. That in his time of triumph he carried his son's image with him. He wanted to show him that he was in his mind and his heart, no matter what was going on in his life.

So he wanted to win, just once more, tonight. He took a deep breath, stretched his skin taut, and plied the razor.

Molly shifted in the vinyl chair and glanced over at Tobie. He'd been dozing off and on for the last hour. Right now he had his head turned to the side with his chin resting on his shoulder. The black hat he was never without covered his lap. She moved to take it away and lower the head of his bed, but he stirred, so she let him be.

Maybe it was just as well that he slept. Charlie hadn't won either of the awards he'd thought were maybes. Worse, he hadn't presented any awards or performed. They hadn't even caught a glimpse of him when the camera panned the audience of big hats and big hair.

Things had quieted down on the floor, too. There had been some commotion earlier, when the awards Charlie was up for had been announced. He was a popular figure with the kids on the unit, having taken the time to stop in and talk to many of them. Even the nurses had found opportunities to come to the door and sneak a peek at the TV. Those who hadn't been fans of Charlie's before his visits were now.

It was going on eleven. Only one category left, for Best Entertainer, the big one. Charlie had never won that one and said he didn't have a prayer of picking it up this time. Not with the competition this year.

She leaned her head back on the chair and gazed at the television through slitted eyes. She barely registered what was taking place on the screen until she heard the whoops and laughter coming from the other rooms.

Then she saw him, stepping carefully in front of others, accepting the back slaps and hugs of congratulations, as he made his way from his seat to the aisle. Midway back in the audience, he'd been seated. He really hadn't been expected to win it this time.

Molly got her first good look at him when he reached the aisle and headed for the stage. She leaned over to shake Tobie awake but saw he was already straightening up in the bed, eyes wide and mouth agape. Glancing back at the TV, she pressed a hand to her chest in an effort to calm the frantic knocking of her heart against her ribs.

Tobie crept on hands and knees to the foot of his bed to get a closer look. "Mom!" he said in a hushed voice.

"I see, Tobie."

The boy sat on his heels, his hands resting on his skinny thighs as he stared. "Mom, did he—"

Charlie reached the presenters and received his award, turned to the audience and doffed his hat. His head was completely bald. Outside the room, Molly could hear the entire Transplant Unit go wild, every child there with various degrees of hair loss and regrowth sharing a special kinship with that gleaming pate up on the stage.

Tobie gave a shout and Molly lurched from her chair to clasp him before he threw himself over the bed rail into her arms. He pounded her back, laughing and crying at the same time. "Mom, look at him!"

"I know, Tobie," she said, her own eyes filling and her voice tight. Over the pandemonium she strained to hear Charlie's words as he dedicated his award to his son and the other brave children on the unit.

Suddenly Tobie stilled and stared again at the television. "He must really love me, Mom," he whispered, awe in his tone. "He looks awful."

Molly clutched her son's head to her breast and gazed at her husband. That depended entirely on your perspective, she decided. He looked pretty good to her.

"What did he say?"

Molly had picked up the phone on the first ring. She'd settled Tobie down for the night and hurried home as soon as she could, knowing Charlie would call her there. The hospital switchboard didn't put calls through to patients' rooms after ten.

"He's very proud, Charlie, and very touched, but what he said was, you look awful."

"Yeah. Well, you can promise him for me that I'll never rub his head again. They've been doing that to me all night. It gets old real quick."

Molly laughed. "Whatever possessed—"

"It bothers me that I can't be there with him. That I can't help you. But I've got a lot of people depending on me at this end. At least now, no matter how far apart we are, we share this."

"It means a lot to him, Charlie. The whole unit went crazy, as a matter of fact." She paused a moment. "I'm glad you won."

"Yeah. It was special. The guys are pleased." She could hear his heavy sigh. "I have to tell you, I've been a bear. There's not a fella in the band still talking to me. Even Harlan walks around with his chin on his chest when he gets near me."

She could guess what had prompted his mood. "I'm sorry, Charlie…"

"Hey, that's all right. Can't have you thinkin' I only come home for one thing."

Thinking just that, she laughed again, but her question was serious. "When *will* you be home again?"

"Aw, it'll be weeks, Molly. We've got dates in Texas, Colorado, we've rescheduled Tulsa. Six weeks, anyway, it looks like."

"Tobie will be home by then."

"I know. I've got two weeks blocked out there with nothing scheduled and I'll guard 'em with my life."

She twisted a strand of hair around her finger. "I've had an idea."

"Uh-oh."

"*Char*lie!"

"Someday I'll have to show you what it does to me when you say my name just that way."

"*Char*lie!"

"Yeah, like that."

Embarrassed laughter bubbled out.

"That laugh's good, too." She heard his low chuckle. "What's your idea, honey?"

"You remember Gail Ramsey and her son?"

"Jeff."

"Yes." He did remember, all right. That was part of his popularity. When he talked to people, he really talked to them.

He hadn't lost the common touch. "The boy was discharged this morning. He and Gail will have to stay in the area for the next three months, though. Charlie, they're really strapped for funds. It's so hard. I remember what it was like to have to watch every nickel and practically beg to get my child what he needed."

He was quiet for so long that she thought she had offended him with her mention of what she had gone through for Tobie. His voice was subdued when he answered. "Molly, I'm rich, but even I can't pay for every fam—"

"No, Charlie, that's not what I meant."

"What, then?"

She licked her lips, trying to decide how best to phrase her request. "I was thinking of a benefit performance to set up some kind of fund…like an endowment. Families could draw on the interest when they needed it. They'd pay it back when they were able, but they wouldn't be hounded for it."

"You're talking a *lot* of money there." He sounded skeptical.

"I know," she pushed on. "But if we had a really *big* name, best in the business, say…"

"Ahh…"

"Charlie, your name would bring in the corporate sponsors. That's where the money is. The law firm I worked for has the contacts…"

"And you can twist arms with the best of them." He sounded like he was coming around. "That may be doable. Let me talk to some people here tonight, see who I can rope in."

"I hadn't even thought of others."

"I've done my share of favors. I've got some chits I can call in. When were you thinking of having this production?"

"You'll be home in six weeks."

"It's going to be a working vacation, I take it," he said, but she could hear the smile in his voice. "See what you can set up over there and I'll take care of my end."

"Thanks, Charlie."

"Give Tobie a hug from me. You know, I was thinking. Doc Morrissey told us his hair might not be the same when it comes in. It might be a different texture or color. Maybe it'll grow back red. Wouldn't that be a hoot?"

She couldn't resist. "Maybe yours won't grow back at all. Wouldn't *that* be a hoot?"

"Ouch! Watch your mouth, woman!"

Molly plowed into her work with a vengeance. Though ordinarily she hated to ask for favors, this was different. This wasn't for herself, and her heart was engaged.

It was easier than she'd anticipated. Charlie's name counted for a lot and the others he'd brought in only added to the allure. Country music was huge and the cause was worthy. Everyone wanted to be a part of it.

The lawyers from her firm donated their time and their Rolodex. Within two weeks she had a venue, concessions, T-shirts, all donated. The hospital administration and civic leaders were on board. Between the arm-twisting she discovered she was good at and the time she spent with Tobie, she had little opportunity to dwell on what was missing from her life.

Only late at night, after that last lingering phone conversation with Charlie, did she lie in her bed and allow her mind to drift. Only then did she allow herself to admit that she missed him. She missed him emotionally, though they did their best to support each other. And she missed his companionship, his laughter, his silliness, even his flares of temper. But she had missed him in these ways for years.

She missed him *physically*. And that was new.

The places on her body that he had touched with his mouth and his warm fingers now craved his touch. She'd learned what longing meant. She longed to turn in her bed and roll against him, and lie with him, skin to skin. To hear his even breathing when he'd sleep, and to stroke him, soothe him, when he couldn't. Her nights now were spent yearning and she wondered—hoped—that he spent his nights yearning, too.

Molly straightened from the packing box she was bending over and shoved her hair off her face. She should have braided it. She'd gotten out of the habit, wearing it to please Charlie.

Hands on hips, she surveyed Tobie's room. The surfaces were cleared of his belongings, the bed had been stripped, most everything was packed. Only the bookcase remained. She started sorting through Tobie's books and games, searching for heavier objects to put on the bottom of the box.

Under his magic kit she found the four bulky volumes, all bound in maroon with gold lettering. Her high-school yearbooks. She hadn't looked at them in ages.

Easing back onto the mattress, she pulled them on to her lap. She opened the one from freshman year first, the only year she and Charlie had been at school at the same time. She turned to his senior-class picture, unprepared for the wave of wistfulness that swamped her.

Even dressed like all the other boys, in tux, formal shirt and black tie, he drew the eye. His hair was long, waving down over his collar. A little different from the style he was sporting now, she thought with a chuckle. His generous smile spread across his face and crinkled his eyes. She traced a fingertip over his mouth, remembering that was the year he'd taught her to kiss and forever spoiled other men's kisses for her.

The photograph revealed him pretty much as he was. Good-natured—*good-looking,* the girls had been all over him that year—maybe a little bit of a ruffian. Among those who knew him then, teachers and students both, the general consensus had been that likeable though he was, he'd never amount to much.

She had never, ever shared that opinion. Her only explanation for their misappraisal of him was that they had never looked in his eyes, where the hunger and determination lurked. She had seen that drive early on and believed he was destined for great things. She'd always thought that, kind as he was to the gawky girl who adored him, he would leave her behind. And so it hurt, but it didn't surprise her when he did.

Only now, she reflected, it seemed that he hadn't left her. She lifted the book and hugged it against her chest, biting down on her bottom lip. *She* had thrown him out of her life, and he had never known she needed him back.

She spread the book over her lap again and flipped the pages to the freshman class. For the first time in many years, she stared at Lucy's picture. The Cochrane mold, female version. High-spirited, sassy, spoiled well beyond what was good for her. But Molly had loved her then, and loved her memory still. She'd been full of pranks and adventure, and Molly's experiences had been so restricted. It wasn't until later, when her exploits turned wrong and dangerous, that they'd drifted apart.

Of all the boys, Charlie had been closest to Lucy. Both in age and spirit. Molly knew, rightfully or not, he blamed himself for some of the wrong turns his sister had taken in life. She could see no possible gain from telling him now that Lucy had kept them apart. He seemed willing to forget the past. She had no reason to complain about his treatment of her.

Molly looked once more at the photograph of her old friend. They had kept each other's secrets as children. She would keep this one now.

Chapter 10

Molly stood and walked across the wooden floor to lean against the porch post. Mrs. Cochrane was nodding over her book in the wicker rocker. Her husband sat on the top step with Tobie, sipping iced tea and regaling the boy with stories of Charlie as a youngster. Molly thought she'd stand by to defend her man's honor if need be.

The Cochranes had driven in that morning from Wheeling. They'd finally been able to meet Tobie, though they had talked to him numerous times by phone. He'd only been out of the hospital a week, and his contacts with other people were still severely limited. Infection could cause a major problem for months to come.

She'd been a little uneasy about Charlie's parents' reaction to her, but she needn't have worried. She had no idea what he had said to them about her, but it was clear they were delighted with Tobie and ready to accept her as a daughter. They were waiting now for Charlie to arrive. The benefit was tonight and then he'd be home—he'd be hers—for two weeks.

"You really shouldn't smoke, Grampa."

Molly's head whipped around to where her father-in-law was shaking out a match, cigarette in hand, guilty look on his face. "Tobie..." she began in a remonstrating voice.

Mr. Cochrane waved her comment off. "It's okay, Molly. The boy's right." He took a long, long drag on the cigarette and then pinched it out, stuffing it back in the pack. "I'd like to quit," he said to his grandson, "but I haven't been able to. Your dad used to smoke, but he stopped a few years ago. Did you know that?"

Tobie shook his head.

"Mmm-hmm. Smartest thing he ever did," the old man continued. He lifted his gaze to Molly. "One of 'em."

"Mom never smoked."

Mr. Cochrane's eyebrows rose and he glanced at Molly over the rim of his glass, clearly unwilling to contradict her if that was what she had told her son, and just as clearly itching to set the story straight.

She made a clucking sound with her tongue. "Oh, go ahead before you burst, Dad." Charlie's parents had let her know how they preferred her to address them, and she was happy to accede to their wishes. They'd been like second parents to her years ago, anyway.

Mr. Cochrane set his glass on the porch floor and cleared his throat. "Your momma did smoke one time." He shot another glance at her. "That I know of."

Molly crossed her arms in front of her chest. "*Just* once," she said.

Tobie, all eyes and ears now, swiveled his gaze from her to his grandfather.

Mindful of his rapt audience, the old man took his time with his tale. "Your dad had a younger sister. She's gone now." He paused for a moment and stared down at the step. "She died before you were born. Anyway," he sighed, "Lucy and your mom were like that." He raised two fingers and crossed one over the other.

"Lucy was full of ideas, not all of them good ones. We had a little tomato patch behind our garage and when the girls were back there, you could be sure they were up to no good."

He took a deep breath. "One day your father caught them behind the garage puffin' on cigarettes Lucy had filched from one of her brothers." He shrugged. "Maybe me, who knows?"

"From Cleeve," Molly said.

"From Cleeve." He acknowledged her with a nod. "See there, I learned something today. Well, like I said, your daddy caught the two of them and lit into them like gangbusters. Said if they were gonna smoke, they should *smoke,* not those timid little pantywaist puffs they were taking."

Molly felt Tobie's eyes turn her way again and she rested her elbow on the arm across her chest, chin in hand, but she didn't interrupt her father-in-law.

"So, he kept lighting the cigarettes for them, one after the other, till they were puffing like locomotives and your momma was as green as this floor." He paused and tapped a finger on the wood for emphasis. "But she got even."

Molly covered her face with her hand, feeling herself go as red as one of those tomatoes from the patch. Tobie stole another quick look. "What did she do?" he asked, entranced.

"She threw up all over his boots," the old man answered with a satisfied grin.

"Wow, Grampa! And he forgave her?" Tobie slapped his hands on his knees, laughing. "He could forgive her anything!"

"Yes, son, I think he could," he said, his grin softening. He looked at Molly over the boy's head. "He was sweet on your momma even then."

Molly met his gaze for a moment, but was quickly distracted by the glint of sunlight on something off at a distance coming up the drive. She felt her heartbeat kick up and the adrenaline jolt through her. Must be Charlie.

In less than a minute the airport limousine pulled to a stop in front of the house. Charlie had flown, while the rest of the band members would be arriving with the buses. He had barely unfolded himself from the car before Tobie, streaking down the stairs, grappled him around the waist.

They removed their hats, laughing and doing a quick comparison of their respective hair growth. Tobie's was still black, though coarser in texture than it had been. Charlie's was black and sleek, not long by any means, but thick, like a shiny fur coat.

Mr. Cochrane's aged knees got him down the stairs a little more slowly, but he gripped his son's shoulder and shook his hand, his love and pride obvious. Charlie climbed the steps to greet his mother with a kiss and a hug.

Then he turned to Molly. She touched his wrist and he pulled her close. Holding his hat beside their heads for privacy, he kissed her. A fairly proper, in-front-of-company kind of kiss. You'd have to be watching real close to catch the slide of his tongue along her lips. But his eyes said, "Later."

They separated, gathered the luggage the driver had left at the foot of the stairs and, with the others, piled into the house.

She hadn't seen Charlie perform live in years. Oh, she'd watched the videos and the television appearances, even the public-service announcements about drinking and driving he'd been involved with since his sister died. But the live performance, just Charlie on a stool with his guitar and his music—she hadn't seen that since they'd split.

She'd forgotten the effect he had on a crowd.

He'd been on stage most of the evening, introducing the various acts and plying his brand of low-key banter. After all, this benefit was his baby, the fund to be named in honor of his son, and these were his friends doing their part to help him out. He'd been tireless in his efforts all night long.

And now it was just him on the stage for some slow ones. The wrenching songs of love and loss that he did so well. Molly watched from what had been her vantage point all evening, behind the curtain to the side of the stage. He'd been able to send her a smile and an occasional wink. He'd even mouthed that she looked pretty at one point—he'd gotten there a lot earlier than she had to rehearse and hadn't talked to her before the show.

She could see him in partial profile, a little from the side and the back. A single spotlight shone on him. He'd started out the evening in one of those flashy shirts with the big splashes of color and the pearlized snaps that many of the country singers affected. The lights were hot, though, and he'd peeled that off some time ago.

Now he wore just a black T-shirt that clung like a coat of paint, black jeans—they clung, too—black boots. Black hat. She watched the swell of the muscles in his back and arms as he cradled and stroked his guitar the way he would a woman. She was close enough to see the trickle of sweat that ran from his hairline down his cheek to be slowed in the stubble of his beard.

He didn't give what could be called a polished performance. Nothing easy, or glib, or superficial. He sang the way he did everything else, with all his heart. Eyes closed, neck veins distended with his effort, his face a study in concentration, he seemed to wrest the words from deep in his soul. The impression he left was one of potent masculinity, raw sexuality, barely contained.

He had this audience eating out of his hand. This crowd of movers and shakers and their glittering women. Not the usual hard-core country fans. But every man here tonight wanted to be him. And every woman thought he was singing just to her.

Molly knew. She remembered how it felt when he had sung just to her. She watched until she recognized the first chords to "Bad for Each Other," the song he had written for her, and then she couldn't watch any more.

She made her way backstage to his dressing room, where she could follow what remained of the show from closed-circuit TV. Covering her face with her hands, she gave herself up to the memories the song evoked. Those early days when she had lost him. Those first years of his success when he'd had a reputation for dancing from heart to heart. When he'd had his pick of bed partners after a show and women clinging to him like the seeds of a stickweed.

How could she live with that? What would she do about it, if that was how he chose to conduct himself? Now there was Tobie. Her doubts and misgivings poured over her in a torrent.

She had no idea how much time passed before she realized the television was showing snow. Not long after that, the door opened and Charlie entered, a smile on his lipstick-smeared face.

"I wondered where you—" he began, then stopped as he saw her face. His smile faded. He glanced at himself in the mirror, grabbed a towel and wiped the bright streaks from his cheek and around his mouth.

"What is it?" he said. He threw the towel on the dressing table disgustedly and followed the towel with his hat.

"Nothing."

"Don't give me that, Molly. Something's got you bent all out of shape."

"This isn't a good time to discuss anything, Charlie. You're tired—"

He'd walked to the door and pushed it shut with the flat of his hand, then turned and sagged against it, eyeing her. "Yeah. I'm tired." His mouth thinned and his eyes glinted. "I'm tired of you lookin' at me, and seein' your daddy."

She stiffened. "I don't." But she did. He was more perceptive than she had imagined.

"Yeah, you do, Molly. You always have." He shoved away from the door and approached her. "I've got something to tell you, and I'm only gonna say it one time, so you listen good."

He had her backed against the dressing table. She pressed her hands on it to keep her balance. He was as angry as she'd ever seen him. A muscle twitched near his eye and his throat worked. His voice was tight, but even, when he spoke.

"I'm not your daddy. *I don't cheat.*" Something in her face must have touched him. His tone softened. "I know what your father was like. I know what it's done to you."

She couldn't meet his eyes. She stared at his throat, willing an expression of control she didn't feel. "My father was a drunk and a womanizer. You have no idea what it's done to me."

He tipped her chin up, forcing her to meet his gaze. "He was those things, Molly, but that's not all he was."

"You're right." She smiled up at him, her voice imbued with a false brightness. "He was a liar, too."

"Molly." He sounded so pained, she looked away. "And I'm those things, too. Is that how you feel?"

She shrugged.

"Dammit, Molly, look at me." She did, her eyes fierce and tearless. "Why will you believe the stories? Why not me?"

"I believe what I see, Charlie."

She knew in an instant she'd gone too far. His expression became shuttered and he backed away slightly. "That's what this is about, isn't it? That last blowup. What we fought about that last time."

"I don't remember," she whispered.

"You don't remember *who,* maybe. But you know it was a woman. It was always a woman."

He strode to the door and locked it, the click echoing loud in the silent room. "You know the saying, Moll, believe *half* of what you see and none of what you hear?" He flung himself into a chair, lounging back, legs spread. "What did you see?"

Her fingers gripped the edge of the table, knuckles whitening. "I don't want to talk about this."

"We have to have this out, Molly. Nothing will be right between us until we do." He lifted his chin and held her gaze. "Come here. Show me what you saw."

She shook her head slowly.

"Then, go. You come to me, Molly, or you go."

"Please, Charlie."

He closed his eyes for a moment, letting out a gut-wrenching sigh. "Come here," he said, finally, lifting his hand to her, beckoning, inviting. "Help me do this, honey. Show me what you saw."

She went to him slowly, reluctantly, slipping out of her shoes along the way. The woman she'd seen hadn't been wearing shoes. He reached both hands out to her as she neared, guiding her over one of his knees, positioning a long, nylon-clad leg on each side.

"So pretty, Molly. Did you wear this dress for me?"

Just for him. She'd bought it with the vision of the approval she'd see in his eyes guiding her choice. A simple shimmering sheath. No froufrou at all. Long-sleeved, scoop-necked, clingy, short. Covered in coppery sequins, the color of her hair. She set her hands on his shoulders and nodded to him.

He smoothed his palms over her hips and nudged her nearer. "Is this the way it was, honey? Is this what you saw?"

She focused her eyes on the wall behind him for a moment, remembering. Then she bent one knee and placed it on the chair between his thighs, close to, but not touching him. Not yet.

One of his hands slid up her arm to her shoulder, fingers hooking in the neckline of her dress and pulling the stretchy fabric down, her bra along with it, exposing her breast with its nipple already beaded, pleading for his lips. He touched his tongue to it, the rough surface abrading, and Molly inhaled sharply, arching. He closed his mouth over her, suckling so strongly it caused his cheeks to hollow, before he moved his face to the warm, sweet valley between her breasts, nuzzling gently. "Is this what you saw, Molly?" he whispered against her skin.

"No." Her answer was a barely audible puff of her breath.

"No," he repeated, his whiskers rasping on her tender flesh. "You didn't see this, because it didn't happen."

She couldn't swear to that. She'd been behind the woman. But she hadn't *seen* it.

He moved his hands to the backs of her thighs and let them glide up under her dress to cup her bottom, his calluses making a scratching sound on her panty hose. His fingers kneaded her buttocks, the tips probing into the moist heat between her thighs until he'd wrung a "Charlie!" from her.

"Is this what you saw?" he asked again.

She squeezed her eyes shut, trying to picture the scene in her mind. But the images blended. The fine hairs that dusted the fingers caressing the woman's bare bottom were red, not black. And one of the fingers bore a wedding ring. Charlie's hadn't. Not then. She shook her head blindly. "No!" she said.

"Show me what you saw, Molly," he demanded.

She took a deep breath and tried to edge the knee between his thighs forward to press it against him. And found she couldn't. *She could not.* His hand had come down to grasp her above her knee so tightly he would leave bruises. His other hand clutched her hip, holding her away from him. His grip was implacable. She could not move against him.

Someone watching from behind her wouldn't know that. That person would see only his hands on her in a seemingly suggestive position.

She opened her eyes and gazed down at the black ones staring up at her.

"This is what you saw, Molly," he said. "This is how it happened. She was coming on to me, and I wasn't having any part of it."

"Oh, no, Charlie." They couldn't have lost so much over something like that.

"You would never ask, Moll. Only accuse. This is what you saw, honey."

She bit her teeth into her bottom lip and a wounded sound escaped her. Tears spilled from her eyes to splash his cheeks, and he let her go.

Shakily she separated from him, straightened her clothing, and walked across the room. Wiping the wetness from his own cheeks, he watched her weep into trembling hands, her sobs tearing at him.

"What else did you see, Molly?" He suspected. God knew, he'd suspected for a long time. He had to find out for certain.

Her sobs became less intense, quieter, but she kept her face hidden in her hands.

"Did you see your daddy?"

She went very still, then raised her head, her teeth set. He had hoped he was wrong, but he knew in that moment he wasn't. He knew, just as certainly, that she hadn't misinterpreted what she'd seen that time.

"How old were you, honey?"

"Nine."

Her quiet word stung him like a lash. God. Nine years old. No shades of gray at that age. Everything black and white, right or wrong. No allowances made for a hopeless, loveless marriage. No understanding for a woman who didn't *like* to be touched in that way and a man who couldn't live without those touches. He'd heard stories of how it was in that house. His mother had worked there. He ached for Molly, and for himself, and for what that ruined marriage had cost them.

He didn't want this distance between them, but he knew she couldn't cross it. Heavily, he rose from the chair and walked to her. He wanted to take her in his arms and hold her, but he sensed she wasn't ready for that yet. She stopped twisting her fingers and spread them, examining her nails, in a gesture he remembered from long ago.

"He'd lie to me, Charlie. All the time. I'd ask where he'd been...what he'd been doing, and he'd lie." She gave a short, humorless laugh. "As if I didn't know. As if every kid in school didn't tell me."

"He was weak, honey, and ashamed. But he loved you. When are you going to let yourself admit you loved him, too?"

She shook her head in denial first, and then she turned her face into his chest, sobbing in capitulation. He wrapped his arms around her, and rocked her, and crooned to her while she cried the tears she hadn't been able to shed that awful night in the past.

As she quieted he lifted strands of her hair and combed his fingers through them, and talked. "He wasn't a bad person, honey. When my daddy was laid off for that spell? You remember? He paid for Lucy to have her tonsils out."

Molly turned her head to the side on his chest and sniffed. "I didn't know that."

He stroked her back and kissed the top of her head. "Mmm-hmm. Half the town had stories like that. He didn't have much left when he died because he was such an easy touch for every hard-luck case that came down the pike. And your momma, too. You remember when she used to go read to the old people in that high-rise for the elderly on River Road?''

She smoothed her palm over his chest. "Yes, I do."

"They weren't bad people, Molly. Just bad for each other." He chuckled low. "It's ironic as hell. That's what they used to say about us."

She lifted her head and looked up at him with that old pagan-god expression on her face. He figured, what the hell? Let her know. "I came looking for you...after we split...but you were gone." She was so still he thought she must be holding her breath. "I talked to your momma." If he'd had any doubts about that incident, her gasp dispelled them. "She never told you?" She leaned back in his arms and closed her eyes, shaking her head.

"Well. That explains a lot." Bringing her head back to his chest, he tangled his fingers in her hair and massaged her scalp the way he liked to do. "She wasn't being cruel, honey. I was a little...tight...that night, which she was gracious enough to point out. I'd been slammin' 'em back, workin' up my courage at the Blue Moon, listening to the folks tell me how wonderful I was. I started to believe them. So, I thought I'd take a hike out to your place. Figured with all this money I was making, how could a woman resist? Anyway, there I was, cocky, brash, full of myself...."

"Not you!"

He chuckled. "You're a little mouthier than you used to be, Mrs. Cochrane. We're gonna have to find a better use for that tart tongue of yours." Her muffled laughter warmed his chest. He continued to stroke her gently. "So, I'd come looking for you, and you were gone. She wouldn't tell me where you went." He paused and his hand stilled in her hair. "I always thought she'd told *you* I'd been there."

"No, Charlie."

He tugged on her hair to make her look at him. "Don't hold it against her," he said firmly. "I had some growing up to do. She knew I'd been sniffin' after her daughter for years. I was her worst nightmare.''

She didn't disagree with him. Just looked a little sad. Like she could use some diversion. As long as it was a night for revealing secrets, he may as well go whole-hog. ''You know, before you threw me out, there had never been any other woman for me. I'd never been with anyone but you.''

Her head jerked back, her big brown eyes widening and her mouth falling open. He'd like to freeze-frame that look. ''You mean—''

''Yeah, that's what I mean.''

Her eyes moved over his face, searching. ''But, that first time…you knew what you were doing.''

''Well, it's not that difficult. Let's just say I took to it a little better than I did algebra.'' Behind her back he linked the fingers on one of his hands around the wrist of the other just above her bottom. ''Besides, that's what big brothers are for.'' He gave her his sweetest smile and watched her eyes widen even more.

''You didn't discuss us with Clee—''

''I didn't tell him *who*. Although,'' he acknowledged with a shrug, ''I think he might have guessed.'' He could see another doubt flicker across her face.

''You were prepared.''

''Honey.'' He rested his forehead against hers. ''We were gettin' steadily more hot and heavy every time we were together. That wasn't the place or the circumstances I'd have picked, but I knew it was only a matter of time. And big brother or no, I did know how babies were made.''

She slid her hand up his chest and cradled his jaw, rubbing her thumb along his bottom lip. ''I saw you with so many girls, Charlie….''

He caught her hand and kissed her palm. ''I was dancing with them, Molly, not sleeping with them.'' He lifted his head and looked her straight in the eye. ''You asked me to wait for you and I told you I would.''

He could see that really surprised her. ''I never meant—''

''Now's a fine time to tell me,'' he said with a laugh. But

he quickly turned serious again. "You have to trust me, Molly. I was true to you before there were any vows between us. You have to think what you're saying about me, what you're calling me, every time you think that I cheat."

She lowered her gaze to his chest, a faraway look on her face. "I know that, but it's so hard, given what you do for a living."

"That's an excuse, Moll. If I sold shoes for a living, you'd be wondering whose foot was in my lap and exactly what it was doing there." She had the grace to blush. "I know you're leery. I understand. But I can't spend my whole life trying to justify myself to you. You have to trust me."

She nodded slowly. "I'll try."

He sighed and decided to broach another topic. Delicately. "I hope Cleeve's learned something over the years. His instructions were sorely lacking."

Her head shot up again and she gave a surprised laugh. "Charlie! You were always—"

"Quick. I was quick." He sighed and sent her a sidelong look. "I've learned it should take more than a minute and a half, though damned if I've been able to demonstrate that to you just yet." He laid caressing fingers on the back of her neck. "Will you let me show you tonight?"

He watched the blush rise from the neckline of that sexy dress all the way to the roots of her hair, and he couldn't help but wonder how far down it extended. Looking at her, he expelled a tight breath of frustration.

"I've got to go back out there and make nice with all these people who want to donate money, Moll." He had a short list of things he'd rather do.

"I should go, too."

He looked at her flushed face. "No. You go home, check on Tobie. I'll make your excuses."

He reached behind her and shoved the clutter on the dressing table aside with his forearm. Then he grasped her waist and lifted her onto the table, stepping between her legs and sliding her dress way up high.

"Charlie!"

"I just want to make sure you'll wait up for me, honey. Did I tell you how much I like this dress?"

"Well, yes…"

"The color's a knockout.…" He spread his hands on her thighs and she tried to bring them together, but he was standing in the way. "And it covers you up nicely." Her legs tightened around him and he liked that sensation real well. He nudged his burgeoning erection against her to let her know that, and with a rush of breath she gave up trying to get rid of him altogether and settled her shoeless feet on the backs of his thighs. He liked that sensation even better.

"Your dress is modest, but…" He edged his fingers under the hem. That was just a distraction, and it worked fine. "Everything is so…" She was totally unprepared when he moved his hands to her neckline, slipped his fingers into the tops of the sleeves and pulled them down her arms. "Accessible."

"Charlie!"

Her bra came away, too—it was just a scrap of a thing, served no useful purpose as far as he could see—and the lush bounty of her breasts was exposed to his feasting eyes. He really didn't play fair. Positioned as they were with him in her way, she couldn't even bring her hands up to cover herself, which she seemed anxious to do. So he did it for her. Well, he cupped her breasts, anyway, and covered her nipples with his circling thumbs.

"*Char*lie!"

"Molly, there's one thing we'll have to agree on. You can't be saying my name like that unless you want to rush this."

His name was on the tip of her tongue again, he could tell, but she bit it back and instead buried her face in the curve of his shoulder. He wanted a taste, just a taste, and then they would stop. He kissed her throat, trailed his tongue down the ridge of his collarbone, nibbled his way over the soft swell below.

She tried to lift her arms and couldn't, so settled her hands at his waist. "Someone might…"

"Door's locked." He bent his head and closed his mouth over the dusky crest he sought. He'd forgotten how soft she was, how warm, the fragrance of her skin. A taste wasn't enough. He swirled his tongue on her and pulled her nipple deeply into his mouth. He felt her arch closer, felt her feet press into his thighs and her fingers dig into his hips. But it was her whimpers, those helpless sounds of abandon wrenched from her throat, that brought him back. He dragged his mouth away from her and lifted his head.

She leaned against the mirror, that red hair intensified by its reflection. Her breasts rose and fell with her rapid pants. She was as aroused as he'd ever seen her. As aroused as he'd ever made her.

She rolled a shoulder toward him, lifting a breast in silent invitation, but he shook his head. "No, honey. We're not gonna do this on a dressing table, in a rush. Not this time. This was foreplay. You've never had enough of it. But you will."

Still, her lips were already parted, puffy and red, as if she'd been biting down on them. Her eyes were already half-closed. It seemed a shame to waste such an invitation. "Just one more kiss, Moll, and then you're going home." He placed his mouth on hers and slid his tongue inside.

Half a dozen kisses later he released her, pulled her hands away from his belt buckle, and tried to steady his breathing. "You okay to drive?" he said, still gasping.

She shoved her tumbled hair off her face and gave a shaky nod, rearranging her clothes and batting his hands away when he tried to help.

"I think we'll sneak you out the back way, Mrs. Cochrane. You're a mess."

She threw him a quelling look. "Well, you've got sequins stuck to your shirt, and I'd give *this*—" her hand caressed the bulge in his jeans "—a little time before you go out there and make a spectacle of yourself."

"You wait up for me, hear?" He grasped her hand and kissed the palm. "I'll walk you to the car."

"Okay. But don't kiss me again."

It was going on one before he was able to bum a ride back to the house. He offered his thanks for the lift, slammed the door and headed for the porch. The house looked completely dark, unless that was a glimmer of light on the second floor toward the back. Their bedroom was dark. Maybe his lazy-bones had given up on him.

He climbed the steps, working the jaw that ached from smiling. He'd had his picture taken with so many people he was still seeing spots. But it was little enough to ask of him, considering all the good this cause would do.

Suddenly he caught a whiff of an acrid scent that made his mouth water. He turned his head to the side and saw a man standing in the shadows against the porch balustrade, the red glow of a cigarette at about chest height.

He ambled over. ''What are you doin' out here, Pop?''

''Aw, I don't want to smoke in your house. Everything's newly decorated. Smells fresh....''

''Did Molly—''

''No! Molly didn't say anything. She's just as gracious as she could be. Don't you go gettin' on her.''

Charlie licked his lips. That smoke smelled real good. ''Could I have a cigarette, Pop?''

The old man exhaled a lungful and looked at his son.

''What?''

''Well, you know how it is. Sometimes one would taste real good.''

Charlie watched his dad rub a finger over his white mustache. A sure sign he was going to get a lecture. The older man cleared his throat.

''Let me just tell you something. I'm smoking out here 'cause this is your house, and that's fine, I don't want to stink it up. But when I go home, your momma says, 'Sam, we've got new carpets.''' He paused and picked a piece of tobacco off his tongue. ''They're nice carpets, by the way, Kick. Thank you very much.''

Charlie lifted a booted foot to the porch rail and propped an elbow on his knee. ''That's okay.''

''Anyway, be that as it may, I can't smoke in my own home.''

He was really getting cranked up about this, Charlie thought, pulling at his lip.

"Driving up here, miserable as the traffic was, she wouldn't let me smoke in the car. She wants me to stop. Man my age. What do you think of that?"

"I think I'm not gonna get a cigarette."

His father looked at him again. "You were smart to quit. Now don't go do something stupid."

Charlie gave a snort. Not likely. He could never seem to get any cooperation. His father stretched and he could hear his old bones creaking.

"I'm afraid I let the cat out of the bag today about Molly's one experience with the weed."

Charlie thought for a minute and started to laugh. "I forgot about that."

"Yeah. Well, Tobie won't."

They laughed together, companionably, then quieted, listening to the night sounds. "She never came to you, did she, Pop?" Charlie asked after a time. The cigarette glowed brighter for a moment before parallel streams of smoke issued from his father's nostrils.

"When you got her in trouble, you mean."

Leave it to the old man to use that old-fashioned phrase. He hadn't heard it in years. But the man was right. It must have been big trouble for Molly.

"Yeah."

His father gripped the railing with both hands and leaned heavily on it. "I raised you better than that, Kick."

Holy Hannah! He was gonna get a lecture on this, too. He shifted uneasily and blew out a long breath. His dad turned to look at him and he felt the tips of his ears burning like he was seventeen again, being told to quit making calf eyes at that little redhead who, no matter how nicely she had filled out, was too young to know her own mind. Around that time he'd gotten the sit-down about responsible young manhood and birth control. The talking-to must have done some good, because Molly was the only woman he'd ever been with where he didn't always take care of that particular necessity himself.

"I've got nothing to say on that subject, Pop."

"Meaning you thought birth control was all covered, so to speak. Well, as you found out, accidents can happen. Even in a marriage, accidents can happen. You have to stick around and be sure."

Charlie twisted to look at his dad. That was the first time the old man ever said anything about birth control in connection with his own marriage. He pushed his hat back, feeling as if the ground was shifting beneath his feet. He'd been born eleven months after Cleeve. Did that put him in the category of a fender bender? He really didn't need this. All he'd wanted was a smoke.

"Did she come to you, Dad?"

"Hell, no." He crushed his cigarette out on the sole of his shoe and tossed it into the bushes. "I'd have been after you with a pitchfork so fast you'd have been lucky to drag what was left of your sorry butt to the altar."

"Yeah, I kinda figured." He sighed, feeling the tension ease from him.

"You think she went to someone?" They stood side by side, staring out at nothing.

"I can't believe she didn't."

"Cleeve?"

"He says no." From the corner of his eye Charlie saw his father tip his head back, reach up, and set one of the pots of impatiens in motion.

"Did you ask *her?*"

"Couple times. Thinking back on what she said, I'm convinced I never got a straight answer."

"Why don't you let it rest?"

"I lost seven years with him, Dad. Eight with Molly. I'd just like to know what happened."

The old man was silent for a long while, watching the pot until it stilled. Finally he spoke. "I think what happened is as plain as the nose on your face. If you don't see it, it's because you don't want to see it.'' He turned to go inside, hands in his back pockets. "I'm going to go spend some time with my wife. Maybe you ought to do the same.''

Chapter 11

Charlie climbed the stairs to the second floor in darkness. She hadn't even left a light on for him, he thought, trying to swallow his disappointment. He came to the door of Tobie's room and went in.

There was a night-light on in here. Maybe that was the glimmer he'd seen from the outside, although this didn't seem like the right spot. He still wasn't real straight on the room arrangement in the old place.

He approached the bed quietly. His son was as restless a sleeper as he was, and he didn't want to wake him. The Stetson rested on the pillow alongside the boy. It looked a little the worse for wear, as if it had been rolled on a few times. Charlie reached to move it and then thought better of it. This wasn't just a hat. It was his presence, his constancy, in his child's life. He kissed Tobie gently and left the hat where it lay.

Moments later he turned the knob to the big room he would share with Molly. The room was deeply shadowed, but pale light slanted into it from the open bathroom door. That must have been what he'd seen outside.

The bed was unmade, but empty.

He'd been in here earlier in the day and was familiar enough with Molly's furniture rearrangement to keep from bumping into things. He crossed to the fireplace and gripped the mantel while he eased his boots off with the bootjack she'd had installed on the hearth. That was a nice touch, he thought as he peeled off his socks. Made him feel welcome.

"Charlie?"

He thought he'd made enough noise moving around the room to let her know he'd come in. Molly really was kind of a modest young woman. They hadn't been in the habit of busting in unawares on each other when they'd lived together summers and breaks. The last thing he wanted to do was turn her skittish now.

"Yeah, I'm here."

She didn't answer. He laid his hat on the chest and noticed her dress draped over the chair next to it, sequins glittering like stars in the faint light. He moved closer and saw her panty hose strewn there, too. And her bra, such as it was. He fingered the silky wisp, wondering where his Molly had ever gotten the nerve to buy such a thing.

He could hear the trickle of running water coming from the bathroom. She'd had plenty of time to shut that door if she'd a mind to. Pulling his T-shirt from the waistband of his jeans, he strolled over and leaned against the jamb.

She was shaving her legs. Such a mundane description for such a mind-blowing scene, some rational portion of his brain registered as his eyes took in the sight.

She seemed to take no notice of his presence. Just continued about her business. She was sitting on the closed lid of the commode, one lovely, slender leg stretched out, her foot resting on the rim of the tub. He watched her rinse her razor under the thin stream she'd left running in the sink. Then she took a long, curving sweep through the foam on her leg and his mouth went dry.

He had a thoroughly unencumbered view of her legs because she was wearing that teddy. It pulled taut across her breasts as she leaned to rinse the razor again and he felt his jeans pull a little more taut. The circle of lace around her thigh seemed to rise almost to her waist when she extended her arm down her leg to take another sweep. He might not be comfortable discussing French cut with a saleslady, but he could surely appreciate the effect.

She was wearing her hair the way he liked it best. Piled precariously up on top of her head, looking like one good tug in just the right place would send the whole mass tumbling. It shimmered in the dim light from the chandelier.

Dim light, Charlie thought, glancing up at that chandelier and then at the wall switch that adjusted its intensity. This wasn't serious leg-shaving light. At one o'clock in the morning, he'd venture to guess, this wasn't serious leg-shaving at all.

He cleared his throat, not sure it was in working order. "Can you see well enough to do that in this light?"

She favored him with a look, finally, turning those witchy eyes that glowed like warmed brandy on him. "I do it mostly by feel anyway."

Oh, my. That's all he needed to hear. This had all the hallmarks of a seduction. Well, hell, he'd play along.

Quickly he stripped off his shirt and tossed it on the chair with Molly's dress. Returning to the bathroom he sank to the floor in front of her, sitting back on his heels, knees spread. He took her ankle in one hand and her razor in the other. She did have a blade in the thing, he noticed. This wasn't entirely for show.

"Let me help you with this." He lifted her leg a little and she gripped the seat with both hands to keep from tipping off.

"You don't need to—"

"It's no trouble at all. I like to feel you."

"Charlie..."

At her mention of his name he took her other foot and placed it very deliberately in his lap, against his crotch, where the arch of her foot accommodated him nicely. "There are some places on a woman's leg," he said, taking up the razor again, "here, for instance—" he touched behind her ankle

"—and here—" he dipped the razor into the concave spot behind her knee "—that are hard to reach. We don't want any nicks."

He rinsed the blade under the tap—warm water, smart girl—and edged a little higher up her thigh, raising her leg a tad more to do so. She pressed her other foot to him for counterbalance, her eyes widening at its effect on him.

"It really doesn't look like you need to do this, Molly," he said, gratified to see her blush and catch her bottom lip between her teeth. He set the razor on the sink, turned off the faucet, and put his tongue to a spot of foam on the inside of her thigh just above her knee.

She slid down a little on the seat, holding on for dear life. "I don't think that's good for you, Charlie," poured out all on one rush of breath. Her eyes widened even more at the response under her foot when she said his name. "That really does hap—"

"I did warn you."

"Well, if that happens whenever somebody says your name, it must be a serious problem for you."

He gave her his lopsided grin. "Not really. There's not another person in the world who calls me 'Charlie.'" That was true. He'd been "Charlie" to her ever since he'd given her the option. It had always been special between them. "'Kick' doesn't have the same effect."

He slid his hand up the inside of her thigh to that sweet juncture. "How high do you shave, honey?"

She inhaled sharply and clamped her legs together, but not before his fingers had insinuated themselves between the snaps of the teddy and found another barrier.

He blinked in surprise. "Are you wearing panties under that teddy, Moll?"

"Charlie!" She gripped his wrist with both hands, blushing fiercely.

"You are!" he said with a laugh. "You're one cautious woman. I thought this was a seduction."

He regretted the words as soon as they were out. Her gaze

skittered away and a disconcerted look crossed her face. "I'm not very good at this, Charlie."

He moved his hands to settle one on each of her thighs, caressing gently. "Aw, honey, if you were any better at this, my heart would stop. My pleasure's a given. Don't you know that? It's your pleasure we're concerned with tonight."

He looked at her uncertain expression a moment more, then rose, went to the end of the tub and turned on the tap. She watched him check the water temperature and adjust it.

"What are you doing?" she asked.

"I'm having a bath." He threw her a quick glance. "You're welcome to join me, if you'd like. I'll help you get the rest of that foamy stuff off your legs."

She pulled in a breath and licked her lips. "I can just use a towel."

He shrugged. "Suit yourself." Then he gave her a long look over his bare shoulder. "Chicken."

He turned his attention back to filling the tub. Watching him reach for the stopper hanging on a chain to plug the drain, she was torn between warring feelings of eagerness and timidity.

They'd been lovers in the past, but there were some things they hadn't done. And this was one of them.

Though they'd lived together for months at a time, there were lines of intimacy they'd never crossed. Maybe in some perverse way, because they'd been friends for so long before they'd been lovers, it had been more difficult for them. They'd been more conscious and considerate of each other's privacy. Charlie had wrestled with his desire for her for so long, perhaps it had been hard to give it free rein. Then, too, they'd both been very young. They'd *both,* she now knew, been inexperienced.

For whatever reasons they hadn't been in the habit of parading themselves in front of each other. And certain touches were, by silent, mutual agreement, reserved for the bedroom. She'd seen him naked and she'd seen him aroused. In bed. And even those poker games, when she'd been a little giddy with wine and he'd coaxed her, had ended up in bed.

If he'd wanted more, if he'd found their relationship lacking, he'd never pushed. And if this proved beyond her, she knew, despite his taunt he wouldn't push now.

But she found that this was a threshold she wanted to cross. She wanted to experience what his eyes and his touch promised. When he finished what he was doing and rose to come back to her, she stood to face him.

He put his hands on her shoulders, slipping his fingers under the straps of the teddy. "Do you want to do this, Molly, or wait for me in bed?"

She raised her face and whispered against his neck, "I want to do this."

He seemed to relax and let go the breath he was holding. He hooked a finger under each strap and guided them down her arms. She helped when the teddy got caught up on her breasts, and in moments it was lying in a pool at their feet.

He brought her arms up and linked them around his neck. The movement caused the tips of her breasts to brush against his chest. She felt herself go weak at the sensation.

"I take back what I said about the panties," he breathed near her ear, just a little unevenly. "Very seductive." He slid his thumbs along the stretchy lace strips that rode high on each hip and were all that joined the meager triangles of fabric front and back. "They match the bra, don't they?"

Her answer was a nod that jiggled her breasts against him. They both gasped.

"Did you buy these for yourself, Moll?" He couldn't picture that.

She hesitated a moment. "I ordered them from a catalog."

"Ah." That sounded like his Molly. "You're no more comfortable in those stores than I am." He took a nibble of her neck. "You'll have to show me this catalog. I'll order you one of everything in it—" his tongue traced the curve of her ear "—just for the pleasure of taking it off you."

His hand moved to the triangle in front, his finger sliding over her where she was moist and he knew it. "Will you let me take these off you?"

She closed her eyes a moment seeking courage, then leaned

back a little and looked up at him. "I'm not going to take a bath with them on."

"Sass," he whispered, his eyes glittering, and he kissed her. Just a slow slide of his tongue into her mouth and out again. He went down on his knees to remove her panties, stopping for a delicate lick to the tip of each breast on the way. He skimmed the panties off quickly and kissed each thigh, then pressed his mouth to the red curls he'd uncovered, so casually his foray there seemed almost unintentional. But Charlie never did *anything* unintentionally.

She was quivering in his arms when he rose to his feet again. He pulled her snug against him to steady her. Burying his nose in the soft tendrils behind her ear, he murmured. "Tell me something, Molly. I want to know. Have you ever come?"

She stiffened with a jerk and he stroked his hands over her back to soothe her. "I know that's vulgar, honey," he whispered. "I'm sorry. I don't know any other words for it. *Have* you?"

She stared straight at the vee where his collarbones met. "Sure, I think so."

He closed his eyes. This was bad.

"It was…" she went on, struggling for words.

He put a single finger to her lips. "Do me a favor. Don't tell me it was *nice*."

She clamped her lips together and slid a glance up at him. That's what she was going to say, all right. He expelled a heavy breath. "Honey, first of all, there's no thinkin' about it. It's like falling off a cliff. If you don't *know,* you didn't."

She frowned at his throat. "I don't remember any cliff."

"That's what I thought." He sighed. "I don't know if you can tell, but I'm strung about as tight as I can get here. This is never gonna work unless you let me take care of you first."

"Charlie—"

"Another thing. It'd help a lot if you'd just call me Dwayne."

She laughed out loud then, breaking the tension somewhat.

"This isn't all your fault," she said when she could, "that I've never..."

"Aw, gee. You've had another lover?"

She looked up into his eyes, her own softening, and laid caressing fingers on the back of his neck. "No."

He dropped tiny kisses over her face as he spoke. "Honey, this isn't a problem, or something wrong. This is just something you've never experienced. A gift I want to give you." She rested her head against his chest and brought a hand down to stroke him there. He had to grab quick to keep it away from his nipple. "I'll never last if we try to...you know...together. Let me show you first."

She mulled that over some moments, chewing on her upper lip. "Char—" She cleared her throat. "Maybe I'm just not very...responsive. Some women aren't."

He looked down at her, a serious expression on his face. Then he tilted her back from him just a little. With one knuckle he circled the areola of her nipple while both of them watched its center tighten up, stiff as a gumdrop. "Somehow, honey, I don't think that's the case here." He wrapped his arms tightly about her, holding her close, where he could feel her breasts move against him with every breath she took. "Now, I don't expect you'll go head-bangin' nuts the way I do, but a little toe-curlin' nuts might be fun to see."

She tipped her head back, staring up at him, eyes enormous. "Are you going to watch?"

He hadn't anticipated this being a problem. "I thought I might. That's a big part of the fun...watching." Her indecision was palpable. "I won't if you tell me no."

She came to a decision, sort of. "I'll make up my mind at the time."

It was his turn to laugh. "You won't be able to make up your mind at the time, I promise you." He glanced back at the tub. "The water's getting cold."

"So am I." She managed a flirty, if tremulous, smile. "Standing here with nothing on." She prodded his chest gently. "You're overdressed."

It was his hands that decided her, finally. The hands that

went to his belt buckle, and undid it, and shoved his jeans down his legs. The same hands that had gripped her bicycle seat to steady her when she would have careened out of control. The same hands that had pushed her bottom up and supported her so she could grasp that tree limb just out of her reach. The same hands that had broken Jimmy Jordan's nose for her when he'd spread that nasty story after she'd stopped seeing him. She'd chastised Charlie for being such a barbarian, but she'd been secretly pleased.

She would take from his hands the pleasure he wanted to give her. She would entrust her life to them. It was so much more difficult to entrust her heart.

He stood before her now clad only in his briefs, which did nothing to disguise his desire for her. She stepped up to him and tucked her fingers into the waistband, stretching it out and over his erection. In just a moment he was as naked as she. "You never used to wear black underwear," she said.

"I'll wear white if you want. I'll go without if you want. You tell me what you want and I'll do it."

"I want to take a bath with you."

He held her hand to steady her as she stepped over the high edge of the tub and he followed. "Uh-uh," he said when she would have seated herself at the opposite end facing him. "You won't be comfortable over there with the faucet and knobs."

He grinned as her eyes pointedly perused his ready body. "I'm not saying you won't get poked, just that you'll like it better."

He settled himself in the water, then eased her down in front of him.

"Oooh! It's very warm," she murmured.

"Too warm?" he asked, and she shook her head. "I made it hot. I didn't know how long it would take me to talk you into this." He watched a fine sheen of perspiration cover her face and the silky tendrils around her forehead curl from the heat and humidity. She kept her back straight when he guided her to lie against his chest. The heat-induced lethargy hadn't invaded her body yet. But it would.

He'd estimated the water level pretty well. It just lapped over the crests of her breasts. She'd feel caresses there even when his hands were occupied elsewhere.

True to his word, he slid his hands along her legs, rubbing off the last traces of the shaving foam. Relaxing a little from his ministrations, she leaned her head back into the curve of his shoulder. His fingers searched the coil of her hair, finding the pin that held the whole mass in place and releasing it. The fiery cascade tumbled over his shoulder and the back rim of the tub.

"You're gonna have to keep your head right there now, honey, or you'll get your hair all wet."

"You planned it that way, didn't you?" she whispered with a catnip smile, her eyes closed, head lolling. She was loosening up nicely.

He wasn't.

He shifted a little, trying to make room for himself where he was wedged tight between her body and his.

She moved to accommodate him. "I'm sorry, Charlie. I didn't—"

"That's all right. Don't pay it—"

"No mind. I know, it's just being a hound," she said, teasing laughter in her voice. She settled back into his arms.

"Exactly." He groaned as he found a spot for himself against her hip. She was getting real loose. Giggly. He traced a finger down her neck, across her collarbone, over the slope of her breast, to where the nipple broke the surface of the water, waiting for him. At his lingering touch a gusty sigh escaped her.

He lifted his gaze from her and was confronted with their reflection in the mirror above the sink. Molly, with her head thrown back on his shoulder, her arms dangling at the sides of the tub, her breasts glistening as the water lapped them.

He laid his hand on top of one of hers, lacing their fingers together and bringing both to cover her breast. Gently he guided her hand upon herself.

He felt her immediate resistance and her eyes met his in the glass, distressed. "I can't do that, Charlie!"

He released her at once, letting her hand swing back to the side. His own remained to cup and stroke her breast. "Then don't," he whispered. "It's not important. I'm just trying to find out what you like."

She bit her lip, turning her face into his neck. "I'm sorry...."

He tore his gaze from the mirror to look at the woman in his arms. What need did he have for a reflection when he held Molly in the flesh? "Don't, Molly. Come on, honey, don't." He brought his hand up to cradle her jaw when she kept her eyes squeezed shut. "We have the rest of our lives to find out what pleases us and what doesn't. Don't be embarrassed."

Her features relaxed somewhat, though her eyes remained closed. With two fingers under her chin, he tipped her face to his and opened his mouth on hers. "Kiss me back, Molly," he whispered, gliding his tongue over her lips. "Kiss me back."

Her lips parted and her tongue met his, tentatively at first, and then with sweet demand. He'd forgotten the pleasure to be had in the sounds of loving. The gentle suction of lips seeking and clinging. The catching of breath after breath-stealing kisses. The soft whimpers that escaped when desire heightened and was too intense to suppress. Molly's sounds of need, yearning.

Swirling his tongue in her mouth, he covered her breasts with his hands and repeated that pattern with his wet palms on her nipples. He lifted his head when her breathing was choppy and shallow, moving his mouth to her throat, keeping his touch gentle though the need was riding him hard, too. He laved the tips of her breasts with cupped hands, allowing the slapping of the water to intensify the sensation until her nipples pearled. Under the water he spread his legs with hers upon them, opening her to him and his questing fingers.

And very slowly he slipped his hand between her thighs and covered her.

She arched to him, her beautiful throat, her slender torso, and below, where his fingers stroked. Her whole body strained for his touch. Her head rolled side to side on his shoulder as without her conscious thought her hips began a rhythmic undulation. An unmistakable invitation.

He slid one finger into her. She was wet, slick, and not from the water. At that realization, he closed his eyes against his own ravening hunger. She was at the point he'd promised her, where no logical decision was possible, but he found himself unable to watch.

He slipped his finger in and out while his thumb explored her wet curls for the only rigid place on Molly's soft, yielding body. The keening moan that poured from her when he found it nearly undid him. He had to still his hand to regain his own control. Molly's impatient thrusts let him know how little *that* pleased her.

He opened his eyes to her then, and saw her sweet need revealed to him, honest and total. He began the motions she craved and watched the deepening flush of desire spread over her. Watched her fingers alternately grip and release the rim of the tub. Watched the frantic rise and fall of her breasts. Watched her in the extremes of her passion as her lips formed soundless repetitions of his name.

And at her peak, when she was mindless, heedless of any other presence down the hall, he covered her mouth with his own and absorbed the cries of her ecstasy.

He held her to him while the last tremors of pleasure shuddered through her. He held *himself* rigid, hoping he'd get a grip, hoping she wouldn't move, hoping he'd manage to get past the next few moments without humiliating himself right there in the tub. She turned in his arms and he almost lost it. Pulling away from his shoulder, hair floating out behind her, she twined her arms around his neck and tried to straddle him. His hands went to her hips when he realized what she was about, but whether to pull her to him or push her away, he couldn't have said.

The water sloshing around them and over the edge of the tub brought him to his senses. "Honey, no! Moll—" Her openmouthed kiss stopped his protests for a moment. Then he tore himself away. "Honey…" He pressed her face into his shoulder. "We've got to get out of here." He grabbed her seeking hand. "Molly, we will drown!"

He helped her to stand, though he wasn't especially steady himself. Holding her close, he reached for towels and half lifted her from the tub. Her hair hung in a dripping mass down her back. "Look what you did, honey," he said, trying to soak up the excess water with a towel.

She put her hands on top of his, halting his motion. "I don't care, Charlie." She took the towel from his hand and let it fall to the floor. "I don't care." Reaching for him, she ran her fingers over his chest, feeling him shake with his desire, his skin so hot he should have sizzled.

His fists clenched at his sides, he closed his eyes, unable even to look at her. "I've got nothing left, Moll. No control, no finesse, nothing. I just need you, honey."

Her hand coasted lower. Her palm closed around him, cupped him, welcomed the thrusts against her he couldn't have held back if his life depended on it. Standing on her toes, she whispered at his ear, "Charlie, it's been so long. I want to feel you inside me."

Those had to be the sweetest words under heaven. As he reached the bedroom, he lifted her still wet body against him and was inside her, his thrust strong and sure, before they hit the bed. He felt her arms and legs go around him, cradle him, and, paradoxically, that seemed to calm the madness in his blood.

Just to be inside her, to feel her moist heat clinging, welcoming, wanting, gave him the measure of control he needed. Raised up on arms propped on either side of her head, he gazed into her face. She was illuminated only by the faint light from the bathroom, but he could tell her eyes were open and looking directly into his. "Molly." The word was a whisper, a groan, almost a prayer.

She put her hands on his upper arms, sliding them along the damp skin, feeling the power contained in the muscle and sinew as well as the vulnerability he made no effort to hide. She lifted her hips to him, inviting him deeper and moaning as he obliged with a push that stretched and filled her even more. Her tender parts were so sensitized to him, just his slightest movement sent pulses of pleasure skittering through her.

He saw her response and marveled at it. This woman who feared she was unresponsive was making herself ready for him again. He knew the subtle hints, the cues that signaled sexual excitement. He'd learned them with other women who were about as subtle as a blow to the head. He'd had a lot to learn, so he appreciated the lessons. But as he looked into the eyes of the woman lying beneath him, even as he recognized the signs of her arousal, he realized that this was utterly different.

This was Molly.

There was tenderness, affection in her expression as well as desire. It tapped a wellspring of emotion in him he hadn't been aware existed. Gently he brought his mouth to hers and probed with his tongue, smiling at the breaking of her breath. He pushed up on one arm and reached for a pillow, then turned her a little, arranging it under her shoulders.

When he rolled her to her back again, she gasped at the position she found herself in. Her neck arched over the pillow, completely exposed to his plundering kisses. Her breasts jutted, inviting the lingering ministrations of his tongue and his teeth. To ease the pressure on the small of her back, she'd raised her knees and set her feet flat on the bed alongside his hips. She couldn't so much as take a breath without his stimulating some portion of her anatomy.

And stimulate and stir and arouse, he did. With his mouth and his hands, his whispers and his groans, his words, vulgar and sweet. And transcending it all, the constant, insistent, drugging penetration and withdrawal.

He watched her, his Molly, as she approached the brink. Her arms flung up above her head, her upper lip pulled back, eyes closed, breath coming in ragged pants, and her belly, her hips rising in rhythm to meet him.

Wanting desperately to take her that last short distance, he withdrew and rubbed himself, slippery with her body's dew, against that swollen knot of sensation at the apex of her thighs. She came apart in his arms, her expression one of ecstasy that was close to pain. He plunged into her once more, pushing her over the precipice. And this time, when she soared, he went with her.

He didn't know how long he'd been asleep, only that his waking wasn't comfortable. The bed was a mess, covers every which way, only one pillow to be found and that one under Molly's back. She couldn't be too comfortable, either. He sat up and ran a hand through hair that still surprised him when he found it so short.

"Molly."

Her answer was a barely audible sigh.

"Honey, this bed's all wet."

She rolled to her stomach. "Don't be grumpy," he thought she mumbled.

He gave a short laugh, got up, and padded to the bathroom. This wasn't a pretty sight either. He slipped on the jeans he'd dropped on the floor, zipped them halfway and left them un-belted. Then he pulled the plug in the tub, shut off the light and left everything else where it lay.

On the way back to the bed he grabbed his shirt from the chair. "Come on, sleepyhead," he said, propping her against himself in a sitting position. He pulled the shirt down over her head.

"What are you doing?" she asked drowsily.

"Now who's being grumpy?" He helped her poke her arms through the sleeves. "I'm paying for eight bedrooms here. I can use a couple of them if I feel like it." He stood and lifted her into his arms.

"Charlie." She yawned widely. "You don't have to be a caveman about this. I can walk."

"Oh, hush." He moved toward the door.

"Charlie! This shirt is gaping," she said, feeling air on her bare bottom. "Tobie might—"

He turned back to the bed. "Grab the top sheet. It's dry."

She did as he told her and wrapped it around herself, gig-gling.

"Now, hush! You're gonna wake him." They eased out into the hallway. Moonlight from the landing windows was sufficient for them to see by. "Which room?" he asked her.

She pointed to a room at the end nearest the stairs. "How about that one?"

He stood for a moment, considering. "That's right above my folks," he said finally.

She laughed into his shoulder. "Charlie, they had nine kids! Do you think we're going to give them ideas?"

"I don't care," he said, laughing with her. "I don't think of my parents in those terms."

"I suppose you believe all that stopped when you were born."

"Well, I'd like to think so, but they had Lucy, so I guess they kept at it."

"Do you suppose—"

"Molly, don't even suggest it."

But she cupped his jaw, turned his face to her, told him with a look that she couldn't imagine a time when she wouldn't welcome *his* touch, *his* kiss. Years wouldn't matter. He was so affected, he had to lean against the wall and kiss her soundly. When he raised his head, their breathing was a little less even and their desire to find a room a little more urgent.

"How about that one?" Molly indicated another door with a nod of her head.

"That's right next to Tobie, honey." He gave her a wicked smile. "You get a little carried away."

She looked chagrined, then pleased. "Oh, are we going to again?" She clasped her arms around his neck, legs swinging.

"Uh-huh. Unless you'd rather sleep." He grinned at her hoot of laughter and opened the door to the room closest to the second bath. This one would do nicely, he thought, his eye catching the gleam of the brass headboard. Good handholds.

He carried Molly into their cocoon and closed the door on the rest of the world.

* * *

He wasn't going to be able to sleep. Here he was in the fat part of the night, wide awake, with a woman who, judging by the way she'd sprawled all over him, considered him just another part of the bed.

He couldn't see Molly, but he could smell the jasmine in her hair where it tickled his nose. He could feel the soft breezes of her even respirations blowing through the hair on his chest. He was conscious of the hand she had snuggled right up into his armpit, and the way her thigh draped over his belly gave him access to her most private, feminine secrets. He was aware of her body's invitation, but too thoroughly drained to respond.

That was the problem.

He'd emptied himself into her, unprotected, without any regard for what her feelings might be on the matter. Oh, he figured that first time, he could plead extreme duress. But not this time. This time they'd shared lingering kisses, leisurely touches, slowly heightening pleasure. There had been time to savor each brush of skin on skin, each contact of tongue to tongue, each sigh, each moan, that built to the mindless explosion they both sought.

And his neglect of any precautions had been deliberate on his part. He just didn't want anything between them.

He'd taken the time to dump the packets in the nightstand drawer in their room earlier in the day. He'd even given a thought to stuffing a couple in his jeans before he'd carried her to this room. Just a thought, and he'd quickly discarded it.

The truth was he'd like to have another child. With Molly. He hadn't given a lot of consideration to the matter before, but the fact remained he'd be thirty-two by the end of the year, and he wanted to be young with his kids. Tobie appeared to be doing fine and as for himself, well, this was the only marriage he would ever enter into.

But he should have checked with Molly.

He cringed, remembering his words to her when they'd married. Questioning her about birth control, telling her he'd take care of it. As if it was too big a responsibility for her to be trusted with. What a pompous ass. He'd been happy enough to let her be the responsible one years ago.

She rubbed her nose into his chest as if it itched and then settled herself again. He wrapped his arms around her and caressed her bottom.

He'd like to be there this time to see her belly swell with his baby. He didn't know the simplest things about Tobie's birth. Did she have morning sickness? Had she breast-fed him? His hand went to stroke that part of her that he'd always considered most especially his. What the heck. He wasn't a selfish guy. He could share.

Another thought shook him to his core. Had she been alone when Tobie was born? Had she gone through labor with no one beside her? He'd seen enough of his kick-butt brothers shaken by that ordeal with their wives to realize it was no walk in the park. Had anyone been there for Molly?

Maybe her mother had softened enough to come up and be with her. He knew women shared a special affinity at that time. Maybe she'd been able to overcome her aversion to that no-good Cochrane boy in order to support her daughter. Charlie uttered a fervent promise that he would never entertain an uncharitable thought about the woman again if she had come through then.

He tightened his arms around Molly and she stirred, patting his shoulder, as if *he* were the one who needed soothing. He made an effort to relax and stared into the darkness. When had it been, exactly, that she had her period? He tried to do the figuring, but math was never his strong suit and counting backward gave him a headache. He'd have to talk to Molly.

"Honey?" He tangled a hand in her hair and she batted her fingers ineffectually against his face. He kissed her fingertips. "I need to talk to you, Moll."

He thought she was still asleep and was going to speak again when she whispered, "What?"

He ran his dry tongue over dry lips. "I didn't use any…when we…made love. I didn't use…any protection." He hissed a breath through his teeth. *Just get it out, Kick.* "I didn't use a condom."

He knew she opened her eyes. He could feel her lashes flutter on his chest. Then he felt her stiffen. Every inch of her, from her fingertips to her toes, stiffened and withdrew from him. God, did she think he was regretting it now? He was really making a hash of this.

"What I mean is—" he put his hands on her back to hold her to him "—I'd like a baby. I want us to have one." Her hand settled on his chest again, combing through the hair. He started to breathe a little more easily. "But it has to be all right with you." Just as he'd felt her stiffen, now he sensed her gradual relaxation. Her thigh came back up over his to wrap around him. Her arms circled his neck and she burrowed her face in the curve at its base. "Would you like that, Moll?"

She didn't answer him directly. Just snuggled in real close, kissed his ear, and whispered, "Go to sleep, Charlie," against his skin. He'd take that for a yes.

Chapter 12

Molly shifted and Charlie woke, missing the warm blanket of her body. He opened his eyes to daylight, though it was still early judging from the long slant of the gauzy shadows in the room. He went up on one elbow to look at his sleeping wife.

Her hair was a bright tangle on the pillow, enticing his fingers to sift through it. Her lips were slightly parted and the fingers of one hand curled near her chin.

He lowered his eyes.

The bedsheet was twisted around her legs, crossing her abdomen just below the shallow dimple of her navel. The rest of her body was bared to his gaze. Crooked red streaks patterned her breasts, remnants of having been smashed on top of him during the night. With a twinge of guilt he noted the flushed areas near her nipples, light abrasions that reminded him *he* hadn't shaved before they'd gone to bed last night. Even with the wrinkles and the redness, she was beautiful.

The flat discs of her nipples beckoned him. They were so sensitive. He knew it would take just a whisper of his breath, just a nuzzle with his nose to bring them to peaks. He'd heard there were women who could be brought to release just from loving attention to their breasts, but that was outside of his experience. It wasn't something he'd ever given much thought to. Before Molly.

In truth, he'd been kind of concerned that his experience with other women would taint what he had with her. But that hadn't happened. She made everything new again. She made *him* feel new again.

She rolled a little more onto her back, bringing her arms up alongside her head, and his breath caught. Her position thrust the lush tip of one breast within inches of his mouth. His response was instantaneous, a heavy rush of hot blood to his loins. Maybe if he was extra careful not to scrape her, touched her only with his tongue and his lips, she wouldn't mind a little wake-up loving.

He opened his mouth to tongue her nipple when a muffled shuffling outside the door caught his attention. Some protective instinct caused him to pull the sheet high over Molly's form before the door opened and Tobie's head poked in. Shaken by the close call, Charlie raised a finger to his lips and waved the youngster away.

With a last rueful glance at Molly and a kiss to her forehead, he slipped from the bed and stuffed himself into his jeans. He stepped quietly into the hall, spotted Tobie using the adjacent bathroom and went to join him.

"Things are probably pretty relaxed around here when it's just you and your mom," he said, "but I know Grandma would appreciate it if you shut the door when you do that."

"Mom appreciates it, too," Tobie answered, frowning as he turned on the water and reached for the soap. Charlie was pleased to see the hand-washing habit had taken root. "I was in a big hurry, Dad."

Not so big that he couldn't make that inopportune stop, Charlie reflected. He caught a glimpse of his face in the mirror. *Woooof.* Bristle city. Maybe it was just as well he hadn't been able to make good on his plans with Molly.

He started for the other bathroom to shave and then remembered the condition it had been left in. Molly's teddy and his underwear on the floor. He thought he'd emptied the tub, but he wasn't even sure about that. He didn't feel up to any questions his curious seven-year-old shadow might have.

Glancing around, he noticed the shaving things on the railed wooden shelf above the toilet tank. Victorian stuff. One of those china bowls with a lump of shaving soap you added a little water to and fluffed up with the brush hanging on its side. Molly had probably gotten it to go with the house, but it looked serviceable. He'd never used anything like that. Always wanted to. No time like the present, he thought, sprinkling water on the soap and swishing the brush over it.

From the corner of his eye he saw Tobie watching him, his tongue caught between his teeth. "You'll have to do this every day, before you know it. It won't seem like such fun then." He picked up the ornate razor and twisted it open. Empty.

Tobie hesitated a minute, then darted his gaze to the mirrored cabinet. "Mom hides the blades on the top shelf in there," he offered.

Charlie laughed. "Good hiding place." He opened the cupboard, found the blades and inserted one. "Does Mom know—"

"I'm not gonna touch 'em, Dad."

Slathering the soap over his face, Charlie eyed his son. "I'll let you try this in a minute, okay?"

Tobie brightened, then poked his finger in the bowl of soap and sniffed it. "Did you and Mom have a fight last night and then make up?" he asked a little too casually.

Charlie halted the sweep of the razor in midstroke and looked at the top of his son's bent head. Had Molly said something to him about that incident after the show? He wouldn't classify that as a fight, and he doubted Molly would have brought it up with Tobie anyway. "Why do you ask?"

The boy shrugged his pajama-clad shoulders. "You started out in separate beds."

Charlie let his breath out through pursed lips. Stood to reason that Tobie would have checked their room first before looking for them elsewhere. It really was too early in the morning to handle questions like this. He was beginning to believe a seven-year-old was something you needed to work up to gradually, not just have dumped on you, awkward questions and all. "No, we didn't have a fight," was all he said.

"That's not to say we never will," he continued after a few moments. "Have words, I mean." He rinsed his blade and glanced at Tobie. "We're both kind of...strong-willed. You appear to be a might that way, yourself," he said with a reproving glance. He took another swipe over his jaw. "But you don't have to worry if you hear us disagree. We're not gonna call it quits." He was a little puzzled at the sullen expression that crossed his son's face until the boy spoke.

"You did once."

Charlie put the razor down and rested his fists on the sink cabinet. He was unsure how much Tobie understood about that period in their lives, if anything. What had Molly explained to him other than if his father knew him, he would love him? "That's...complicated," he said, the words sounding lame even to his own ears.

"That's what *she* said," Tobie answered, rolling his eyes toward the bedroom where Molly still rested.

For the first time since he'd met his son, Charlie felt prickles of irritation with him. He was criticizing Molly, albeit indirectly, and Charlie didn't like it. He found himself girding for her defense, something he'd never thought he'd do over this issue.

He straightened and rinsed the rest of the soap from his face, then grabbed a towel from the rack and wiped his jaw. "Come here," he said to Tobie and lifted him onto the cabinet in front of the mirror. He picked up the soap bowl, added a little more water and gave the brush to the youngster. "Slather."

The boy swished foam all over his face, snorting when he got some up his nose. Charlie took the blade out of the razor, put it back on the high shelf and handed the razor to Tobie. "Here. Let's see how you do."

Tobie slid the instrument over his cheek and it skipped in a few places.

"Okay, there, let me show you," Charlie said, circling Tobie's shoulders with his arms and placing his hands over his son's. "You have to stretch the skin taut, or the blade will skip and you'll get nicked."

They watched each other, father and son, in the mirror, sizing each other up. The one wondering how much he should trust, and the other how much he should reveal.

"This spot, especially, can be tricky," Charlie continued, tilting Tobie's chin up and touching a finger to his Adam's apple. The boy made a few swipes over the area. "It gets bigger as you get older. You're gonna get hung up on it a couple times, I guarantee, before you remember it's there."

Charlie looked into his son's eyes in the mirror. They were identical to his own, yet so different. Tobie talked with his eyes, the way Molly did, while he tried to keep his feelings hidden. Did a pretty good job of it, too, if the past was any indication. She hadn't known what she meant to him.

He handed Tobie the towel and then settled his hands on his shoulders. "I'm going to tell you something about your momma," he said. He held the boy's gaze in the reflection. "There was never a time, not a minute, from the moment she knew you were on the way, that you didn't come first with her. She never made a decision without thinking what was best for you. I won't listen to you say a word against her."

Tobie's gaze faltered and he frowned down at the towel in his hands. "*You* didn't want me?"

Charlie exhaled a tight breath. "I didn't know about you." He put the towel aside and closed his hands over Tobie's. "There was never a time when I wouldn't have wanted you, but there might have been a time when she didn't know that."

Tobie sagged back against his father's chest and turned his head from the mirror as if impatient with reflections and images. He looked directly into Charlie's eyes, his own tolerating no evasion. "Do you love her?"

Well, that came in on his blind side. Took him back a bit. His first impulse was to conceal his feelings, to make light of it. But one look at his son's face stopped him. The time for such shenanigans was long past. Tobie was asking an important question and he deserved an honest answer.

Charlie was reminded of something his father had said years ago, during one of those lectures that had proved more influential than he would ever have guessed. The best thing a man could do for his children was love their mother and let them know it. Both his heart and his mind were in agreement on this one.

"Yes, I do," he said simply.

Tobie gave a firm nod of what appeared to be satisfaction, picked up the razor and rinsed the rest of the soap off of it. Hearing a floorboard creak, Charlie glanced back over his shoulder and saw Molly, clad in his black T-shirt and a bedsheet, skittering down the hall to their room. He set his shoulders across the doorway, blocking Tobie's view. But the sight brought to mind a further concern.

"One other thing we have to talk about, Tobie." He helped the boy scramble off the sink top and watched him replace the shaving things on the shelf. "If you need me or your momma during the night...you don't feel well, or you're worried about something...you can come wake us." He paused and licked his lips. "But you have to knock, okay? Before you open the door, you have to knock—*hard.* Understand?"

Tobie appeared to digest those words for some moments, then settled his hands on his hips and gave his father a level, indulgent look. "I'd like a brother," he said.

Charlie laughed, flabbergasted. "Well, we'll see what we can do."

He'd barely recovered his cool when he saw Molly leave the bedroom and approach them, setting him back on his rear again. She was wrapped in a deep green robe—velour, he thought—that looked as soft as she felt. She'd done the best she could with her hair, he supposed, but he hoped she'd give it some more attention before they had to face his folks. Despite that, she looked a lot more rested than she had any right to be after the night they'd shared.

"How are my men this morning?" she asked, smiling

widely. Tobie grinned back and stuck out his chin. "O-o-o, smooth," she murmured, caressing his soft cheek.

Watching, Charlie found himself tempted to stick out his jaw like some pathetic mutt, tongue lolling, begging for her touch. With an effort he tore his gaze from her and addressed Tobie. "What would you like for breakfast?"

"Grampa promised to make buckwheat cakes," Tobie answered. "I've never had those, Dad," he continued, looking a little doubtful. "Is he any good at it?"

With those words, Charlie saw the morning take a decided turn for the better. He was going to be able to cadge some more time with Molly after all. He wouldn't be surprised if the old matchmaker had planned this all along. "Your grampa makes the best buckwheat cakes this side of the Rockies. He'll let you help, too, and not just set the table. Why don't you go find him?" He winked at Molly. "Tell him we'll be down in a bit."

Tobie took off down the hall toward the staircase. "Don't wake your grandfather if he's not up," Molly called after him.

"He'll be up," Charlie assured her. "Runs in the family."

She turned back to him and they faced each other, the air between them charged with memory and anticipation. Molly moved first, raising her hand to his cheek and stroking gently.

"Smooth," she whispered, and Charlie suspected that she didn't mean his jaw. He pulled her further into the bathroom and shut the door behind her, locking it. Her eyes darted around the space and then settled on him. "Have you showered yet?" she asked, confronting him with the mixture of boldness and innocence he hoped she'd never lose.

His own gaze quickly took in the room. This bath was as small as the other was large. Probably had been a linen closet before it was converted. The shower stall, especially, captured his attention. It would hold one person comfortably if he didn't try to turn around. He caught Molly eyeing it and glanced again at the tiny square footage, just rife with possibilities. "No," he said in answer to her question.

Mustering her courage, she took a deep breath and put her hands to his belt buckle, undoing it. Moments later she inhaled even more sharply. "Oh, Charlie! No underwear at all," she said with a *tsk.*

"I was in a big hurry, Moll," he muttered, stealing Tobie's excuse. He dropped his hands to the zipper to assist her where the going got tricky. "Careful, there," he began, but then Molly opened her robe and words failed him.

He was feeling as loose as a well-oiled hinge. If he were an engine, he would purr. If he were a kettle, he would whistle. If he were a clock, he would chime.

And if he didn't pay more attention to this checkers game, he was going to get his clock cleaned. By a seven-year-old.

It was difficult, though, keeping his mind on the game, what with Molly flitting around the kitchen, fixing him a second grilled cheese, then waltzing back to the table, spatula in hand, to offer her two cents worth.

His folks had left for Wheeling earlier that morning. They'd planned to stay a week, but his mother said she feared she was coming down with a summer cold and didn't want to risk exposing Tobie, so they'd left after only three days. Charlie secretly suspected that his parents had wanted to give this newly formed family some private time to bond. Much as he enjoyed their company, he wouldn't give them any argument on that score.

Molly sashayed back to the table and slid the grilled cheese from the spatula to his plate, then remained standing behind his chair, massaging his neck. He bent his head and rolled his shoulders, giving her better access. She'd been doing this more and more over the past several days. Finding excuses to touch him. To brush her breast against his arm in passing. To stroke his shoulder. To meet his eyes for just a moment and then touch him everywhere with hers.

This was apart from the bedroom touches. Those were enough to steal his breath just thinking about them. They'd even gotten a little bit fancy the past couple of days. More than a little bit. He didn't think he'd be suffering unduly anymore, those times when she was indisposed.

Truth to tell, he was a happy man. He had a wife he loved

like crazy who not only welcomed, but sought, his embrace. He had a son who could give lessons in courage and fortitude. Yep, he was as content as he could ever remember being.

Except for this checkers game.

God, he hated to lose, and he was really taking a beating here. It didn't seem natural for a kid Tobie's age to be planning four moves ahead, but that's what he was doing.

Even as he held the thought, Charlie was swamped by an overwhelming sense of déjà vu. He'd been beaten this way before. He had a sudden acute recollection of bumping bony knees with another seven-year-old under another kitchen table. Molly'd never been any great shakes at poker, but checkers was another story entirely.

He lifted his gaze from the board in time to see Tobie sneaking a peek at something above and behind him. He glanced over his shoulder and, sure enough, there was Molly, talking with her eyes.

"Aw, hey!" he groused good-naturedly. "No kibitzing. He doesn't need any help." He caught her hand as she started to move away. "I'll play with you later."

She did the eye-roll thing, indicating Tobie, but the comment seemed to slide right past the boy. With a final gentle squeeze to Charlie's neck, Molly picked up the used dishes and strolled off toward the sink. "Watch him, Tobie," she said, laughing the laugh that turned Charlie inside out. "This is where he accidentally upsets the board."

Charlie gave a beleaguered snort and made a move.

"Uh-uh, Dad. You have to jump me."

Now, this was a rule he'd never understood. He could see as well as the next guy what was going to happen when he made that jump. It was a lot like asking the condemned man to sharpen the guillotine blade. He made the jump.

Thwack, thwack, thwack. "Crown me."

"Don't tempt me," Charlie said, laughing with his gleeful son. "I don't suppose you know how to get a man out of a double corner," he offered hopefully, surveying the wreckage.

Tobie's answer was an ear-to-ear grin, but Charlie scurried for the corner anyway.

"It's not quite the same," Molly gasped, coming up from drowning waves of sensation.

"No?" Charlie murmured. He bestowed a last lingering lick to her nipple before raising his head.

"Well, it's very nice," she breathed, arching to him involuntarily, even in the aftermath of her fulfillment.

Charlie winced. "Honey, I thought we'd come to an understanding about the use of that word with regard to my lovemaking."

She huffed, her breathing still erratic. "I mean it's very, very, *very* nice." She put a hand to his cheek, touched by the tenderness in his expression the lamplight revealed. Charlie liked to make love with the light on and she found that now, she did, too. "But it's not the same."

"You appeared to be having a good time."

She covered her mouth with the back of her hand to muffle her laughter. "How could you see?"

His black eyes flashed devilment. "I was reading your body language."

She laughed again, softer this time, feeling the heavy languor that always followed his loving settle into her limbs. A pleasant drowsiness was overtaking her, but she couldn't give in to it just yet. She was getting better at reading body language herself, and Charlie's was communicating his needs loud and clear.

"How was it different?" he whispered between the kisses and nips he dropped on her shoulder.

She shrugged the shoulder he was nuzzling and turned her face into his cheek. The stubble of his beard rasped her lips as she spoke, causing them to tingle. "I can't explain exactly. Just...different. Less..." She trailed her tongue around the curve of his ear and was rewarded with a muffled groan. "Intense. More...all over. Let me show you." She pushed against his chest, seeking his nipple.

He grabbed her hand and laughed into the pillow. "It won't

work, Moll. I'm about as primed as I can be, but, trust me, it won't work."

"No?" Her fingers strayed into his hair, still short, but growing in thick and luxuriant. She loved touching him there. At that thought, she smiled to herself. She loved touching him everywhere. She loved him.

"No. You women have got us guys beat in the 'all over' department. With us, it's a lot more…" He lifted his head, gazing at her with mischief-filled eyes. "Focused."

He was giving her the same look he had when they were children and he'd tempted her into some silly monkeyshines. Only now his temptations were adult in nature. Love play. And she was as powerless to deny him as she had been then.

Not that she had any wish to deny him. Nothing in her life had ever felt as right as lying here with him in languid abandon. Sharing tender caresses and whispered nothings, hot, devouring kisses and fevered strokes, and love words far too explicit for other rooms, other ears. Sharing these with the man she was committed to, heart and mind, body and soul.

Years ago he'd taught her the ways she could pleasure him. Where to put her hands and how to move them. Now he coaxed her beyond her shyness, her reticence, to show him what pleased her. And she acquiesced, not only for the exquisite pleasure his touch brought, but also for the look in his eyes when he gave it. Though he'd never said the words she longed to hear, seeing that look, she was coming to believe that he meant them.

But he was watching her now with hot eyes. He was past teasing, past play, the hard evidence of his desire burning high against her inner thigh. She shifted slightly, nestling his blunt tip against the part of her he had made so thoroughly ready for himself. Bringing his ear down to her lips, she murmured, "If you could manage to get yourself…focused…I'd love to feel you inside me."

He moved over her then, covering her, looking directly into her eyes while his body began its penetration. She cupped his face in her palms, tracing his taut features with gentling fingers. A lift of her hips brought a catch of his breath and a ragged "Moll!" torn from his throat. She pulled his head down to her, opening her mouth and her body to him, feeling his tongue slide past her lips even as his rigid shaft pushed into her.

With his thrust she felt herself quicken again, surprised that it could happen so soon. Her breathing picked up, keeping time with the pace of his entry and withdrawal. She hugged him with her thighs, flattening the soles of her feet on his hair-roughened calves and rocking to his rhythm.

He pushed up, bracing himself with his arms extended on either side of her head, and stared down into her face. She watched him struggle, his eyes heavy-lidded, his nostrils flaring with each heaving breath, to hold her gaze through the tumult of sensations that racked him. Deliberately, her hands stroking the sweat-slick skin of his chest, his flanks, his tight buttocks, she whispered the carnal words she knew would inflame him, and she gloried as his control shattered.

With a raw sound that could have been a curse, or a plea, or some mindless variation of her name, he poured himself into her. She saw his face contort into an expression she might have mistaken for agony had she not shuddered with the same sweet, sweet release. Cradling her lover, she gave herself over to the ecstasy.

For long moments any thought, any purposeful action was impossible. Only when each breath was no longer an effort, when her arms and legs again answered to her volition, did she turn her head and find that Charlie was asleep.

Restless as he was, she seldom saw him sleep and she cherished the moment. He lay heavy upon her, pressing her into the mattress, but she welcomed his weight. She studied his face on the pillow beside her. He appeared peaceful, relaxed, boyish—the way she remembered him best. It was as if the years they'd been apart had contracted in some way, becoming small and vague and distant, while the time before those years and the present stretched into a continuum. She could barely remember life without him.

But she would soon be without him again. They had only five more days of this private Eden before he had to return to the road. Five more days before she surrendered him to the crowds. The adulation. The temptations.

She tried to reach across his body to switch off the lamp, but he stirred, mumbling her name, so she left it on and ran a hand along the warm skin of his shoulder to soothe him. In his sleep, he called for her. Only for her. All the times she'd seen him preoccupied by other cares, heedless with passion, or simply distracted, she had never heard another woman's name cross his lips.

Holding him to her, feeling him still joined with her, though no longer aroused, she felt the first fragile tendrils of trust entwining her to him.

Charlie draped one arm over the open door of the refrigerator and surveyed the contents. No bacon, no eggs, no juice, not even a slice of bread for toasting. Molly said she'd duck out later for groceries, but there was still breakfast to contend with. Looked like it was going to be oatmeal.

Yech.

The little fellow at his elbow didn't seem any too happy about that either, he thought, catching a glimpse of Tobie's glum expression.

Straightening, Charlie shut the fridge door and opened the freezer above it. "Let's see what else we can dig up," he said, pulling out the cardboard cylinders he found.

"Ice cream, Dad!" Tobie piped up, brightening considerably. "For breakfast!"

"This is just to whet our appetites. You're still gonna have to face the oatmeal." He took down a bowl for Tobie and shuffled through the silverware drawer for spoons. "Let's see what we've got…peach…and strawberry."

"I don't like strawberries, Dad."

"No?" Charlie questioned, scooping some peach into the bowl and handing it to his son. "Why not?"

"It's those black specks all over 'em. Makes it feel like another tongue in your mouth." Tobie said that with a grimace and a little shiver.

For just a moment Charlie thought maybe the kid was putting him on, but the shudder seemed genuine. "I guess it's an acquired taste," he said with a laugh as Tobie took a seat at the table and plowed into his ice cream.

Charlie put a pot of coffee on to brew, then settled himself against the counter, ankles crossed, and dug into the strawberry. They ate in silence for a few minutes, Tobie stealing an occasional glance at his father.

"She's not gonna let you eat like that," the boy said, finally.

"Like what?" Maybe Tobie meant the fact that he was barefoot and bare-chested. Females could be fussy about such things at mealtime. Although last night when their activities had caused them to work up an appetite and they'd eaten leftover lasagna in bed, Molly hadn't raised any objections to his wearing just the corner of a sheet across his lap. But then, she'd been similarly attired and *he* hadn't raised any objections, either.

"Right out of the carton like that," Tobie explained. "She says it looks like a pig at a trough."

Charlie laughed outright. That sounded like Molly. A trace of her mother reared its prissy head every once in a while. "Well, it's really not good manners, but this is the last of the carton. Let's keep it under our hats."

"Keep what under your hats?" The woman under discussion sailed in and Charlie inhaled the fresh scent of soap and jasmine. She stopped in front of him, and he felt her warm hands settle on naked skin at his waist as she tipped her face up for a good-morning kiss. It wasn't her first kiss of the morning either, not that he was counting.

"Mmm, strawberries," she murmured, licking her lips and noting the carton. "For breakfast?"

"We're trying to work up an appetite for oatmeal."

Grinning, Charlie scooped out a spoonful of ice cream and slipped it into her mouth. "Tobie doesn't like strawberries." The bright color that rushed to her cheeks and the mirth dancing in her eyes told him she knew why.

"I suppose we'd better start to worry when he changes his tune," she replied with a sultry chuckle. He sucked in a breath, feeling her palm drift across his belly and the pad of her thumb dip into his navel before she moved away.

Molly poured two mugs of coffee and left one on the counter next to him while she busied herself measuring out the oatmeal and preparing breakfast. Charlie disposed of the empty ice-cream container, sipped his coffee, and watched her efficient motions. She was barefoot, like he was, her long legs encased in faded blue jeans. On top she wore a loose-fitting, long-sleeved shirt, tails tied at her waist. With a double take he realized that was *his* blue-striped button-down, unless he was greatly mistaken. No wonder he could never find it.

Though the shirt was less figure-hugging than the T-shirts she often wore, the gentle sway of her breasts indicated she'd dispensed with a bra entirely. Again. To his surprise—and delight—she'd taken him up on his suggestion to go without around the house.

She'd surprised him a lot over the past two weeks. She was everything he could imagine in a lover. Watching her placidly stir the pot on the stove, he pictured her as she'd been only hours before. Her hair a radiant curtain swirling down around them in the pale dawn light. Her breasts just brushing his lips in a teasing dance as she straddled him. Her emotions as bared to him as her body. In years past she'd been generous to him with her body, but she'd never shown this freedom, this wildness, this abandon, and he wondered at what had brought about the change.

He suspected he knew, at least in part. And it had little to do with technique, or finesse or experience on either side. When they'd been together in the past, there had been no talk of marriage, of commitment, of permanence.

He'd accused Molly of stiff-necked pride, but the truth was, he had his pride, too. He hadn't offered marriage when he'd considered himself a step down for her. He'd wanted to wait until his faith, and hers, in himself had paid off. Until others looked at him the way she always had. Until he could come to her with more than the mill grime underneath his fingernails.

But first had come the distrust, the misunderstanding, the

shouting and the ugly words. Then he'd been gone, and events had conspired to assure they never reconciled.

So he'd never mentioned marriage. And for all that she teased him about being a nineties male, Molly was an old-fashioned girl. Though she'd never said in so many words, he couldn't pretend he didn't know where he stood with her. She might dismiss the lack of men in her past with excuses about a busy life, young child, single motherhood, but the reality was simpler than that. He'd known it intuitively when she was seventeen, and it was as true and pure now as it had been then.

Molly didn't sleep with a man she didn't love.

He was a little humbled by the knowledge and a little ashamed he couldn't make a similar claim himself. He doubted that she would be much comforted by the idea that the women in his life had been Molly substitutes—a fact he was none too proud of, but a fact all the same.

Molly glanced his way, a question in her eyes, as if wondering at his prolonged silence. He pushed away from the counter and set bowls and spoons on the table.

"What do you say we do some fishing today, Tobie, while your momma goes shopping?" Charlie asked, taking a chair alongside his son. He watched Molly approach and spoon the cooked cereal into the bowls, then return the pot to the stove. "We could catch some crappie, bass...." He broke off as Molly set applesauce and cinnamon on the table. Leave it to her to make even oatmeal special.

Molly took their mugs to refill them and Charlie turned to find his son regarding him with an expression of utter horror. "She's not gonna let you talk like that," the boy breathed in hushed tones.

"What?" Charlie mouthed in return, rapidly replaying his last words through his mind. Granted, his thoughts could sometimes use cleaning up, but, generally speaking, he was pretty careful about what came out of his mouth, especially around Tobie. Judging from the look on the kid's face, he'd let fly with one of the biggies.

He looked to Molly for help and saw her at the counter

adding milk to her mug of coffee, a hand cupped over her mouth and her shoulders shaking. Suddenly it dawned on him what he'd said to cause Tobie's consternation.

"You mean *crappie!*" He was barely able to get the word out. He saw his son's eyes dart uncertainly from him to Molly. "Tobie, it's a fish. Looks to me like some elements of your education have been sadly neglected," he said, laughing with Molly as she took a seat at the table.

"We prefer bass in this house," she said primly, but mischief gleamed in her eyes.

They ate in a silence punctuated by quiet laughter and the disgusted shaking of Tobie's head. Evidently he was finding the behavior of the adults too juvenile for words.

"If you're going fishing," Molly said as they finished, "make sure Tobie keeps his—"

"Boots on. I know," Charlie finished for her. He was acutely conscious of the precautions they still had to take to protect Tobie from infection. "And, lucky me, I get to bait all the hooks."

"You get to clean all the fish, too." She grinned at him as she rose to take their dishes to the sink. "I refuse to handle anything that can look me in the eye while I prepare it."

"I'm gonna need a reward, then." He caught her hand when she returned to the table and reeled her into his lap.

Their heads spun at the sound of Tobie's spoon clattering into his bowl and the scrape of the chair legs on the wooden floor as he pushed back. "If you two are gonna do mush," he muttered, "I'm goin' to watch TV."

Charlie waited until the boy was out of sight and earshot before he sidled his hand up under Molly's shirt. "*Nice* chest," he whispered into the V of her open collar.

She giggled into his hair, sliding her hands over his naked shoulders. "Don't you ever think of anything else?"

"Well, it's hard." His fingers found her nipple, which beaded at the first gentle stroke.

Her hand dove for his lap. "Again!"

"Ahhh!" he gasped, grabbing her wrist. "I don't think so! You've worn me out. Honey, I'm tapped."

"Well, that would certainly be a change." She laughed a little breathlessly and rested her chin against his forehead, feeling herself go weak as he played her nipple between thumb and forefinger.

He nuzzled the edge of her shirt aside, his tongue trailing over the slope that was gradually becoming more exposed.

"*Char*lie!" She brought a hand to his jaw in what was meant to be a gentle shove, but became a caress.

With the last remnants of good sense he possessed, Charlie scooted his chair a little away from the table and adjusted Molly so her back would be to the door if they got company. Then he chinned her shirt aside and her nipple popped free, begging for the attention of his tongue and teeth.

"Maybe I'm not in such bad shape, after all," he mumbled against her fragrant skin between teasing licks. "I could be coaxed...."

"Charlie...we..." She arched to him, her hips beginning a rhythmic rocking in his lap.

"Let's go upstairs, Moll." He buried his face between her breasts and his hand between her thighs, cupping his palm over her mound through the denim. "Let's go upstairs and do mush."

"Tobie..." Her fingers gripped his hair as if grasping at the last dematerializing strands of her sanity.

"He knows to knock." He pressed his middle finger against her sweet spot and was rewarded with the gush of her breath at his ear. "Come on, Moll."

"Oh, Charlie...please...we can't..."

It penetrated his foggy brain that she was pushing at his chest, though not very forcefully. He eased back, stilled his seeking hands, settled them at her waist, and looked at her.

She was so ready. He could persuade her. But this was good, too. This self-denial, this restraint, this forbearance.

They'd had some experience with it in recent days. They knew what to expect. The hunger, the edge, this wait would lend to their passion, when tonight, after long hours of hot looks and discreet touches, he would shut that bedroom door and press her against it. She would go wild for him, so eager, so aroused they'd barely make it to the bed, wouldn't care if they didn't.

"Okay," he said. "Later," he whispered on her mouth, taking delicious liberties with his tongue while he did so. "I'll take care of Tobie. You go upstairs…finish dressing—" his hand moved to cup her bare breast and gently squeeze while he gave her a pointed look "—before you go to the grocery store."

"Charlie!" She laid her cheek against his, laughing. "You're such a—"

"Barbarian. I know. Just humor me, okay?" He released her, helped her to stand, steadied her when her legs were still wobbly, watched her walk away.

He had her heart. He knew that. But he'd had her heart years ago and it hadn't been enough.

What would it take to win her trust? To convince her his commitment ran as deep as hers? That there were corners of his soul, closed to everyone else, that only she could enter. What else would it cost them, before he did?

Tobie squirmed as Molly hugged him too fiercely, and she eased up a bit. Together they watched the airport limo till it disappeared among the trees.

As goodbyes went, it hadn't been too bad. Molly and Charlie had both been strong for Tobie, and he'd been a little subdued, solemn, but not weepy.

Of course, she and Charlie had said their personal goodbyes the night before. All night. Charlie said he could sleep on the plane. He could sleep on the bus. Hell, what difference did it make, he didn't sleep anyway. And they didn't want to waste a minute.

So their loving had been playful, raunchy at times, tender at others. Thorough. And when they'd discovered there *was* a limit to the times they could tell each other physically how much each would be missed, they had just lain together side by side, awake, but silent. Molly's hand, spread on Charlie's chest, rose and fell with his breathing. She felt his fingers, tangled in her hair, making tiny circles on her scalp the way he liked to do, even when they were teenagers, even before they'd been lovers.

Finally, they'd risen and she'd watched him put on his public persona again. A little more glitter, a little more strut than he'd displayed the past couple of weeks. They'd gone downstairs and she'd fed him breakfast before Tobie joined them. Then, dry-eyed, she'd kissed him and watched his rangy, loose-limbed stride carry him away from her.

When the limo disappeared from view, Tobie turned to her. She hunched down, her face on his level, and met his eyes. He pushed his hat back with his thumb, a gesture she'd seen his father perform countless times. Black eyes crinkling at the corners, he smiled at her.

"He's pretty cool, Mom."

Trying to keep her chin firm, her lips from trembling, she smiled back. "Yes, he is."

"Do you s'pose he'll bring me one of those belt buckles like his next time he comes home?"

She laughed with genuine amusement and hugged him close.

Like father, like son.

Chapter 13

Molly watched Dr. Morrissey draw the last blood sample from the catheter in Tobie's chest. She helped her son slip his arms into his shirt as the doctor peeled off gloves and labeled the vial.

"You keep that hat on when you go outside, Tobie?" Morrissey asked.

"Yep, I do," the boy answered and Molly had to smile. He didn't sleep with the hat on, but that was about it.

"Where'd you get those sharp-looking boots?"

"My dad," Tobie responded with obvious pride. "He's bringin' me a buckle with my initials stamped on it next time he comes."

"Is that so?"

"Yep." He eyed the doctor hopefully. "I've been taking my medicine without complaining and eating lots of green stuff."

Morrissey favored Tobie with one of his rare smiles and looked to Molly for confirmation. She nodded her assurance.

"Well, Miss Colleen will have a reward for you. Why

don't you go see her? She'll give you the July calendar with the dates marked for your checkups, too.''

Tobie scrabbled from the examining table and scooted out the door before Molly could even offer any assistance.

''His energy level appears to have picked up,'' the doctor commented dryly.

''Yes,'' Molly agreed with a laugh. ''I'm glad he's able to be outdoors more.''

Morrissey indicated for Molly to take a seat. She did so and sat tensely, watching as the physician scratched some notes in Tobie's record in his crabbed handwriting. After a few minutes he looked up, as if just remembering her presence.

''The hat's good,'' he said, picking up on a previous thought. ''With the medication he's on, it's important that he avoid exposure to the sun. He'll need to wear long sleeves outside, even with the weather getting hot.''

''I understand,'' Molly replied. ''He doesn't object.'' She shrugged and looked away. ''Too much.''

Morrissey ruffled the papers he held, referring back to some lab reports. ''His blood picture is showing considerable improvement. No sign of rejection.'' He lifted his head and looked at Molly. ''His color's good, too. And he's gaining weight.'' He cleared his throat. ''I think we can allow him some playmates now. Selectively. Not in groups, certainly, but one at a time.''

Molly let out a long breath and clasped her hands in her lap. ''He's really missed a couple of his friends. That's been the hardest part for him.''

''Try to screen the children. I know that's hard. But there's less going around that we need to worry about this time of year.'' He made another note in the chart, speaking as he did so. ''Tobie seemed to enjoy his father's visit.''

''Oh, yes.'' Charlie had come with them for Tobie's checkups while he'd been in town. The rapport between the two had been obvious to everyone.

Morrissey put the chart aside and fiddled with his pen. Molly sensed he was uncertain about broaching a subject, but she couldn't imagine what. The man was nothing, if not direct.

"I was happy to see the two of you getting along so well."

She glanced at him sharply. That was a strange comment, even from Morrissey. "How do you mean?" she questioned.

"I'm afraid I might have been a little...rude to him...when we met. Naturally, I was surprised to find out who he was. Anyway, I told him how important it was for Tobie's well-being that you two...be agreeable." He gave her a curious look. "He never mentioned that?"

She shook her head, uncertain that she could utter even a single word. The muscles in her face seemed to have gone numb.

"Well." He made a dismissive gesture. "It's clear you get along fine." He gave her an abashed smile. "He's not what I expected."

"Yes," Molly said, finding her voice. She couldn't have been more stunned if he'd kicked the chair out from under her. "He surprises a lot of people."

She and Tobie left a short time later, after filling a prescription at the in-house pharmacy. Later, she remembered little of the ride home or Tobie's chatter. Dr. Morrissey's words and their implications crowded her mind as she gripped the steering wheel and maneuvered the familiar streets.

Charlie'd been *told* to get along with her.

Could so much of the past weeks have been an act? He'd undergone an operation for his son. He'd shaved his head for his son. She didn't doubt for a moment that he would die for his son if the situation demanded.

And Charlie was used to performing. Time and again she'd seen him assume the facade his audience expected. How difficult would it be to pretend some degree of affection for the mother of his son? To convince a woman who was so pathetically eager to be convinced?

She remembered his behavior when she first confronted him with the knowledge of Tobie's existence. His anger, his antagonism, his insistence on marriage despite that.

When had she noticed the change in his attitude? Sometime

before the transplant, surely. Even before they'd married. He'd been considerate, tender—with no trace of the anger he'd shown earlier—on their wedding night.

She pressed her lips tightly together and focused on the road, trying to force her disquieting thoughts from her mind. What useful purpose would it serve, nurturing such doubt? But, like a splinter imbedded under a fingernail too deeply to be removed, her suspicion nagged. And it hurt.

Molly cut a slice of apple pie and handed it to Lisa. Outside the bay window of the breakfast area, Tobie romped with Lisa's son, Ryan, on the jungle gym Charlie had erected under the pin oak. One of the advantages of Tobie's being able to have visitors was that Molly could have them, too.

Ryan had been playing with Tobie most of the morning and she'd invited Lisa to stay for lunch and chat. They'd worked together at the law office for several years and their boys had been in day care together before they'd started school. Now they all had some catching up to do.

Up to this point conversation had centered on the mundane—talk of people and events familiar to them both—but Molly sensed Lisa's understandable curiosity, simmering for so long, was about to reach full boil. She refreshed their coffee cups and took a seat next to her friend, where they could keep an eye on the boys.

"You really are a deep one, Molly," Lisa remarked, her gaze on the children. "I mean, the resemblance is so obvious, but *Kick Cochrane!* Who would ever have guessed?"

Molly sipped her coffee and remained silent, not knowing how to respond. She hadn't expected anyone to guess.

"Why didn't you ever say?" Lisa turned her head toward Molly sharply, concern written on her face. "Did he leave you in the lurch when he found out you were pregnant? Is that what he's like?"

"No!" she answered quickly, coming to his defense. "He didn't know." I thought he did, she finished to herself. But she was unwilling to reveal to an acquaintance something she had never told Charlie. "His success was so sudden."

"I suppose," Lisa agreed, shrugging offhandedly. "And then there were the women." She took another bite of pie while Molly held her breath, hoping she would drop that line of inquiry. No such luck.

"Although, as I recall, the paternity suits never amounted to anything, did they? He doesn't have any other children?"

"No." She doubted whether Lisa would have had the nerve to ask such a question if Charlie had been an engineer or a plumber. He'd warned her that some folks always considered it open season on those in the spotlight. There had been two suits, both of them without foundation. One of them was lodged by a woman he couldn't even remember meeting, bizarre as that seemed. Some people became fixated on celebrities and imagined all kinds of things, Charlie told her. She had no reason to doubt him. Whatever else he might do, he would *never* deny a child. She knew that now.

"Still," Lisa continued, oblivious to Molly's lack of enthusiasm for the conversation or choosing to ignore it. "He's so-o-o attractive. And those eyes...I've always thought he looked a little...wild...dangerous." Lisa glanced at Molly expectantly, as if seeking confirmation.

Molly had to laugh. "Well, I've known him since he was nine years old. I don't think of him that way." Probably it was difficult to see a person in that light when you'd engaged in cherry-pit spitting contests with him.

"He must be *very* different from what he was at nine," Lisa maintained. "Or even at twenty. All that money. The glamour, the fame."

"No. Not really." That's what had struck her most about Charlie. He didn't care about the trappings of success. They hadn't changed him. His needs were simple. Well-worn jeans, a decent guitar, some quiet time to write, an occasional beer. And his family.

All the rest was a job. More high-profile, better paying than most. But a job.

"He's the same," Molly said. "Just the same."

* * *

"Where're we headed?" Charlie reached overhead to dim the reading lamp, swiveled his chair and propped his bare feet on the bed.

"Morgantown." Harlan had stopped in the bus to discuss the next week's itinerary and stayed to talk. Charlie was reluctant to see him leave. He had the feeling it was going to be a long night.

"Would that be West Virginia or Tennessee?" Sad to say, one was the same as the other for all he got to see of the towns. He'd do radio-station promotions, interviews, squeeze in a visit to a hospital or a residential facility if he could, catch a nap, sound-check, do the show, try to unwind, then it was back on the bus and on to the next venue to do it all again.

"That would be Kentucky, Kick. Kentucky." Harlan yawned around a chuckle.

"Am I keeping you up?" He figured he was, but Harlan was too good a friend to say so.

"Nah, that's all right."

They both heard the rumble of the bus engine as it roared to life, the groan of the gears, the wheeze of the brake when it was released. Harlan made to rise.

"I'd better get back to the band bus—"

"Nah. Stay. You can bunk on the sleeper in the forward room. Unless you'd rather..." But Harlan was already easing his long frame back into his chair. Charlie flicked the intercom to alert the driver. He turned again to Harlan when he finished. "Shooter make it back?"

"Yeah." The older man rubbed a hand over his face. "He was wasted. Didn't try to smuggle any women on the bus anyway."

Charlie answered with a grunt. "It's not the women I'm concerned about. It's the girls...."

"I know. He doesn't show much judgment when he's hittin' the bottle—"

"Which, here lately, is all the time." Charlie drummed his fingers on the arm of the chair. "Did you talk to that fella— the studio musician—while we were in Nashville?"

Harlan raised his eyebrows and sighed heavily. "Yeah. I thought we had a chance with him. He'd love to play with us, Kick, but he doesn't want to go on the road. Hell, he records with half the big names. He's making real money. He's got a couple little kids and he doesn't want to live like a nomad."

Charlie closed his eyes and leaned his head back into the chair. He could relate to that. The road had stopped being fun a long time ago. He wanted to settle down. He wanted to wake up in the morning next to Molly's red head and know what town he was in. He'd like to know what was going on *in* Molly's red head right now. She'd been just a little bit distant the last couple of times he'd talked to her. Three weeks apart, and he could feel her slipping away.

He clasped his hands over his chest and spoke without opening his eyes. "I've been thinkin'...when we knock off for the holidays this year...around Thanksgiving." He opened one eye and peered at Harlan. "I've been thinkin' maybe we'd stretch it out. Not tour next year, I mean. How would you feel about that?"

Harlan puffed his cheeks and blew out a long breath. "You've been on the road pretty steady for the last eight years. I've only been with you for six, and I'm tuckered. You won't get any argument from me."

"What about the others?"

"Hell, they'll miss the gravy train." He shrugged his shoulders. "But they won't be hurting. Tell you the truth, I think we all could use the break." He gazed out the window as the bus merged onto the highway. "Maddie and I could use some extra time together," he said more quietly, almost to himself.

Charlie came alert, rolled his head on the chair back to look at his friend. "Are you and Maddie having problems?"

Harlan propped an elbow on his knee and rubbed a finger over his mustache. "Ah, you know how it is. Females get these ideas in their heads...."

"Even Maddie?"

"Even Maddie." He laughed humorlessly. "I don't know who she thinks would be interested in this old bag of bones."

Charlie relaxed again, closing his eyes. "Well, tell you what, Harlan. If it comes to that, I'll vouch for you."

"Thanks." His laughter was more genuine. "I'd do the same for you, Kick."

"Yeah." If it comes to that.

"Mom."

Molly came awake by slow degrees, not sure if she dreamed the voice that seemed to come from a distance.

"Mom," it came again, insistently. She wasn't dreaming the hand tugging on her arm, nor its heat. Raising her head from the pillow, she strained to see the small form next to the bed, silhouetted in the faint light from her open bedroom door.

"I don't feel so good, Mom."

She was up like a shot, her hands going to cradle Tobie's cheeks. Hot and dry. She put the inside of her wrist to his forehead. He was burning up.

"What hurts, Tobie?"

She switched on the bedside lamp, and he squinted and turned his head, but not before she caught the glassy look to his eyes. His face was flushed.

"My head. That light hurts my eyes, Mom."

His voice sounded weak and a little stuffy. She thought she'd caught him wiping his nose on his sleeve a couple of times during the day, but she figured it might be an allergy, with him being outdoors so much.

God. She'd figured wrong.

Mentally, she kicked herself. Charlie'd been gone a month. Had she been distracted? Inattentive?

Already she was reaching for the phone and punching in the number Dr. Morrissey gave to his patients where they could reach him, day or night.

She knew what he would tell her. His words only confirmed it. Meet him at the hospital without delay.

* * *

Charlie said a few final words to his agent and dropped the phone receiver into its cradle. With a look of satisfaction, he crossed his feet on the standard-issue hotel coffee table and turned to Harlan. "The new album and the first single from it both finished number one on the country charts this week."

"Hot damn. You've still got it, Kick," the older man responded, helping himself to another slice of pizza. "I swear that tune's a real weeper. You could wring tears out of a sumo wrestler."

Charlie laughed, but basked in the honest compliment nonetheless. Harlan was no bootlicker. He'd be the first to let him know if he was losing his touch. "That's got me a little worried, to tell the truth. I think we ought to release the fourth cut next. It's more upbeat. We don't want folks thinkin' we're only good with the hankie set."

"Tell you what," Harlan countered. "We're gonna have to do a better job with that cut than we did tonight. It sounded a little flat."

"Yeah," Charlie agreed, picking the olives off his pizza. "Needs more of a backbeat. We can work it up." At a knock on the door he turned his head and checked the clock. Almost one. He threw a questioning look at Harlan, who only shrugged and rose to answer.

Charlie lifted his feet from the table and pushed himself up from the couch when his brother walked in with a girl who very obviously needed the supporting hand Beau had clamped on her elbow.

"Lookee what I found on the bus," Beau said by way of an introduction.

Harlan and Charlie exchanged glances before Charlie directed his attention to his brother. "Shooter?"

Beau nodded. "He promised this young lady he'd bring her to meet you. It appears he passed out before he got the opportunity."

Looking at the girl, trying to judge her age, Charlie could only hope the guy had passed out before he'd had an opportunity to do anything else. With Beau's help, she made her way on wobbly legs to the couch where she plopped down, caught a glimpse of the pizza and put a hand over her mouth. Harlan quickly closed the box and shoved it out of sight.

"Were you at the show tonight?" Charlie asked the girl.

She nodded and gazed at him with that moony, calf-eyed look. What the hell, he was just a *man*. If he lived to be a hundred, he'd never understand that reaction.

"Did you drive?" God help us all. She wasn't driving home, that was for damn sure.

She shook her head in response, but that seemed to upset her touchy tummy. She put one hand to her midriff, and the other grasped the arm of the sofa as if trying to make it stand still.

"She came with friends," Beau offered helpfully. "Monica and…" He looked to the girl for assistance.

"Celeste." She had a lot of trouble with the "*s*" sounds in that name, Charlie noticed.

His brother folded his arms across his chest and went on. "It appears Shooter promised her a ride home, too."

Charlie glanced sharply from the girl to Beau. "Where is he?"

"On the bus. He's tanked, Kick. He's not goin' anywhere."

"Isn't someone gonna be missing you?" Charlie turned his attention back to the girl. She seemed to have a lot of trouble with that question. He gestured impatiently with his hands.

"You know. Family. What time were you supposed to be home?"

She shifted her gaze around the three of them, then looked shamefacedly down at her hands. "I told my dad…" She swallowed hard. "I was staying at Monica's. She's going to cover for me."

Charlie hooked his thumbs through his belt loops and stared at the girl. God save him from teenage daughters. He wondered if there was any way to ensure that Molly gave birth only to sons. If what he recalled from sex-ed class was accurate the determining factor for that rested squarely in *his* court. He let out a long breath and shook his head. "How old are you, young lady?"

She had to consider that question for a while, too, but Charlie didn't think she was lying. "Sixteen," she said finally.

That effort seemed to use up the last of her reserves. Her hand went to her mouth again and her eyes darted frantically around the room. Charlie pointed the way to the bathroom and cleared a path for her as she made a dash.

"She's legal in this state, Kick," Harlan said quietly over the sounds of her retching.

Charlie turned on his friend. "Don't hand me 'legal,'" he muttered under his breath. "She barely knows her own name. She's in no shape to consent to anything."

"And Shooter was in no shape to perform anything, Kick," Beau put in. "I'm sure nothing happened. She was dressed just like she is now. He was passed out. That's why she came looking for somebody."

Charlie placed his hands on his hips, his mouth flattened to a thin line and his black eyes fierce. "He's gotta go. I don't care if we've got a replacement for him or not. He's done."

The other men offered no argument. They all watched as the girl, looking very pale, made her way back to the couch. When she was seated, Charlie said, "I'm gonna call your daddy."

He wouldn't have thought she could get any whiter, but she did. "I wish you wouldn't do that," she said, a panicky expression on her face.

Charlie squeezed his eyes shut and scratched a hand through his hair. It turned *his* stomach to have to ask, but in this day and age, it was necessary. "Does he hit you?"

She looked at him like *he'd* hit her. "No!" she answered with a huff. Blinking down at the floor she continued. "He's going to be so disappointed in me."

O-o-oh, he knew what she was feeling now. *One time* he'd driven the pickup just a little bit tiddly and his dad caught him. He'd eat glass before he'd see that expression on his old man's face again. "Well, maybe you'll think real hard next time before you do something so disappointing," he said without a lot of sympathy.

She raised her eyes to his pleadingly. "Couldn't you just—"

"No. Either I call your daddy, or I call the police and they call your daddy. Now give me your number."

She wrote the information on the hotel stationery in a wavering, childlike hand and gave the paper to Charlie. "You sound old," she said sullenly.

He gave a humorless laugh and watched the other men turn their heads to hide their smiles. "Gettin' older by the minute," he agreed, picking up the phone.

When he finished he spoke to the girl once more. "You can lie down in the other room until your father gets here." He watched her walk away, wiping her eyes, and then turned to Harlan. "Keep a lid on things. We're gonna go have a talk with Shooter."

Grabbing his hat, he left the room with his brother.

Molly walked alongside the stretcher as Tobie was wheeled to his room. With his admission, things had happened very quickly. He'd been probed, palpated, percussed, auscultated, x-rayed and stuck—in record time. An antibiotic now trickled its long, winding path through the clear tubing into his chest. Tobie slept, exhausted, both from his illness and the procedures necessary to put a name to it.

They had a tentative diagnosis. Sinusitis. Something most people shrugged off, or treated for the discomfort it caused. But for someone with a compromised immune system, such as Tobie, this was serious. Life-threatening. For him there was no such thing as a "common" cold.

She waited, biting her nails, outside the door to his room while the hospital staff transferred him from the stretcher to the bed, attached whatever needed to be attached and saw to his comfort. She would spend what remained of the night at his bedside.

Dr. Morrissey approached and, seeing his slow step, his sagging shoulders, she wondered briefly how he could bear to do this day after day. The victories were still too rare, and so hard won.

He stopped next to her, leaned one hand against the wall behind her and clasped the stethoscope hanging around his neck with the other. ''We're not sure what bug is causing his problem,'' he said without preamble. ''I've asked for an infectious disease consult. Tobie's getting a broad-spectrum antibiotic. We should know within hours, a day at the most, whether he'll respond.''

Molly nodded, totally incapable of a verbal reply.

''He's got some immune function, Molly. He's not completely without reserves anymore.''

His words were meant to reassure her, she knew. But they had the opposite effect. He had never, in all the time he had been treating Tobie, called her by her first name. His dropping of that last formality showed the measure of his concern.

Before she could frame a response, he continued. ''Have you called his father?''

''Oh my God,'' she whispered past bloodless lips. Sagging against the wall, she put a hand to her face.

He looked down at the floor and then back to her, his expression grim. ''I don't want to alarm you,'' he said, pausing for a moment while she struggled for control. ''But I think he should be told.''

She covered her mouth with both hands, swallowed hard, and nodded stiffly. Morrissey brought his hand from the wall to her shoulder and gave a gentle squeeze. ''You can use the phone in the office.''

He walked with her to his cubbyhole on the unit and shut the door softly when he left to give her some privacy. She sat for a few moments, clenching and unclenching her fists to try to stop their trembling. As it was, she had to punch the number Charlie had given her three times before she could get it right. He was staying in a hotel tonight, she remembered from their conversation earlier. She should be able to get through to him directly. The phone rang twice, three times.

''Hello?''

A woman's voice. She must have gotten the number wrong anyway. ''I'm so sorry,'' she said, glancing at the wall clock. Two-thirty. It was an hour earlier where Charlie was, but still very late to be waking the wrong person. "I must have dialed wrong. I'm trying to get in touch with Charlie Cochrane..."

"Who? Oh, *Kick.*"

Molly heard recognition in the voice. She felt as if she had opened a door onto blackness and stepped into an abyss. "Is he there?" she asked, aware that she couldn't conceal her disbelief, her shock. Seconds passed, as if the woman were actually *searching.*

"He...he had to leave...for a while." She sounded half-asleep, or half-drunk. Or both. "He should be back soon." Apparently that was meant to be helpful.

Molly took a deep breath and squared her shoulders. "Can you give him a message?"

"Sure."

That eager-to-please tone again. This was unreal.

"It's very important." In a few terse words Molly gave the information and hung up. She sat for some time, unblinking, staring at the phone.

Then, summoning all of her will, she struggled for composure and went to sit with her son.

Charlie opened the door to his hotel room, past weary, closing in on stuporous, in time to hear the girl's father tell her, no, she couldn't ask for Mr. Cochrane's autograph and she wouldn't be allowed to keep it if she got it. He decided straight away that he liked the man.

He introduced himself and shook hands, sparing a glance for the girl sitting very subdued on the couch. She'd remember this night for a long time to come. If her head had cleared any.

Father and daughter rose to leave, Harlan holding the door for them, when the girl lifted her chin suddenly and turned to Charlie.

"A woman called," she said, "while you were gone."

Charlie shifted his startled gaze to Harlan, disbelieving.

"I don't know anything about this. I was in the can, Kick. Not five minutes."

His fatigue giving way to dread, Charlie addressed the

youngster. "What'd she say?" What else could happen this god-awful night?

With obvious effort the girl strove to collect her thoughts. "She said...Tony...?"

"Tobie," Charlie provided, gritting his teeth.

"Yeah." She rubbed a hand across her brow as if that would clear the fog, while Charlie fought the urge to shake her. "She said he had a...crisis?" She looked at him blankly. "You're supposed to meet her at the hospital."

Charlie felt as if he'd been gut-punched. He turned to Harlan who stood, hands spread, an apology on his lips, and interrupted him.

"Get me a flight."

Chapter 14

Molly watched as the brilliant orange beam piercing the slats on the hospital window blind widened and paled, even as the room around her grew brighter. The sun was coming up.

It hurt to close her gritty eyes, and her shoulders were stiff from holding them hunched. She hadn't slept at all. The old terror had returned. The unspeakable fear that Tobie would slip away from her forever while she slept unaware.

A nurse Molly hadn't seen before came into the room to check Tobie's IV and hang another of those small plastic packets of fluid containing the antibiotic. She smiled at Tobie when he roused as she took his vital signs and listened to his chest. Molly observed her every move with unwavering scrutiny.

Tobie drifted off again quickly. The nurse smoothed his sheets and turned to Molly. "His temperature is down a little," she said in a low voice.

"He's getting better?" She knew anxiety suffused her words. She felt so useless amid the procedures and techniques and contraptions that sustained her son.

"He's holding his own."

A noncommittal response if she'd ever heard one, Molly thought as the nurse adjusted the blinds and left the room. Caring though the hospital staff were, they didn't share the desperate, single-minded intensity of her hope and her fear for Tobie.

Only one person did.

She needed him with her.

There. She'd said it, if only to herself. Admitted it. Through the endless hours of the night, she'd kept the flood tide of her thoughts of his betrayal at bay behind the seawall of her will. Now they spilled over, swamping her, choking her. She pressed a fist to her mouth, rocking disconsolately, as her tears flowed.

Damn him. And damn her treacherous heart.

She needed—wanted—Charlie.

Molly sat quietly, absorbing the silence and the peace. Tobie's nurses had told her she could grab some breakfast while they gave him his bath and did their physical evaluation. She had chosen instead to duck into the little chapel in a wing off the unit.

She couldn't pray, not really. She'd started out angry, accusing, decrying the unfairness of Tobie's situation. Then she'd progressed to bargaining. *I will be a better mother. I will overlook my husband's transgressions if his presence makes Tobie happy. I will never ask another thing for myself.* At the moment her thoughts were reduced to a single plea, repeated like a mantra, over and over. *Let Tobie live.*

Charlie slid into the pew alongside her. She knew it was Charlie, though she didn't raise her head to look at him. From the corner of her eye she spotted the jeans, the boots, the hat he set on the bench next to him. "Are they still busy with him?" she whispered, dispensing with any other words of greeting.

"Yeah." He kept his voice low, too, though it echoed in the small confines of the hollow room. "Another five minutes, they said. Morrissey's there."

She stared at her fingers, clasping and unclasping them, waiting. She didn't have to wait long.

"What happened, Molly?"

Her shoulders slumped as she let out a breath. "I don't know. He was fine. More energy. He'd been able to have a few friends over. I told you that."

Her eyes still downcast, she watched him spread a long-fingered hand over each knee and tried hard not to think about where those hands had been. What they'd been doing. The two of them would deal with that later.

She licked her lips. "Maybe he picked something up from one of the children. I noticed he was a little stuffy yesterday. Maybe I was...inattentive...neglect—"

The hands on his knees clenched. "Don't do this, Moll. Don't second-guess yourself. *No one* could take better care of him than you. I don't blame you. Don't blame yourself."

She didn't respond. He made an impatient sound and grasped her chin, twisting her head to face him. "Look at me!" he growled.

She did, her eyes wide, hurt and despair shining in them.

He relaxed his hold immediately. Cupping her jaw in his broad palm, he touched the tip of one finger to a tear at the corner of her eye. His voice was gentle, but determined, when he spoke again.

"We're not going to lose him, Molly."

She nodded weakly, angry with herself that words from him could reassure her, but reassured all the same.

After a time they rose to return to Tobie's room. On the way Molly pondered what had struck her during that brief glimpse of Charlie's face. His fear and concern were plainly revealed. Unshaven, eyes red-rimmed, he looked older, haggard, the creases around his mouth and eyes deeper.

It took longer to register in her mind how he didn't look.

He didn't look guilty.

Charlie rolled his head back and around on his shoulders, hearing the crackle as the kinks worked themselves out. Morning had given way to afternoon and Tobie still slept.

He'd wakened a few times to take something to drink and complain, but he'd seemed a little disoriented, and that scared Charlie more than anything. His temperature wasn't normal yet, but it hadn't spiked again the way Molly said it had when he was admitted.

Wait and hope. Filled with restless, impatient energy, Charlie had never been any good at that.

In the chair next to his, Molly got some much-needed sleep.

He glanced her way in time to see the elbow she had propped, chin in hand, on the wooden armrest slip and jar her awake. She blinked a few times and then settled back into the same precarious position. With a loud sigh Charlie nudged his chair closer to hers and nestled her head against his shoulder.

He tangled his fingers in her hair and pressed a kiss to her brow. The first kiss either had given the other since he arrived. He laid his cheek on the top of her head and tried to swallow his bitter, bitter disappointment.

Neither of them had mentioned that phone call. Instead, like the elephant in the living room nobody wanted to acknowledge, they'd just kind of tiptoed around it.

He tried to see things from Molly's point of view. She had a problem with trust. Understandably. He knew he should explain. But what if she didn't believe him? What, then? He didn't think he'd be able to stand seeing her shift her gaze away, suspicious, skeptical, unwilling to look him in the eye.

Hell, the situation would be funny, if it wasn't so sad. He tried to picture his own mother in like circumstances. If she called his father's hotel room in the middle of the night and a female answered, there'd be hell to pay, for sure. Come to that, he doubted there'd been a single instance, other than when his mother was in the hospital adding to the family, that his parents had spent a night apart.

Given the way he made his living, he and Molly wouldn't have a marriage like that. They had to deal with the separations. All the more reason that their relationship had to be based on trust. A trust it seemed impossible for her to extend.

"Dad."

He glanced over at the bed to see Tobie leaning on the side rail, clear-eyed, an urgent expression on his face.

"I gotta pee, Dad."

Charlie smiled. "No, Tobie. It just feels that way. You've got one of those tubes in. Goes into a bag. See here?" He tried to reach the bag, but couldn't without disturbing Molly. Using the toe of his boot, he lifted it a little away from the side of the bed so Tobie could get a look at it. The nurses were in periodically, measuring the contents, observing, nodding meaningfully, writing something on that clipboard hanging at the foot of the bed. Charlie didn't know what to make of it. Looked like pee to him.

Tobie peered over the rail, then picked up the sheet, took a gander at himself and shrugged. "Did you bring me my buckle?" he asked, already off on another tangent.

Charlie laughed out loud. "Not this trip. I'm workin' on it."

Tobie gave his father a more thorough appraisal. "You don't look so hot, Dad."

"Well, you're lookin' lots better."

Charlie was saved further criticism when Dr. Morrissey walked in, pleased to see his patient so animated. Molly stirred and rubbed her eyes while he checked Tobie over.

"I think we've got this bug on the run, Tobie," Morrissey said, more for the benefit of the boy's anxious parents. He turned to address them. "We'll continue the course of antibiotics, but he's showing a good response."

Charlie gripped Molly's hand and felt her answering squeeze. For the first time since that moment in the chapel, their eyes met. And, for the first time since his arrival, she smiled at him.

She'd sounded very young.
The thought nagged at Molly. That was the one piece of the jigsaw puzzle that didn't slip easily into place, that had to be forced. And in the forcing caused the whole picture to buckle.

Sitting there in the hospital room, listening to her men

snore softly, she had plenty of time to think. Plenty of time for that thought to nag.

She'd played games with Tobie until he figured he'd beaten her enough and decided to take a nap. Sprawled awkwardly in the vinyl chair next to her, Charlie slept the almost co-matose sleep of the exhausted. The blameless? The innocent?

She didn't know. But the very fact that she harbored doubts about what had gone on the previous night counted for some-thing.

She'd sounded very young.

Not just the quality or tone of her voice, although they had given the impression of a girl still in adolescence. The *way* she expressed herself, her inflection, her eagerness to please, all suggested someone still in her teens.

She'd sounded very young.

And that flew in the face of everything Molly knew about Charlie. She remembered vividly how he had wrestled with his desire for her while she was still in school. She cringed, recalling the times she'd all but thrown herself at him, and he'd held back. Not all that many girls in her class had grad-uated virgins. But she had.

So had Charlie, if she were to believe what he said. And she found, despite the lessons gleaned from her own family life, that she was inclined to.

The truth of the matter was, when you came right down to it, Charlie was a bit of a prude. He had a very strong sense of what was proper. He didn't hit on fans, easy as it would be for him, and he didn't bother to hide his disgust for stars who did. He didn't consider women prey. He preferred a re-lationship with a partner, an equal.

Still, last night there'd been a young woman in his room who knew who he was and awaited his return. What expla-nation could there possibly be?

You would never ask, Moll. Only accuse. Charlie's words came back to lacerate her. How many times had she lashed him with her suspicions, rejecting his denials, until finally the denials ceased? What had it cost them? And their son? And what of the new life she had only begun to suspect grew within her?

A nurse stepped into the room with Tobie's dinner tray and set it on the over-bed table when she saw he was asleep. She spoke a few words to Molly, glancing frequently at Charlie. She had started for the door when she saw him wake, and paused.

"Mr. Cochrane?"

He looked up at her, still trying to get his bearings.

Hesitating just a bit, the nurse went on. "There's a little girl…down the hall. You haven't met her yet." She stopped again, as if questioning the wisdom of her action, but continued. "She's getting her transplant tomorrow. She's a big fan, Mr. Cochr—"

But Charlie was already pushing himself to his feet. "Sure," he said.

The woman's smile lit her face. "You can't go inside, of course. Just speak to her from the door. It'll mean so much."

He nodded, running a hand over his prickly jaw. "Is there something I could use..?" He made a shaving gesture along his cheek.

"Oh! I'll get you one of our prep kits. It has a razor."

She left briefly and returned with the kit. Charlie went into the bathroom while the nurse waited, talking quietly with Molly.

When he emerged, tucking his shirt into his jeans, Molly was amazed anew at his ability to transform himself. Gone were the fatigue, the weary eyes, the slumped shoulders, as gone as the whiskers on his freshly shaved cheeks. For a little girl who needed cheering up, his shoulders straightened, his black eyes glittered, his smile flashed. Very few people were privy to the discipline he exercised over himself to carry off that effect.

Molly knew she was one of the privileged. He winked at her, grabbed his hat and followed the nurse from the room.

Molly sat in stunned silence, recognizing the truth at last. Certainty settled over her, cold and crystal clear. He was a genuinely kind, good man. For all his success, the essential man remained unchanged. The values he'd been raised with were the ones that shaped his behavior still.

He'd been her friend long before he'd been her lover. He, more than anyone, would know how infidelity would cut. And he would *never* deliberately hurt her. He'd told her so, in a lover's vow, on a sad, sultry night almost half her lifetime ago. *I swear...I'll never hurt you that way.*

For too long she had allowed the letdowns and disappointments she had suffered at the hands of others blind her to his worth. She could only hope that her eyes hadn't been opened too late.

When Charlie returned a few minutes later, the toll taken by his mission was clear. He tossed his hat on the bedside table and sagged into his chair, drained. Reaching for his hand, Molly laced her fingers with his.

With the tip of one finger she traced the long, elegant bones on the back of his hand until he fixed his gaze on her, a question in his eyes. *You would never ask, Moll. Only accuse,* she heard again. She inhaled deeply and asked at last. "Are you going to tell me what happened, Charlie?" Attempting a brave smile, she only managed half of one. "What that girl was doing in your room?"

Surprise registered in his face, and hope battled wariness in his eyes. But he answered evenly, in a calm voice. "She's a fan. She was at the show last night. One of the fellas in the band got her skunk drunk." He shrugged disarmingly. "She was just a kid, Moll. I felt responsible for her."

Yes, you would, Molly thought, and nodded.

"Anyway, I left her to sleep it off while I went to talk to the guy."

"Shooter."

"Yeah." His eyes narrowed on her. "You remember him."

"I remember you mentioning he was trouble."

"Well, he's gone now." He rubbed a hand over his jaw tiredly. "He's talented. If he gets himself cleaned up, he might have a future. But he doesn't have a future in my band."

He paused for some moments, still eyeing her warily. Finally, he said, "Harlan was there. He didn't hear the phone."

Molly felt his fingers tighten around hers. He looked away and his voice was tight, too, when he continued. "You can talk to Harlan, if you want. Check my story. He's as honest as milk is white."

She pulled in a breath and lowered her gaze to their joined hands, ashamed, *ashamed* that he felt the need to offer her that. Swallowing hard, she shook her head. "So are you, Charlie." She looked into his eyes as she whispered the words she'd always thought impossible for her. "I trust you."

His smile broke over his face like sunshine, chasing away the caution, the fatigue, the strain. That devilish gleam was back in his eye as he tugged on her hand and hauled her into his lap. "Well, I've been here the better part of a day, and you've yet to greet me properly."

Holding her chin in his hand, he pressed a kiss to her mouth. A sweet kiss, full of the innocence of a first love and the confidence of a mature one.

It quickly developed into something more.

His tongue probed insistently past her parted lips, taking full possession of the lush, warm recesses protected by them. His kisses left her breathless, dizzy. Coming up for air, laughing against his cheek, she gasped, "I hardly think this is a *proper* gree—"

"Shut your precious mouth and kiss me," he muttered, his seeking mouth closing over hers again.

She did just as he told her.

"Moll…" he threatened.

"You told me to shut my—" That was as far as she got. Locked in his arms, she forgot teasing, she forgot "proper," and lost herself in the heady oblivion his kisses brought her.

They enjoyed each other for long, blissful moments, until a sound very much like a "Sheesh" came from the direction of the bed. Two pairs of guilty eyes turned that way to see Tobie, arms dangling over the bed rail, an appalled expression on his face.

He looked from one to the other, his revolted gaze finally

settling on Charlie. "Did you have your *tongue* in her mouth?" He made it sound as if a slug would be preferable.

"You must be seein' things, Tobie," Charlie answered through his chuckles. "Why would I do a fool thing like that?" he countered, while Molly buried her laughter in the front of his shirt.

It just wasn't right.

Charlie stabbed at the stop button on the recorder and tossed the pick away. He folded his arms over the smooth wood of his guitar and rested his chin on them, hissing a disgusted breath through his teeth.

He and Molly had stayed with Tobie the night before and well into the afternoon of the following day. They would have remained longer had not the staff informed them rather firmly that Tobie was out of danger and he was more cooperative with his regimen when they weren't constantly around. As a result, they'd gone out for the only decent meal either of them had eaten in over twenty-four hours, then come home and crashed.

At 2:00 a.m., Charlie was wide awake and of a mind to love Molly breathless. She'd just rolled over and muttered something unintelligible, but hardly encouraging. So, he'd summoned more gallantry than he'd known he possessed, slipped into his jeans and come out here, into what they now called the music room, to wrestle some more with this tune.

The words were fine, he liked the melody, the *mood* was all wrong. He couldn't express the mood. He'd slowed the tempo, fiddled with the rhythm. Nothing. Right now, he was staring at the glass panes that revealed the blackness of the night at the same time as they reflected his image back to him in the dim lamplight. He knew from long experience that when it came to composing, staring at the wall was just part of the process.

He saw her reflected in the glass before he heard her come up behind him. She was belting herself into a silky, cream-colored robe he hadn't seen before. Apparently Molly was getting a little less sensitive about spending their money.

"That's pretty, Charlie...." she murmured as she walked past him, trailing her fingers over his naked shoulder in a way that told him it was going to be a long night and he was going to love every minute of it.

She was lookin' mighty pretty. The robe hugged her curves the way a road did a hillside, and shimmered with a luster second only to her skin. He'd never known another woman with a complexion like Molly's. Right now, it had a rosy glow as if she'd just stepped from a bath. Her hair was piled up, too, the way she wore it in the tub. He wished he had known. He wouldn't have been wasting his time with this damn song.

Still, he'd caught her phrasing. That little suspension at the end that indicated an incomplete thought. "That's pretty, Charlie," he repeated, *"but..."*

She slid him a sidelong glance, and compressed her lips into a pouty expression. "It wants to be in a minor key in the worst way."

He made a sound, half laugh, half groan. Sonofabitch, that was it. That would supply just the melancholy note he was looking for. It would have come to him eventually, maybe six months down the road. But she was always so good at this. She might dance like an ostrich, unless you knew just how to hold her—which, fortunately, he did—but music was in her blood.

"Show me." He indicated the piano with a tilt of his head.

She sat on the bench seat primly, closing the robe carefully over her legs. Then, with a deep breath, she put her fingers to the keys. She didn't need any coaching. She never forgot a tune once she'd heard it, and transposing in her head was a cinch.

Charlie heard his song come to life under her hands. Tinkling out in a two-fingered melody. Well, she was playing chords, so it took more than two fingers. But that was it. It was a wrap.

He rapidly found his attention drifting. The footwork she was doing with the pedals had caused the robe to part, revealing a long length of shapely leg. No nightie anywhere in sight. If she was looking to distract him, she was doing fine.

"Are you listening?" she asked without turning her head.

"Are you wearin' anything under that robe?"

"Charlie!" She did turn then, throwing him that slanty-eyed look over her shoulder that told him, whatever she'd like him to believe, she only had one thing on her mind. His one thing was beginning to take serious notice.

The melody segued into an old tune, one from his first album, lighthearted, easy. "Are you wearing anything under those jeans?"

Charlie smiled from ear to ear, and picked up the tune on his guitar, cradling the instrument the way he'd cradle her. Soon. "I asked first."

Her shoulders stiffened a little, and she stared straight ahead, but he knew she saw his reflection in the glass, just as he saw hers. "Yes, I am."

"No, I'm not."

She hit a clinker then, a rarity for Molly. With a laugh and a shake of her head, she gave up and closed the keyboard cover.

"Come over here," Charlie said. "Sit by me." He swept the papers off of the ottoman in front of him, clearing a place for her, and watched her approach. His whiskey-eyed woman was more adventuresome than he'd ever dreamed, but she liked to be coaxed, wooed, courted. She liked the slow buildup, the steadily escalating tension. He was finding, more and more, so did he.

She sat, her knees closed between his spread ones, her hands folded in her lap, her eyes dancing around the room. His fingers stroked the guitar strings, one finger, one string at a time. That drew her attention, finally, and her gaze settled there.

"It's not...uh," he cleared his throat, "an inconvenient time of month...or anything?"

To his surprise she looked uneasy. She moved her hands to the front edge of the ottoman and curled her fingers around it, still not meeting his eyes. "I don't think we'll have to worry about that for quite a long time."

It took a minute for her meaning to sink in. He felt as if

the air had been sucked from his lungs. "Already!" he croaked with more shock than tact.

Her gaze did dart to his then for just a moment and, reading her dismay, he could have bit his tongue. "Well, I...uh...haven't been to a doctor yet." She was trying to smile, but it was a struggle. "I haven't taken any tests...." Her eyes flicked to his again and she ran her tongue over her lips. "But I've only been this late one time." She gave up on the smile altogether and bit down on her lower lip to still its trembling. "I thought you'd be pleased," she said in a quavering voice.

He felt like the worst kind of heel. "Aw, honey, I am." That came across mealymouthed, even to him. *That's real convincing, Kick. You sound like an idiot.* "What I mean is...I'm scared to death."

That got her attention. She looked at him, dumbfounded.

"I know what you're gonna do, Molly. You're gonna give me a skinny, little, redheaded girl. Every time she scrapes her knees, my heart will bleed."

She looked at him with a blank expression for some moments, raised her eyebrows and shrugged, as if to say, "Oh, that's all." Then she laughed, a hoot that would have roused the house if there had been anyone else around to hear it. "Seems only fair to me...considering what I've had to contend with the last seven years."

He wasn't going to get a whole lot of sympathy on this score, he could tell. "Well," he admitted. "He is a chip off the old block."

She gave that throaty laugh. "Chip, my eye. He's a boulder." Her smile gentled as she reached out a hand to cup his cheek. "You'd make a wonderful father for a little girl, Charlie," she whispered, then added playfully, "and a much better coach for me than Margot was."

"Margot?"

"My roommate, from college. Senior year?"

"Oh, yeah. Tiny thing. Dark," he recalled. "Whatd'ya mean, 'coach'?"

"You know, during labor."

"Ahhh," he said, trying not to think too hard about what coaching entailed.

"Margot meant well, but she was awful. Kept hyperventilating. The nurses had to give *her* a paper bag to breathe into." Molly laughed at the memory.

"Your mother..?"

Seeing his expression, Molly turned serious again. Still cupping his jaw, she traced her thumb over his lips. "She came up to stay with me for a few weeks after Tobie was born...to help me out. We were never really close, Charlie, but we weren't estranged...there at the end."

"I'm glad." He was surprised to discover that he was glad.

"She loved Tobie."

He nodded. He had one more promise to keep. Not another uncharitable thought about the woman as long as he lived. That was going to be a toughie, but he'd try. For *this* woman, he'd tackle just about anything.

"I love you, Molly...somethin' awful," he whispered.

She looked as if she might cry, but a corner of her mouth quirked up. "For someone who's so good with words, it took you long enough to get those out."

"I'll tell you every day, Moll. I've been telling you most of my life. You haven't been payin' attention."

He leaned forward over his guitar, closing the distance between them. Tilting his head he fitted his lips to hers, his fingers on the pulse beat in her throat that quickened under them as he murmured against her mouth, "I love you...I love you...I love you," so softly she couldn't hear the words, only feel them. The way, in all truth, she had felt his love surround her, embrace her, enfold her for much of her life.

With what he considered awesome restraint, Charlie refrained from deepening the kiss. Instead he eased away from her, watching her expectantly, waiting.

She regarded him with dazed, unfocused eyes. Then confusion flitted across her face. Finally, came the dawn, and she went all huffy-puffy, as he knew she would. "Oh, *Charlie!* I love...I've *always*...how could you think..?"

He just waited.

"I love you," she said finally, simply. "I've loved you since I was six years old. You know that."

"Yeah, I do." He gave her his sweetest smile. "But it's nice to hear."

Only one question remained unresolved between them. The one he hesitated to raise, dreaded to pursue, wasn't sure he wanted an answer to. But he wanted Molly to have this chance and he knew she'd never bring it up herself.

"Who did you go to, Moll? Which one of my meddlin' family did you tell about Tobie? Who didn't help you?"

She was taken aback at first, her chin snapping up, her eyes wide, startled. He thought she would deny it. Wanted her to deny it.

But she didn't.

She squared her shoulders and looked him straight in the eye, hers unflinching. "You're right," she said. "I did go to someone. And we've made our peace." Her voice was very firm, despite its softness. She leaned forward, closer to him. "I will never tell you—" she emphasized her words with a shake of her head "—so don't ask me."

He opened his mouth to protest, but she pressed her fingers to his lips. "Families aren't perfect, Charlie. We love them anyway. *You* taught me to accept that."

He moved his head slightly to speak. "Moll—"

"No, Charlie." She was implacable. "There's enough blame to go around. The truth is, I didn't come to you myself until I had no choice." She clasped his wrist where it lay atop his guitar. "We can't get those years back. We can only put them behind us."

He dropped his gaze to her hand upon him. He felt obliged to try just once more, though the fight had gone out of him. Raising his eyes, he studied her calm expression. "You gonna make me wonder...all my life?"

She seemed to sense his willingness to let it go.

"You can do that, if you want...." she answered with a one-shouldered shrug that left the shoulder bare except for a skinny strap.

She was wearing the teddy.

"Seems like a big waste of time to me." Another shrug and the other shoulder was bare. Except for that strap.

"Or…" With that word she rose to her feet, the robe sliding down her arms to pool over her hands where they worked to undo the belt.

"You can come see…" The robe parted. She slid her hands around to her back, over her bottom, and held the garment there. The motion revealed all to Charlie. The thrust of her generous breasts, the slender waist, the flare of her hips, the long, long legs. If there were any changes to her body because of the baby, he couldn't tell. He'd have to get a closer look. Warmth radiated from her, and the scent of jasmine, and woman.

He reached to touch her and she shied abruptly and moved away from him. Giving him a sultry smile, she nudged one strap down off her shoulder, then the other, and turned her back to him. Slowly, slinkily, she strolled toward the stairway to the upper level, dragging the robe behind her across the carpet. Each step revealed more of her graceful anatomy as the teddy slipped steadily downward.

"You can come see if I still wear panties under this teddy," she finished, so sure of herself she didn't even glance back to see if he was coming.

Charlie watched her go, his head swimming in her wake. Then he laid his guitar down, put his questions aside forever, and followed her.

Epilogue

"Look at those legs, Dad. She's got legs like a chicken. How's she ever gonna walk on those?"

"Well…" She did have legs like a chicken. She had fingers like parakeet feet, too. And a belly like a little meat loaf. So what, exactly, was the appeal here? What was it about her that made his chest go tight every time he looked at her?

"Chickens can walk."

Pretty lame answer, granted, but he'd just discovered he'd gotten more than he bargained for when he offered to change the first diaper of the day.

"E-e-ew."

"Yeah. Get me some wipes."

He tried to control the squirmy bundle while he waited for Tobie to come back and caught himself talking to her in that silly, high-pitched tone people used with babies. She gave him a drooly smile. No way was that gas. The past couple of weeks he'd been more and more happy about his decision not to tour this year. He wouldn't have missed this for the world.

The last months had had their ups and downs, but taken as a whole, it had been the most contented period of his life.

Tobie's transplant had taken beautifully, he was sturdy, and there'd been no more major scares.

And Molly. Well, Molly was Molly. Fire and laughter. Sweetness and sass. She'd tolerated her pregnancy fairly well up until the end there, when she'd gotten a little out of sorts. His brothers had coached him on how to coach, but it would be a while before he'd want to go through that again.

"I'd really like a brother." Tobie had returned with the wipes.

"I wouldn't bring that up just yet," Charlie mumbled around the safety pin he had clamped between his teeth. "Your momma didn't get a lot of sleep last night."

He had something to do with that. Molly'd gotten a clean bill of health, and she was in the mood. So he'd kept her up, showing her how much he'd missed doing things just "regular." How was he to know this little pixie was going to want to eat every hour on the hour all night long? His heart was in the right place, but there wasn't much he could do to help Molly with that particular task.

This was a hell of a job. She was doing the bicycle bit now, and he was rapidly coming to the conclusion that he didn't have enough hands.

"Hold on to that foot, Tobie. Don't let go."

"Do you s'pose her hair will ever look any better, Dad?" One could only hope. At the moment she had an orange fuzz-ball of a head. Hair stuck straight out. It lacked *wave*. "Your momma took a lot of teasin' about her hair when she was little. Look how pretty it is now."

"It's *red*."

"Yeah, it is." Maybe he was the only person in the world who thought it was beautiful. He'd always liked it.

"She's sure a tiny thing, Dad," Tobie said on a serious note. "She's gonna need lookin' after."

"She's lucky she's got a big brother." Charlie silently uttered what he figured was every parent's prayer. That his children would always love each other. "You can let go of that foot, now. We'll get her into this…jumpsuit, or whatever the…heck you call it."

His thoughts ran to his own childhood. When Molly decided on this name, maybe that's what she'd remembered. He'd been resistant, at first, but she'd insisted. Though they'd never raised the issue again, he knew what she was doing. And maybe she was right. Maybe following her own convoluted logic, it made sense. She was telling him in no uncertain terms that if she could find it in her heart to forgive his sister, he could, too.

All he knew is that every time he looked at this child they had made, he felt some of the healing Molly intended.

He zipped the playsuit up to his daughter's chin and cradled her wriggly little body in his big hands.

"Come on, Lucy-girl. Let's go see Momma."

* * * * *

This summer, the legend
continues in Jacobsville

*Diana
Palmer*

A LONG, TALL
TEXAN SUMMER

Three **BRAND-NEW** short stories

This summer, Silhouette brings readers a special
collection for Diana Palmer's LONG, TALL TEXANS
fans. Diana has rounded up three **BRAND-NEW**
stories of love Texas-style, all set in Jacobsville,
Texas. Featuring the men you've grown to love from
this wonderful town, this collection is a must-have
for all fans!

*They grow 'em tall in the saddle in Texas—and
they've got love and marriage on their minds!*

Don't miss this collection of original Long, Tall Texans
stories...available in June at your favorite retail outlet.

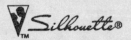

MILLION DOLLAR SWEEPSTAKES
OFFICIAL RULES
NO PURCHASE NECESSARY TO ENTER

1. To enter, follow the directions published. Method of entry may vary. For eligibility, entries must be received no later than March 31, 1998. No liability is assumed for printing errors, lost, late, non-delivered or misdirected entries.

   To determine winners, the sweepstakes numbers assigned to submitted entries will be compared against a list of randomly, preselected prize winning numbers. In the event all prizes are not claimed via the return of prize winning numbers, random drawings will be held from among all other entries received to award unclaimed prizes.

2. Prize winners will be determined no later than June 30, 1998. Selection of winning numbers and random drawings are under the supervision of D. L. Blair, Inc., an independent judging organization whose decisions are final. Limit: one prize to a family or organization. No substitution will be made for any prize, except as offered. Taxes and duties on all prizes are the sole responsibility of winners. Winners will be notified by mail. Odds of winning are determined by the number of eligible entries distributed and received.

3. Sweepstakes open to residents of the U.S. (except Puerto Rico), Canada and Europe who are 18 years of age or older, except employees and immediate family members of Torstar Corp., D. L. Blair, Inc., their affiliates, subsidiaries, and all other agencies, entities, and persons connected with the use, marketing or conduct of this sweepstakes. All applicable laws and regulations apply. Sweepstakes offer void wherever prohibited by law. Any litigation within the province of Quebec respecting the conduct and awarding of a prize in this sweepstakes must be submitted to the Régie des alcools, des courses et des jeux. In order to win a prize, residents of Canada will be required to correctly answer a time-limited arithmetical skill-testing question to be administered by mail.

4. Winners of major prizes (Grand through Fourth) will be obligated to sign and return an Affidavit of Eligibility and Release of Liability within 30 days of notification. In the event of non-compliance within this time period or if a prize is returned as undeliverable, D. L. Blair, Inc. may at its sole discretion, award that prize to an alternate winner. By acceptance of their prize, winners consent to use of their names, photographs or other likeness for purposes of advertising, trade and promotion on behalf of Torstar Corp., its affiliates and subsidiaries, without further compensation unless prohibited by law. Torstar Corp. and D. L. Blair, Inc., their affiliates and subsidiaries are not responsible for errors in printing of sweepstakes and prize winning numbers. In the event a duplication of a prize winning number occurs, a random drawing will be held from among all entries received with that prize winning number to award that prize.

5. This sweepstakes is presented by Torstar Corp., its subsidiaries and affiliates in conjunction with book, merchandise and/or product offerings. The number of prizes to be awarded and their value are as follows: Grand Prize — $1,000,000 (payable at $33,333.33 a year for 30 years); First Prize — $50,000; Second Prize — $10,000; Third Prize — $5,000; 3 Fourth Prizes — $1,000 each; 10 Fifth Prizes — $250 each; 1,000 Sixth Prizes — $10 each. Values of all prizes are in U.S. currency. Prizes in each level will be presented in different creative executions, including various currencies, vehicles, merchandise and travel. Any presentation of a prize level in a currency other than U.S. currency represents an approximate equivalent to the U.S. currency prize for that level, at that time. Prize winners will have the opportunity of selecting any prize offered for that level; however, the actual non U.S. currency equivalent prize if offered and selected, shall be awarded at the exchange rate existing at 3:00 P.M. New York time on March 31, 1998. A travel prize option, if offered and selected by winner, must be completed within 12 months of selection and is subject to: traveling companion(s) completing and returning of a Release of Liability prior to travel; and hotel and flight accommodations availability. For a current list of all prize options offered within prize levels, send a self-addressed, stamped envelope (WA residents need not affix postage) to: MILLION DOLLAR SWEEPSTAKES Prize Options, P.O. Box 4456, Blair, NE 68009-4456, USA.

6. For a list of prize winners (available after July 31, 1998) send a separate, stamped, self-addressed envelope to: MILLION DOLLAR SWEEPSTAKES Winners, P.O. Box 4459, Blair, NE 68009-4459, USA.

And the Winner Is...
You!

...when you pick up these great titles
from our new promotion at your
favorite retail outlet this June!

Diana Palmer
The Case of the Mesmerizing Boss

Betty Neels
The Convenient Wife

Annette Broadrick
Irresistible

Emma Darcy
A Wedding to Remember

Rachel Lee
Lost Warriors

Marie Ferrarella
Father Goose

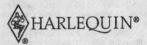 

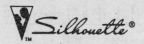

**Special Edition and Intimate Moments
are proud to present**

Janet Dailey Award winner
RUTH WIND

**and three new emotionally gripping
tales of love...**

The Forrest brothers—as wild and untamed as the
rugged mountains they call home—each discover a
woman as special and true as the Colorado skies. But is
love enough to lasso these hearts...?

Lance Forrest—left town
years ago, but returns to Red Creek in
MARRIAGE MATERIAL (SE#1108, 6/97) to a
son he never knew...and finds an unexpected love.

Jake Forrest—lived his whole life by a code of
military honor...until that honor failed him. In
RECKLESS (IM#796, 7/97), he comes home to find
peace...and discovers a woman for his heart.

Tyler Forrest—has raised his son, alone, in the quiet of
the Colorado mountains. But then his solitude is
invaded by the most unlikely woman...who thinks he's
HER IDEAL MAN (IM#801, 8/97).

THE LAST ROUNDUP...
Three brothers travel the rocky road to love
in a small Colorado town.

Available at your favorite retail outlet.

COMING NEXT MONTH

#793 AN UNEXPECTED ADDITION—Terese Ramin

Intimate Moments Extra

When single mom Kate Anden and widowed dad Hank Mathison got together to talk about parenthood, things somehow led to the bed…and now *another* little bundle of joy was on the way! These veteran singles were making room for baby…but would the unexpected addition to their families bring them together—or tear them apart?

#794 MOMMY BY SURPRISE—Paula Detmer Riggs

Maternity Row

Prudy Randolph should have known better than to think that one night of passion with her ex-husband could change the past…and his paternal instincts. But it did affect their future, and now she had precious little time to heal his aching heart…and prove that little *miracles* really do exist!

#795 A MARRIAGE TO REMEMBER—Cathryn Clare

Their marriage was over—or so Jayne believed. But when an attempt on Nick's life robbed him of his memory, they went on the run together… and fell in love all over again. But could Jayne trust this changed man with her heart, or would the old workaholic husband reclaim the man she had come to love?

#796 RECKLESS—Ruth Wind

The Last Roundup

Soldier Jake Forrest was recklessly running from his past, seeking shelter from the memories that plagued his mind. Small-town doctor Ramona Hardy offered him more than just sanity and hope in her protective embrace. She gave him love…and vowed to prove to him that it really could conquer all.

#797 THE TWELVE-MONTH MARRIAGE—Kathryn Jensen

Newlyweds David and Carrie have just solved all their problems. Wedded bliss? Not exactly. David got the wife he needs to keep custody of his children, and Carrie got the children she's always wanted. Now there's only one thing threatening their twelve-month arrangement…*love!*

#798 STRANGER IN HER BED—Bonnie Gardner

T. J. Swift thought he had found the perfect apartment…until the supposedly dead—and very attractive—former tenant showed up to resume residence! Sparks flew, but if Robin Digby and T.J. didn't get to the bottom of this whole mystery—and fast—they just might end up getting burned!